HARD IRISH LUCK

LUCK

THE WELDON SERIES: BOOK THREE

USA Today Bestselling Author

BY JENNIFER SAINTS

Published by Novels Alive Publishing, LLC

Copyright Information

This is a work of fiction. All of the characters, organizations, and events portrayed in this novel are either products of the author's imagination or are used fictitiously.

ISBN: 978-0-9824863-7-5

More Titles by Jennifer St. Giles

Trevelyan Series Writing as Jennifer St. Giles

Mistress of Trevelyan

His Dark Desires

Killdaren Series Writing as Jennifer St. Giles

Midnight Secrets

Darkest Dreams

Silken Shadows

Shadowmen Series Writing as Jennifer St. Giles

Touch A Dark Wolf

Lure of the Wolf

Kiss of Darkness

Bride of the Wolf

Silent Warrior Series Writing as J.L. Saint

Collateral Damage

Tactical Deception

Weldon Series Writing as Jennifer Saints
Wild Irish Ride

Smooth Irish Seduction

Hard Irish Luck

Frankly, My Dear Series as Jennifer Saints
Cocktail Cove

Upcoming Releases
Hot Irish Lass (Weldon Brothers - Book 4)

Down Easy Street (Frankly, My Dear - Book 2)

Fly Me to the Moon (Frankly, My Dear - Book 3)

Find Jennifer Online:

www.jenniferstgiles.com

@jenniferstgiles

https://www.facebook.com/pages/Jennifer-St-Giles/153382491356980

Dedication

I dedicate this book to all of my readers everywhere, whose encouragement and support made writing *Hard Irish Luck* possible during some trying moments. I want all those who enjoy my stories to know just how much your emails, and reviews mean to me. Writing is a solitary job, and to hear from you makes it all worthwhile.

 Many thanks and happy reading,

 Jennifer Saints, Jennifer St. Giles, JL Saint

Acknowledgments

My thanks to Rita Herron, my long-time writing pal and sister in the struggle of publishing for helping me stretch beyond the box when my mind only wanted to vegetate. Huge hugs and thank you to Dayna Linton and Tierney Linton for their input and for helping to make this plot zing. To Sean Linton for his grammar guidance. To Annette for her constant barrage of hunky inspiration. To Jacquie, Wendy for keeping my rear-end off of the ground no matter how badly I drag. Onward and upward! To all of the GALS who make writing Sexy and Southern so much fun! And to Tim Parrish whose best five seconds, I won't be forgetting, your humor inspires.

Hard Irish Luck is more than just a sexy story, it is a story about those who lived through hard times and struggled to rise above them. It is a story of love, forgiveness, and hope.

May God give you...For every storm a rainbow, for every tear a smile, for every care a promise and a blessing in each trial. For every problem life sends, a faithful friend to share, for every sigh a sweet song and an answer for each prayer. – Irish Blessing

The one thing we can never get enough of is love. And the one thing we can never give enough of is love. – Henry Miller

CHAPTER ONE

"We're screwed." Bleary eyed and muttering, Jared Weldon stumbled across the spacious living room, giving the bottle of *Macallan 18* on the coffee table a wide berth. This morning's "hair of the dog" urge was stronger than ever and he had to be at church in less than an hour.

Maybe it was a good thing he was being forced to go back to beer. The expensive crap kicked his ass harder every time he tangled with it. His sensory circuits were under attack. Music piped from the condo's sound system. Gulls over the Savannah screeched. A passing tanker honked a warning to a Sunday boater and the way-too-bright sun stabbed daggers at him from across the Inter-coastal. The jackhammer throb in his head doubled.

Fishing the remote from the couch, he activated the window blinds, killing the sun's glare then silenced the seductive tones of Luther Vandross oozing over the condo's sound system. Vandross turned chicks on and both he and his twin James, were all about that. The music usually played all night, not only setting the mood but effectively drowning out each other's bedroom activities.

He followed the trail of discarded clothes to James's bedroom door, grimacing at the odor of stale booze and left out food hanging in the air. Damn, the line of clothes seemed to go on and on. Either he was seeing double or what's her name had had on more than he thought when he saw her all over James last night.

Jared winced. But then, his own date, April, had had his full attention. At least from the neck down. Or was her name June?

Hell, maybe that's why she left in a huff. Who was named after a month of the year anyway? There were twelve of them, too easy to get it wrong.

He knocked on James's door and thought it was just as well that April-June had left. He hated morning-afters. Hated pretending the sex was great and that he was looking forward to round two. Hated getting phone numbers he'd never call. Hated that by the next weekend both parties would be on the hunt again.

"Wake up, bro! The ceremony is in forty-five minutes." Getting no answer, Jared pounded harder. Nonstop. Something he knew pissed his twin off to no end.

James snatched open the door, naked, and ready for a fight. "What the hell?"

A mirror image of himself, James looked just as rough and wasted as Jared did. And not for the first time Jared wondered what in the hell had happened to them both. Somewhere over the past eighteen months they'd lost their ass in more ways than one.

"The ceremony for Jake and Jason is in forty-five minutes and we lost the bid for the Drake Hotel renovation. E-mail came through this morning."

"We had that bid in the bag. How in the hell?"

"Who else? Those damn vultures from across the river again. McKenna Construction."

"Santa baby, I'm cold." The purr floated from inside the bedroom.

James winced.

"Santa baby? Really? It's July."

"What can I say? I come bearing gifts and she's Aussie. They like their Christmases hot."

Jared couldn't see the bed from where he stood, but the ceiling fan whirling with a pair of red fur-trimmed thongs hanging on a blade told a story that he wasn't about to ask the details on. "We'll talk later. Meanwhile, move ass." He nodded to the bedroom. "Make that plural. We've got less than forty minutes to be at the church."

James grumbled. "I'll hurry. Don't know why we've got to swear before God and country that we'll take care of Jake and Jason. Jackson and Jesse know were good for whatever it takes. Nothing's going to happen to them anyway."

"I agree. Something about getting hitched and downloading a kid has scrambled their brains."

Thirty minutes later a suited, limping James smacked a kiss on his Aussie then climbed shotgun into Jared's Porsche. Jared spun out of the parking lot trying to gauge how much time it would take to get to the church. He loved the feel of speed, precision, and power at his fingertips.

Suddenly, a pang of reality gripped him by the short hairs.

Without the Drake job he and James would have to cut things to the bare minimum, which meant this ride had to go back into the leasing company tomorrow and he'd have to eat the penalty.

The crash in the economy had killed the momentum of Weldon Estates, their high-end housing development on the Savannah River. New building had slowed to a crawl and Shamrock Construction needed another job to meet payroll for their crew.

James buckled in. "Elbow me if I drift off during the ceremony."

"Christmas last all night?"

He grunted. "Remind me to think twice before sleeping with a Pilates expert again."

"You said flexible was right up your alley."

"Flexible is one thing. Planking during sex is another. And by the way, it does *not* prolong an orgasm. Nips the sucker short. I've got kinks in places I didn't even know I had. "

"I'm sorry I asked."

"I'm sorrier."

"Do I look as hung over as you?"

James squinted his way. "All I see is a blur, but no worries. There's a sinister plot afoot anyway."

Jared frowned at James's incoherent jump in subjects. He hoped his brother could keep it together during the church ceremony. "Agreed. McKenna Construction's has practically put us out of business. There's something off about the whole thing. I cut that bid to the bone."

"McKenna? What does he have to do with our nephews?"

"What sinister plot are you talking about?"

"Not long before Jesse and Jackson asked us to do this, I overheard mom complaining to them that we weren't just living high on the hog, but we were living on a high *wild* hog and she'd wrung a hole in her dishrag. I've a feeling this ceremony is a way to hog-tie us back to Earth. Be good examples for our nephews and stuff."

"Hell, why didn't you say something?" A vise squeezed Jared's conscience.

"I figured it would blow over. It's not like we're screwing our lives up like Jesse and Jackson, right? We're just doing what bachelors do. Enjoying playing the field, home run after home run."

"Right." Jared couldn't argue with that logic. Both Jesse and Jackson had run the rough edge of nowhere and had barely escaped its dark side. Still, finding out that he and James had worried their mother as badly as Jesse and Jackson had didn't sit well in his gut. Either that or his whiskey binge was turning him green. He upped the AC and sucked in a deep breath.

"You okay?" James squinted his way again.

"No. We've got mortgage and payroll due shortly and no job. The only possible bright spot is that couple coming tomorrow to see our spec house. But even if they buy, we'll only be out of hot water temporarily. "

"Then we'll cash in the last CD and make damn sure we get the bid on that new bank they're building north of town."

Jared shook in his head and winced at the increased throb in his temple. Was he having a nightmare? Or was James that much out of it lately? "Reality check, bro. We cashed the *last* CD *last* month. And the bank job? Let's just say that when Jesse carted Alexi off from marrying Roger, I don't think the Holsteads are interested in dealing with the Weldons on any level."

James groaned. "We cashed the last CD?"

"Yeah. Remember? We discussed it the Friday you and what's her name were heading out to Vegas for the weekend."

James upped the AC. Now gulping for cool air, too. "Shit. And I blew ten grand on that trip. Why didn't you ream my ass?"

Jared shrugged. "Thought we'd be fine. Always have been before. At least until that McKenna outfit moved in on our territory. How in the hell are they underbidding us?"

"I don't know. As you said, our bid was to the bone."

"Bet you anything they're using illegals for labor." Jared
turned onto East Bay Street and headed north passing through
Savannah's historic district. He loved his hometown. The history.
The architecture. Its Old World flavor was like a good aged
scotch, rich and mellow. He loved the fact that he and James
added to that flavor with the quality of their construction and in the
designs of their housing development. They did each job with
pride and each house plan they'd developed borrowed some of the
look and features of Savannah's historic homes and plantations.
The thought they could lose everything they'd worked so hard for
was soul sickening.

James nodded his agreement. "Using illegals and substituting
lower quality material when no one is looking seems to be the only
way they can undercut us. We should check with our guys and see
if they know any of McKenna's crew. Couldn't hurt to ask a few
questions."

Jared smacked his palm on the steering wheel as he hung a
right toward the church. "Damn right. It's time we take this bull
by the horns before it gores Shamrock Construction into
bankruptcy. Somehow I'm going to find out what McKenna's
game is."

"If we can prove they're up to no good, then we can get the
Drake Hotel bid back."

"Good point. After church today, I'll go check out their last
job."

"You mean after the BBQ. No way dad will let us skip-out
again. We missed the last family shindig."

"We did?"

"Yeah, remember yachting with those party heiresses?"

Jared groaned as he pulled into the church parking lot. "You mean that trip we swore we'd forget ever happened."

"That be the one." James opened his car door.

Blinking bleary-eyed at the bright blue sky, Jared cautiously stepped out of the Porsche and gauged the distance to the entrance. Lightning bolts out of the blue did happen. "Bringing that weekend up before walking into church is just asking for God to strike us dead."

James rolled his eyes, but glanced at the sky and picked up his pace anyway.

That weekend he and James had cruised with rich and infamous jet-setters. The very sketchy memories of booze, drugs, and orgy-like sex had left them both knowing they'd never cross the drug-using multiple-partner line again. The old adage "when in Rome do like the Romans" only worked out well if you want to be Roman. Jared walked into church in a cold sweat, feeling he'd pass out in any second. The smiled plastered on James's green face said he was feeling the same.

Jesse and Jackson were standing just inside and from the instant glint in both their gazes, Jared knew his and James's hangovers were readily apparent. Their older brothers walked over and slapped him and James hard on the back.

The jackhammer in Jared's head worsened. Jesse grabbed his arm, leading him toward the sanctuary. Jackson strong-armed James.

Jesse was livid. "The ceremony starts in five minutes. Not only are Jackson and I going to beat you and James to a pulp for this, but Lexi and Nan can't wait to dig their nails into you both, and behind them are Mom and Dad. Couldn't you two have stayed sober for just one night?"

Jared regretted not having that "hair of the dog" drink this morning. "Relax. We're here and we're sober," he muttered.

Jesse's returning gaze cut deep. "You're barely sober and as for being here, you're not. In fact you are so far gone I question whether you could do anything to help Jake were something to happen to me."

Jared stumbled. Not from the booze, but from the gut-slicing pain in his heart. It wasn't Jesse's doubts that hurt, it was the ugly truth behind them. Jesse's grip tightened and Jared sucked in a deep breath. He stepped into the church and saw the "Come to Jesus" meeting facing him in the look in his parent's eyes. There was hell to pay and it was coming out of his hide today.

He couldn't say he didn't deserve it, but knowing that did nothing to ease the bite and the shame. Jared glanced at James and knew without a doubt Jackson had cut deep, too, but rather than contrite, James looked pissed, as if he'd just had an injustice shoved down his throat.

For once in their close-knit life, Jared found no solace in the fact that he and James were in the dog house together. His world was in such a state that he wouldn't wish it on his worst enemy, but somehow he'd led James down this road to ruin. If memory served him right, he'd been the first one to start blazing their bachelor's trail. James had just followed suit and was thoroughly enjoying the status quo.

Not even God could stop the train wreck that was about to happen today.

The organ blared. The congregation stood and Jared blinked at the sun piercing through the churches arched windows as it highlighted an empty cross and cast the pastor into shadows. The pastor spoke and Jared's mind scrambled for a foothold in quicksand as more and more of his and James's wild nights streamed like an X-rated movie in his head. He wasn't sure how much time passed but when Jesse gripped his elbow, he knew the moment had arrived. He and James were led to the front of the church and then faced the congregation. All eyes were on them and Jared had little doubt that a scarlet letter was stamped in the middle of his forehead.

"Dearly beloved, we are gathered today not only to celebrate the gift of life, but to reaffirm our commitment to family. The love a parent has for their child is a deep and abiding one. It is a love that sacrifices and it is a love that never rests in its desire to provide and secure the best possible future. The greatest gift a parent can have is the assurance there are others within the child's life who will care for the child should they be unable to do so. Today Jesse and Alexi Weldon and Nancy and Jackson Weldon have chosen Jared and James Weldon, brothers and brothers-in-law of whom they have a high regard for, to take a special place in the lives of their children, Jake and Jason. This ceremony marks that faith and commitment."

The pastor moved from the shadows and stared him right in the eye. "Jared Weldon."

"Yes," Jared said, his voice worse than a frog croak. A cold sweat started in his gut and spread. He locked his knees to stay upright but could do nothing to stop his head-to-toe quivering.

"Do you swear before God, this congregation, and your family to take a special lifelong interest in your nephews, Jake and Jason? To be there for them in life and to help guide them morally and ethically as they develop into adults?"

Jared swallowed the choking lump in his throat, sure he was about to die on the spot. The phenomena of spontaneous combustion suddenly seemed completely plausible. He blinked the blur from his vision and found Alexi and Nan were standing before him. In their arms were his chubby nephews, blue eyes bright and slobbery grins happy. Alexi put Jake in the crook of his left arm and Nan put Jason in the crook of his right arm. They were so small, so innocent, so trusting, and so helpless. The thought of their lives resting in his hands blew his mind.   He'd been skating over the surface of life, free as a bird, but in that moment the ice broke and he plunged beneath into the icy water of reality. Terror ripped through.

He nodded several times but was incapable of saying the "I do" he'd been instructed to respond. After an uncomfortable moment the pastor zeroed in on James.

"James Weldon. Do you swear before God, this congregation, and your family to take a special lifelong interest in your nephews, Jake and Jason? To be there for them in life and to help guide them morally and ethically as they develop into adults?"

"I do," James replied, loud and clear. Instead of coming over and taking Jake and Jason from him as planned, James pitched forward in a dead faint and face-planted the altar.

From the expression of his family all staring at him, Jared concluded that train wreck was too mild a description for the situation. Nuclear explosion was a more apt description.

Jared prayed hard, but for some reason God didn't instantly beam him up to heaven, instead he left him squirming in hell. He didn't need a "hair of the dog" drink this morning. He needed the whole damn bottle.

CHAPTER TWO

"Woof!"

"Slow down, Pebbles. You're shaking the steps."

Her tenuous concentration broken by the fact that two hundred pounds of slobbery St. Bernard and the zaniest woman in the South were about to descend on her, Roxanne "Rocky" McKenna quickly stood and stretched her long legs. She slipped a robe on over her sun-kissed skin and prepared for the onslaught. Used to be drugging sunshine, fresh air, and yoga after her routine morning swim could clear the cloudiest horizons. Not anymore.

Either life's troubles or her suppressed hormones reared a disturbing head.

"Thought I'd find you up here. I brought you Intense Chai this morning. Next best thing to an orgasm to start your day."

Rocky laughed as Desmond "Dessie" Langford and her huge pooch breached the privacy of her rooftop garden. Between the riches of Hilton Head, South Carolina and Savannah, Georgia lay a swampy land of everything under the sun from The Golden Bunny burlesque joint to the Lazy Cow Café.

At fifty-five, Dessie, a Marilyn Monroe look-a-like, was still the queen of the Golden Bunny. *Moves Like Jagger* had nothing on her. In Dessie's world, liposuction and silicon fixed what the Good Lord taketh away with age and when the gray hair moved south, she went Brazilian—a waxing luxury that Rocky herself, upon coercion, found she enjoyed.

Wearing a hard hat on the job all day made her enjoy the sleek, cultured feel of being smooth and sexy all over. Maybe more than she should.

The best two moves of her life had been her divorce and moving in next door to Dessie and Pebbles. Well, Pebbles was still kind of up in the air. The monster dog was delusional. Thought she was a lap dog and did her best to crawl one paw into any available lap. Rocky did a lot of standing when Pebbles was afoot. Reaching down, she nabbed one of Pebbles balls left from her last visit and tossed it down the stairs. Pebbles took off in a house-shaking rush after the ball that would likely bounce down all three flights and take her a good five minutes to find.

With Pebbles out of the way, Rocky took the mug of hot tea Dessie held out and inhaled the cinnamon and spice before sipping. "The best."

"Nope only second best. Orgasm is the best. So when are you going to ditch your ivory tower and let your hair down, girl. All this Zen meditating in the nude and Fung Shu-"

"Feng Shui," Rocky said.

"Whatever all this is," Dessie waved at the rooftop garden. "It don't make up for having a man while you're young enough to enjoy him. As I see it, you've let your ex steal three years of great sex from you. Maybe even more than that since it must not have been all that great with him or you'd be itching for a good fix by now."

"It's not like there hasn't been anything else going on."

"Sorry, luv. I'm not discounting your father's illness, but you were in this state *before* his stroke. It's been a month now and who knows how long it will be before he recovers."

If he recovers. Rocky mentally said what she knew Dessie was too kind to say. After skipping a beat Dessie continued. "You need to get out and meet people. You need a man."

A large splash from below alerted them both that Pebbles had found the pool and would return soaking wet.

Rocky rolled her eyes and drank more tea. She wasn't about to give Dessie an inch to hang her with. Truth was Rocky had more than an itch, she had a fever, but she damn well was not going to give into it, no matter what the temptation. Thus the meditation. Not that it helped a whole lot. The heated thoughts that wiggled their way into her mind kept her in a state of need.

But hormones had landed her on the wrong side of love more than once and she refused to give into them ever again. Next time she tangled with a man, she'd connect with his mind first and make sure he was Mr. Right before anything else happened between them.

She arched her eyebrow and turned the tables. Dessie only dished out advice when she had a problem and didn't know what to do. "So who has your thongs in a wad today?"

"That obvious, huh?"

"Only to those who love you. Now give it up. What's ailing you?"

"The new bouncer at the Golden Bunny. OMG he's Robert Redford redone and melts me with one look."

"So?"

"So he's too young. I may purr and scratch, but cougaring ain't my thing. Trouble is he doesn't want to take no for an answer. Come save me. You really ought to swing by the club and meet him today. He's got great sex written from head-to-toe of his hard body."

"Not going to work, Dessie. I'm not going to let your Chai Tea seduce me into another man-mistake. I work with hard-bodied men day in and day out and married one, that doesn't necessarily make a man great. Might even be just the opposite. I have to stop by the office to set up a few things for the new job tomorrow and then I'm going to see Da today anyway."

Dessie put her hand to her forehead as if she might faint. "I've wasted years of my life. Haven't you heard a word I've been saying, Rocky? There're men who've got brains, brawn, balls and heart, but you aren't going to find him up here and you aren't going to find him in the nursing home either. You work too much. You need to get out and date."

"Job pays the bills. Besides, I'm not that bad. I dated Cam Phillips after Newsline did the segment on Building-A-Future." The free summer work camp she held every year to teach area kids the basics of building and how to use tools had garnered national attention after she'd won a local humanitarian award. The well-known anchor had been interested in her for a time.

"That's been over a year ago. He flew in from LA three times over two months. You kept him at arm's length and as soon as a gossip monger splashed your picture in the paper with his, you sent him packing."

"Like Da said from the start, I'm a private person. I wasn't about to become chum for the sharks."

"I think your father didn't want you leaving the hole he pegged for you to live in and sabotaged that relationship before the first date. I like your dad, but did you ever have a choice about what you wanted in life?"

"It doesn't matter. I like being in construction. Building things, improving things, making the world around me a better place."

"Just make sure you haven't locked yourself in a prison. And give your Da a hug for me while you're there."

They both heard Pebbles bounding back up the steps.

"I will. Thanks for the tea," Rocky made a quick exit to the metal stairs spiraling into her house and Dessie turned to meet Pebbles who proceeded to shake, rattle, and roll water in every possible direction. Dessie laughed and bent down, hugging Pebbles' enormous neck—a show of true love if there ever was one. Rocky smiled.

Her smile widened an hour later as she arrived at McKenna Construction's main office. Even though the office was closed on the weekends, she thankfully saw Maggie Dupree's Mini Cooper parked out front. Rocky didn't have a moment to waste and had had everything possible sitting on go. To win the bid, she'd promised to have the renovations done in an impossibly short time. She'd read a local magazine article on the hotel's new owner, Tiffany Parker Bentley, and known that hard-driving efficiency would appeal to the Clinton-like feminist. For once, the fact that Rocky was a woman operating in a man's world had worked in her favor instead of against her. With Maggie's help this morning, Rocky could quickly send the emails and faxes to put the Drake Hotel job in motion and have more time with her father.

Maggie started out last summer as a volunteer at Rocky's Build-A-Future camp then signed on as the McKenna Construction's receptionist and soon became invaluable, not only helping Alice Owen, their longtime secretary, but also serving as a go-to-woman for jobsite offices and paperwork, saving Rocky lots of time. And when Rocky had to move her father's things from his apartment after his stroke, both Alice and Maggie had made the task bearable.

She entered the air conditioned building and for a brief moment her breath caught at the disorder until she realized the books from the shelves and the drawers from the cabinets were in neat stacks and not ransacked as they had been one day last month. The office had a home-like appearance to its furnishings and decor with book shelves and comfortable sitting areas to each room, a central kitchen/break room, and a jungle of plants.

"Maggie?" Rocky navigated her way through the front office. After a moment she heard a door shut then the click of heels on the hardwood floors.

"Rocky?" Maggie called out. "Bugger me, you gave me a fright."

She appeared in the doorway of Rocky's office, better known as the Rainbow room because of the fairytale murals of rainbows and a unicorn riding princess, Rocky's mother, Keira, had painted on the walls of the onetime playroom. Rocky had been coming to the office since an infant. The furniture had changed from crib to tea party table to desk, but Rocky had kept the paintings, something she was glad she had done after losing her mother to cancer five years ago.

Rocky shook her head and smiled. Only the Brits could make bloody, bugger, and bollocks attractive adjectives. "I came in to put the Drake job in motion. This looks like a project."

"A bit of belated spring cleaning." Maggie waved her hands toward the mess and joined Rocky in the reception area. At forty something with strawberry hair that hung somewhere between curly and straight and designer black glasses that somehow missed being stylish, the buxom woman had "hard life" written on her wrinkled brow. She'd lost her mother at an early age, and from occasional comments, Rocky got the idea Maggie's father had passed her around to distant family members after that, so unlike the stable home Rocky had had.

"A project I do not envy. Is Alice coming to help?"

"No need. I can handle the dust mites better than her asthma can."

"Good point." Rocky frowned at the disorder. "I can help after I take care of a few things."

"And have you miss time with your Da? Wouldn't have it. Besides I get more work done by myself. Any change in his condition?"

"Yes. No. Maybe?" Rocky sighed. "It could be wishful thinking on my part, but it seems to me that there are moments lately where I swear he's aware and he's trying to tell me something. His expression becomes intense and I feel as if his hand grips mine. It gives me real hope that damage from the stroke isn't as severe as they think."

"Good to hear. What can I do to help you? I could use a break from cleaning."

"If you're sure."

"Quite."

"Okay. You can send faxes while I do the emails."

Maggie winced as she looked toward the Rainbow room. "Hope you can get to your computer. Your office is a bloody mess. I'm not only cleaning the shelves but vacuuming under them as well. You won't believe the cobwebs."

"Heavens. I don't even remember the last time that was done; likely before my mother became ill seven years ago. Cleaning is not my forte, but hand me a hammer and I'll work all day." Rocky entered her office and saw that Maggie hadn't overestimated the situation. Everything had been moved. She navigated around the vacuum cleaner and the stacked file cabinet drawers to get to her desk then moved the furniture polish and cleaning rags to unearth her files for the Drake Hotel job.

"I suppose that works," Maggie said, following. "If you give free reign to the cobwebs then you can always use a hammer on the spiders."

"Talk about overkill." Rocky wrinkled her nose. "After that visual, I think I'll hire a cleaning lady."

Maggie laughed. "Or bribe your friends. Let me know if you need help, luv. Meanwhile I'll take on those faxes. You're really moving fast on this job. Any special reason?"

Rocky handed her the list. "I promised I'd have the renovations done in record time. We can't afford any delays or we'll be in trouble. Odd thing about reputations, it takes forever to build a good one, but then one mishap and it goes down in a heartbeat."

Maggie took the file and then made the climb for the door. "Money's the same way," she said before she left. "Forever to get it and then you bloody lose it and nothing goes right."

"True," Rocky said and as she sent out the messages that would put Monday's agenda in motion, she realized most of life was like that—forever to build then lost in a second. Dreams, love, relationships…health. For a man in his late fifties, her father had been in good shape. He ate right, exercised, and only indulged in a good scotch on special occasions.

Thanks to Maggie, Rocky made it to the nursing home in good time and settled in to her usual place at his side and told him about Pebbles's latest exploits, knowing he'd enjoy hearing about them. He believed that the only "real" dogs in the world were the ones that weighed more than fifty pounds. After Pebbles, she turned the conversation to his pride and joy. McKenna Construction.

"We're going to stay in the black, Da. We won another bid. This one is for the Drake Hotel job. So you don't have to worry. It's all going to be all right." Swallowing the lump of emotion knotting her throat, she forced a smile as she searched his watery blue gaze. At a hefty six-five, she never thought Rory McKenna could ever look small and vulnerable, but he did.

The stroke had taken him from man to invalid in minutes, leaving a hole in her universe as big as the Milky Way. She tucked the blanket higher on his burly chest and clasped his hand in hers. Persistent Vegetative State...Locked in Syndrome...the doctors were still determining his condition. From all that she'd read about brain stem strokes, the prognosis of a patient could be difficult to predict. And while recovery miracles did happen, they weren't likely and they weren't often.

She wished she could do more. More than just pray. More than just keep McKenna Construction going. She wished she could go back and...what? *Take back their last argument so she might have been with him as usual the night he had his stroke?*

They'd fought over whether or not to have a more in-depth documentary done of her Building-A-Future summer camp and instead of going to his place for dinner, she'd come home to stew. Maybe Dessie was right. Maybe her father had been afraid of her leaving. He'd been against her doing the news show with Cameron last year, too.

She leaned in close, searching. His expression seemed more intense again, but he wasn't looking at her. He stared straight ahead. "You know you'll never lose me, Da. I'm not going anywhere. I love what I am doing. I love running the company. Was that what you were worried about?"

His breathing increased, as if he were suddenly running a race. Rocky's heart squeezed with concern. "Da? What's wrong?" She felt his pulse. It was steady but his skin seemed hotter than usual. He coughed.

She was in the middle of praying he wasn't coming down with pneumonia or something when she heard the words. "Keira. Unforgivable. Stop. Pray."

It took a moment for her to realize her father had spoken. At least she thought he had. As she studied him, looking for evidence, she began to think she'd imagined it. His gaze had become unfocussed again and his expression slack. His breathing had slowed to normal.

She clasped his hand tighter. "Da?"

Nothing.

"Da?"

"Any change?"

Rocky jumped at the question and bit back a groan of disappointment. "Uncle" Pat stood in the doorway. His Irish lilt and deep voice were similar to her father's. Her father had grown up with Patrick Brady in Ireland and they'd immigrated to America back in the early 1980's. Pat was her father's best friend, their business partner, and her ex-father-in-law. As a young woman she had bought into the dream her father and Pat had had, of her and Collin Brady running McKenna Construction together. That hadn't worked out at all and there were still after-divorce potholes that made the road bumpy for everyone.

"Were you just talking to someone in the hall? I heard my mother's name and some other words. I thought Da had spoken."

Pat looked shocked and moved to her father's bedside, studying him closely then shook his head. "Wasn't me talking, but it doesn't look like Rory has either. Ya sure ya heard something, lass? Was it wishful thinking?"

Rocky frowned. She and Pat had argued whether or not to keep her father alive via a feeding tube. Pat didn't want to see her father in this state of limbo forever and she'd wanted to do everything possible to keep him alive. She'd gone with the feeding tube and with every other measure that could be taken to keep him alive. She wanted her father back.

Had she imagined the words? If she had, she wouldn't have imagined the words she'd heard. Her mother's death was too painful for him and they'd avoided talking about her.

Tears stung her eyes as she clasped her father's hand tighter. "Da had to have spoken, Uncle Pat. This is an answer to prayer."

Pat called the nurse who came and checked her father. Barely able to breathe, Rocky waited while the nurse made a neurological assessment and took her father's vital signs.

After finishing, the nurse shook her head. "I'm not seeing any change in his condition, Miss McKenna. But I'll make a report on the chart that he spoke to you and let the doctor know in case there are any tests he wants done."

"Thank you," Rocky bit her lip as the nurse left. She'd hoped for an additional indication that her father's condition had improved. She almost felt let down and close to tears.

Pat set his hand on her shoulder. "If he spoke, he'll speak again. I'm worried about you, lass. All you do is work."

She shook her head. "There's no 'if', Uncle Pat. He spoke. He's been trying to tell me something important. I've felt it every time I've come." She clasped her father's hand again. "Da, what do you mean *Keira unforgivable? Stop pray?* Why would mum be unforgivable? Why would you stop praying?"

Pat inhaled and coughed, drawing her attention. She'd known him all of her life, but their relationship had become business only in the three years since the divorce. Still, she could tell from his flushed cheeks and wincing frown that he was guilty of something. "What are you not telling me?"

Pat looked sadly at her father. "I don't know what to do. Rory had secrets that he wouldn't even share with me and he made me swear upon my mother's grave not to tell ya until he was gone. After the construction office was broken into last month, he gave me a box to keep. He said it was Keira's wish for you to have the box after Rory died. I also know your father's attorney has stuff he's supposed to give ya, too, but not until Rory passes on."

Rocky stared at her him as she held onto her father's hand. A surreal tingling crawled over her. Something her mother had left for her that's been sitting hidden for five years? Why? Why would her father withhold anything about her mother? Why wait until her father dies to tell her? "I'll call the attorney in a minute. What's in the box?"

"That man is not going to be happy with me. I don't know what is in the box, Lass. It's sealed. I put it in a safety deposit box at the bank. I can bring the box to you tomorrow afternoon. I have a meeting with the concrete suppliers in the morning."

Rocky wanted immediate answers and she wasn't getting anything but frustration. "Why haven't you said anything before?"

"I swore to Rory I wouldn't. I'm still not sure I'm doing the right thing. I don't think he expected that he'd end up like this though. So if he is trying to tell you something about your mother, maybe the box will help."

Confusion and hurt warred with her love for her parents. She didn't understand why they would have done this. Why the secrets? Why leave her things to be opened only after their deaths? Why would her mother be unforgivable and beyond prayer?

"I knew something was wrong," she said, almost angry. "Da was frantic when he walked in and saw the office had been ransacked. He went immediately to the safe and appeared relieved until he opened it and went through the contents several times. After that, he seemed distracted and worried. A week later he ended up like this. Did he lie to the police when he told them nothing was missing?"

Pat shrugged. "I don't know what all was in the safe. Since Collin was cut from the company, there are some business matters that I just leave for you and your father to handle. Less tension all the way around." He sighed and studied her sadly.

"Don't say anything about him." Rocky stiffened her back. *Here it comes again. His apology for Collin's behavior. How he wished things were different. How Collin was different now.* She didn't care how long Collin Brady had been on the wagon. And she didn't care how sorry he was. Everyone thought her hard and unforgiving because she'd forced Collin from the company and she let them think that. She didn't have the heart to tell his father or her Da the "real" man beneath Collin's charm.

Pat sighed. "I won't. I've realized you and Collin are a burned bridge. I still think of you as my daughter, lass. I'm sorry my son hurt you."

She could see that Pat was still hurting from the split. "I'm sorry things are the way they are."

"I know you are and I'm worried about you. You've cut yourself off from everyone since the divorce. You need to get out and be young again. The crew's throwing a birthday party for Mack at Sally's tonight. It couldn't hurt for you to stop by for a few minutes on your way home." He chuckled. "And it would do the new boys good for you to take them down a notch or two, if you're still queen of the eight ball, that is."

Rocky bit her lip. She hadn't played pool since she'd come home from a job early and found Collin and some bar hussy in the pool room, and it wasn't the billiard balls in play either. She'd moved out the next day, but not before she'd disassembled the pool table and burned it in the backyard. "I'll be staying here. Seeing if Da speaks again."

The weight of the world settled on Pat, his shoulders slumped. "Don't answer now, lass. Think about it at least. You know Mack and your dad got on pretty good as of late. Maybe he might have an idea about what had Rory so worried."

Rocky nodded and swallowed hard. Her divorce from Collin and her father's help in forcing Collin out of the business had put a rift between her father and Pat. Pat turned to leave, but then swung back. "I mean it, lass. You're young and beautiful. Life is too short. Don't waste any more of it on hurts from the past and us old geezers. Rory will either heal or pass in God's own time and there's not much you can do to change that."

Pat left before she could respond. Part of her realized that he was right. Seeing her father was important, but being at his side every spare moment wasn't necessarily going to make him recover faster. If he did recover.

Stepping to the window for good reception, Rocky called Steve Vance, her father's attorney. She received a voice mail that said he was away on business until Tuesday. As directed, she left a message for him to call her back. She let him know that she knew her father had things for her. She told him that her father had tried to tell her something important and couldn't. Then she suggested that knowing what her father wanted her to have after his death might help him now.

Rocky stayed with her father throughout the day and by evening time, there had been no change. She went over and over in her mind what her father was referring to, trying to remember some point in her parents' lives where there'd been a rift great enough for her mother to be unforgivable and beyond prayer, but came up blank. The more she thought about it, the less sense her father's words made. Her father had loved her mother deeply until her dying breath. There was nothing unforgiven between them. By the time dark descended, her gut was a knotted mess of questions with no answers. She decided to take Uncle Pat's suggestion to see the crew at Sally's Roadhouse, hoping Mack could tell her something.

CHAPTER THREE

"*It's never been this bad* before," Jared said under his breath, as he sat on the picnic bench next to James. The condemnation and tension hanging in the air was thicker than the BBQ smoke and choking the life out of the "after ceremony" celebration. "Why in God's name did you go and pass out? I didn't realize you were that fried or I would have left your ass with the planking Aussie."

White-faced and more wretched than ever, James continued to stare at his untouched plate. "It wasn't that. Swear to God himself," he whispered, voice raw. "I don't know what in the hell happened, Jare. I was standing there, looking at everyone. You holding Jake and Jason, Alexi next to Jesse and Nan beside Jackson, and vowing on my life that I'd do whatever it took to care for the tykes, when all of a sudden Jesse and Jackson disappeared as if Scotty had beamed them up to the Enterprise. Something bad is going to happen to them, Jare."

Jared couldn't believe his ears or his eyes. James's hands were shaking and he'd turned from white to a sickly shade of green. "James, bro. You're losing it. You're tripping after the night we had, a hallucination brought on by extreme pressure and you're blowing it way out of proportion."

James turned and stared at him head on, his blue eyes bleaker that Jared believed possible. "No. I'm not. It's happened before."

Jared leaned in close. "What do you mean, it's happened before?"

"Our graduation party? Remember we were all standing there getting ready to have our picture taken? Do you remember who was with us?"

"Of course, Cal…Tyler, and Steve… and you passed out a second after the picture was taken."

James nodded. "The same thing happened then. Tyler and Steve completely disappeared from my vision. They died that night in a car accident."

"Surely you don't believe that."

James nodded.

"You've never said a word."

"What the hell was I supposed to say? I see future ghosts? It all sounds so impossibly insane, but I've always wondered if it wasn't some sort of premonition."

Jared shook his head and glanced across the yard to where Jesse and Jackson were grilling more chicken with their dad, John Weldon, who'd declared himself to be "Gramps" the day Jake was born. All three men were laughing, eyes bright and smiles confident. They were clearly on top of the world and seemingly invincible. Jared thought what James had said was beyond the realm of believable and, like he said, totally insane. Jared knew that in his head, but seeing his twin so shaken and burdened brought the sharp edge of doubt cutting through his mind.

Hell. James did not scare easily. But to believe him just wasn't something Jared could wrap his mind around. Yet now that the seed had been planted, he couldn't blow it off either. There was only one thing to do – tackle this thing head on.

He made sure Alexi and Nan were occupied. Emma Weldon, now known as "Grams," had Jason and Jake in her lap. She sat in the middle of a baby pool she'd bought, laughing at the boys splashing up a storm. Alexi and Nan stood ready to lend a hand should Emma need it.

Jared grabbed James's arm and hauled him up. "Come on."

"What?" James pulled back.

"We're telling Jesse and Jackson and Dad. That way everyone can make up their own mind."

"But…"

"But what? If they think you're crazy, it's better than them thinking you're drunk. And if they don't quite think you're crazy, it's better for them to be forewarned. Wouldn't you want to know if someone thought you were going to be in trouble?"

James exhaled as if sucker-punched. "I guess."

All three men stopped laughing at their approach. The glare in their eyes meant there was still hell to pay for this day's events. Jared jumped in the deep end, headfirst. He kept his voice low. "James has one hell of a problem that you three need to know about. The reason he passed out this morning wasn't because he had a hangover or cancer and is going to die tomorrow, but because he thinks he had a premonition that Jesse and Jackson are going to die."

Everyone stood frozen, which was saying a lot. Between Jackson's medical experience and Jesse's military, there wasn't much they hadn't seen or faced in life. James gasped for air and bent over as if he was going to pass out again. Jared caught his twin's arm in support. "Go ahead and tell them about what happened before."

James stammered out his story, staring at the ground.

Jared watched as his older brothers' expressions turn from skepticism to concern. Not necessarily for themselves, but because they realized James really believed in his promotion. Their father sat in a nearby lawn chair as if his legs had given out from beneath him. All eyes turned his way.

John grabbed a handkerchief from his shirt pocket and dotted his brow then rubbed his chest as if he had a sudden gas attack.

"What is it, Dad?" Jackson leaned in, scrutinizing as if a patient just walked into his office. "You can't think this is for real. James has made a connection in his mind between an incident and a tragic accident. That's all."

John shook his head. "My grandfather died when I was ten. I don't remember much about him, but I remember he came from Dublin, he could drink whiskey with the best, and he knew when a man's time was up. One day he'd say God bless so-and-so and keep them in His care. Then the next day the man would up and die. Happened three times that I know about."

James collapsed on the ground with a groan.

Jared ran a harried hand through his hair, seriously worried about everyone. Jesse and Jackson were bouncing their gazes between James and their dad, clearly trying to decide who was more insane.

What started out as a way to solve a problem had suddenly mushroomed into a disaster. Jared couldn't believe it. "Christ, you never mentioned this before. You were supposed to tell him he was off his rocker and there was nothing to worry about."

"James *is* off his rocker and there is *nothing* to worry about," Jesse said forcefully as he glanced over at the women and boys. "And not a word of this gets repeated to anyone. Are we all clear on that? We'll discuss this another time and meanwhile, Jackson and I will—"

"Proceed with every caution," Jackson muttered.

Everyone nodded, grasping onto Jesse's firm line of sanity.

This morning Jared didn't believe the world could get any more off kilter than it was. He was wrong.

Jackson continued. "Meanwhile, it looks to me as if James has come down with a bug, so you need to take him home to rest."

It was clear to everyone that James wasn't capable of keeping it together a minute more. Their father's revelation had pulled the rug of reasonable doubt out from under James and he looked as if he was free falling into a black abyss.

Jared hoped to God that nothing did happen to Jesse and Jackson, because Jared knew James wouldn't survive it. The next little bit passed in a blur as he shouldered James out to the Porsche, with their mother fussing and dishing out advice for the flu.

Somehow, as he headed back into town, the financial problems they faced seemed almost insignificant.

"I can't go back and sit in the condo," James said. He sat staring at the road, horror fixed in his eyes. "I need a drink."

It was on the tip of Jared's tongue to say booze was the last thing either of them needed, but he clamped his mouth shut. Maybe now wasn't necessarily the minute to turn over a new leaf. "What do you want to do?"

James shrugged. "Got a text from Dan that some of the McKenna crew will be hanging out at Sally's Roadhouse. Might as well checkout the competition."

"Good idea. It's early yet. Why don't we go visit McKenna's last job site. See what kind of work they did then head over to Sally's?"

James agreed; his relief to have something besides his premonition to think about was evident. They didn't speak during the rest of the drive. Nor did they say much upon arriving at the job site. The stone, three-story office building was impressive, a combination of stylish design and expert craftsmanship.

"When did they finish this job?" Jared asked as they got out of the car.

"Two days ago according to the social media buzz."

Jared shook his head. You couldn't tell that it had just been built. There were no telltale scraps of building materials, or a coke can, or a hamburger wrapper anywhere in a seeable radius. As they walked around the building, Jared became more and more impressed with what he saw. "I have to say the workmanship appears to be top-notch. Of course, only time will tell if the materials used were sub-par or not."

James grunted. "And there was no way to know if illegal labor had had a hand in the construction unless we'd been on the site."

"True. That has to be how they're cutting us out of the market."

James turned a three-sixty. "I think I'm ready for that drink now."

They left the job site no longer riding the same high-horse they'd arrived on. Jared headed to Sally's Roadhouse with a worried frown that he soon shook off. They'd find out how McKenna was cutting corners soon enough. After a day like today, he needed to relax.

It had been a while since they'd hit the peanut-shelling beer joints. It would be a good change from the swinging, upscale clubs of late. They pulled into a full parking lot and walked into a hoppin' place. Seemed as if every nobody in town was out tonight. He and James got the usual double-take as they settled at the bar.

Before he could even order a beer, the first thing Jared saw was the backside of a woman. She was shooting pool on the other side of the bar. Her heart-shaped ass was nicely framed by stonewashed jeans and topped the longest pair of legs he'd ever seen. Men surrounding her were moaning, groaning, hooting, and hollering as she dominated the pool table.

He watched her every move. Svelte, classy, and determined, she angled the cue this way then that way, completely absorbed by the game, unaware of the attention. She had her long black hair pulled back in a ponytail, wore a conservative-sized black T-shirt and as far as he could tell, had no makeup on her sun-kissed skin. Attention wasn't what she was after. At least not compared to the polished and painted women he'd been through recently.

"I can't believe it," James said.

"She is something," Jared added, forcing himself to look at his brother just to prove the woman hadn't cast a spell over him. James's confused frown as he glanced up from the gleaming bar, clued Jared in that they weren't on the same page. He nodded toward the woman. "I'm talking about her. What can't you believe?"

"Christ! I'm going through the biggest crisis of my life and you're checking out the local meat market?"

Jared clenched his jaw. James's words set him off. Without the distraction of the job site, James had fallen back into his premonition funk. "Bro, I'm telling you now. Don't go reading more into what Dad said. It was just an old story a ten-year-old boy believed."

"How can I not?"

"Think about it. When we were ten, Jackson and Jesse had us convinced there was a serial killer in the old saw mill. Remember? We saw that fisherman slicing open a trout in a nearby creek and we both peed our pants running home from the place. We didn't sleep for a week and nobody could convince us the guy wasn't a killer. Jesse kept telling us it was just a story he and Jackson made up.

James grinned. "Dad tanned both their butts for it, too."

"Yeah. But what did it take for us to finally believe it wasn't true?"

"We never did."

"Exactly. Nobody could tell us differently. We moved on, grew up, and eventually forgot about it. Now, Dad was ten when his grandfather died. He's going to believe stories told about him whether or not they make sense. And even if it is true, it doesn't make any real difference in your situation right now. Does it?"

"What do you mean?"

"You either have premonitions or you don't and think you do. Jesse and Jackson have been forewarned and knowing them, they aren't going to blow off what either you or Dad said. Jesse's a freaking security expert. He'll treat this like he would any threat to his family."

"You think so?"

"I do. In fact, I will call him later and tell him exactly that."

James shrugged. "I don't know. Part of me feels like I should be hounding their every step just so I can be there to stop whatever is going to happen from happening."

"Come on," Jared motioned for James to follow him.

"Where are we going?"

"Out front so we can call Jesse and Jackson and tell them how you feel and to find out whether they are taking precautions or not. If they are, then we're putting this premonition stuff to rest for the night and coming back in for a beer. If not, we'll see." He glanced back at the woman, but couldn't see her through the gathering crowd.

After five minutes on the phone with Jesse, James was convinced there wasn't anything more he could do. Jesse had cancelled his upcoming business trip and had a security detail on himself and Jackson.

"I'm warning you—you'll be on your own for a bit, bro," Jared told James. "Before I leave here tonight, I'm getting that woman's number or my name isn't Weldon."

James raised a brow, looking more like his usual self than he had all day. "Maybe I'd better take a second look at her. I haven't seen you this determined in a long time."

"Look is all you can do. She's mine," Jared muttered. There was one negative to having an identical twin. If a woman was attracted to one then odds were she'd be equally attracted to the other. It always left a little doubt.

They'd lost their premium seat at the bar, much to Jared's frustration and had to settle for a table across the room, which put a kink in his brow and had him grumbling at James over it.

"If you remember, the reason we're here has nothing to do with picking up chicks. We're supposed to be scouting out McKenna's crew."

"I said I was getting her number. I didn't say I was…have you even looked at her," Jared glared at James. "She's not that type."

James spewed his beer mid-sip. "You haven't even spoken to her yet and you already know what type she is? Come on, what's gotten into you? Do you hear yourself?"

Jared opened his mouth, then shut it. There wasn't anything he could say. There wasn't any rationale or reason to the vibe he got from her. It bothered him that James couldn't see it. Alan Jackson was crooning over the sound system about being in love with a woman whose name he didn't even know.

"I will warn you that you aren't the only guy in the room focused on her," James added.

"No duh. There're ten staring at her play pool."

"Not them. That guy back there."

Glancing over his shoulder, Jared's hackles rose. A man in the back corner was staring daggers at the woman. It was more than obvious that he had a bone of ill content to pick with her.

"He's looking like possession is the law and that he has every right to possess her," James said. "I don't need any beam-me-up-Scotty's premonition to predict that. Something bad is about to happen."

The guy downed his drink and staggered to his feet. Jared braced himself and turned his gaze on the woman. He had to know what this guy meant to her and he had his answer the moment she caught sight of the guy heading her way. Fear and anger. She was afraid of the man approaching, but not too afraid to turn her back on him.

Jared watched as the woman tossed the cue onto the pool table and pointed her finger at the men around her, clearly accusing them of something. They all stood, shaking their heads in denial. Two of them moved toward the approaching man, who promptly shoved them aside.

Jared stood and James grabbed his arm. "This isn't your business. Men get shot for sticking their nose where it doesn't belong. Sit down. She's not alone."

Two more men split from the group and went to head the guy off. They were close enough for Jared to hear them talk.

"Go home, Collin," the larger man said. "You weren't invited and Rocky doesn't want you here."

"Stay out of it, Mack. This is between me and her."

"Afraid not." The man named Mack moved to block the guy and that's when the fight broke out. The guy threw a punch, Mack ducked, and the punch caught a biker upside his tattooed head. Chaos spread like wildfire.

"Shit." James grabbed Jared's arm again. "Let's get out of here."

Jared pulled free. "Not yet."

Cut off by the fray, he saw the woman backing into a corner and headed her way. People shoved and hollered. Beer bottles flew, along with bar stools. Women yelled and men shouted. He knew she was tall but hadn't quite realized how tall until he got closer. Six foot at least. She had her gaze focused on one man. The man who'd started the fight. The man who still looked bent on getting to her, but was happy to knock a few others out on the way.

"Watch out!" Jared dove her way. Wrapping his arms around her, he brought her crashing down with his best offensive tackle, as a flying bar stool smashed into the wall where she'd been standing. He grabbed the heart-shaped ass he so admired and twisted to take the brunt of the fall. Splintered pieces of wood rained down on them.

Jared's pulse kicked up about ten notches. Just an adrenaline rush. It had nothing to do with the scorching feel of her long, lean but curved, just-right body plastered to him or the thick-lashed, narrowed green eyes, the color of spring clover, staring at him. Her curtain of dark hair fell about them, framing her face that could only be described as beautifully determined. Her sun-kissed skin glowed like warm honey and an even sweeter-looking, lush mouth softened her dominant nose, chin, and brow. She smelled of citrus and coconuts, making him want to lick just to see if she tasted that way, too.

The fear was still there in her gaze, along with surprise.

Jared spoke, hoping to reassure her. "I don't know who that jerk coming after you is, but I do know two things. He doesn't deserve to be in any universe you're in. And I'd do just about anything to take that fear out of your eyes." He slid his hands up from her delectable bottom to pull her tighter to his chest. "Please tell me he isn't your husband."

She blinked at him a moment before she exhaled and whispered. "Ex. He's my ex."

He brushed back a wave of hair that had fallen across her face. It was like heavy silk. "Best news I've heard all day. I've half a mind to kiss you and show him you've moved on to bigger and better things."

She arched a skeptical brow. "I've lost my mind, because I've half a mind to let you."

"Two halves make a whole," Jared whispered. He leaned up slowly, giving her plenty of time to back off before he claimed her full mouth. Explosive didn't come close to describing everything that coalesced in a kiss that moved from sweet to spicy with a stroke of his tongue.

The bar fight, the advancing mad-as-hell ex, the very fact that he needed air to breathe, completely disappeared from Jared's consciousness. All he could think about was the woman in his arms kissing him like there was no tomorrow.

CHAPTER FOUR

Rocky's heart sped. She went from questioning Mack about her father, as she dominated the pool table, to having Collin come after her, and lying in the strong arms of a stranger who wasn't like a stranger at all. It was as if she were free-falling into a dark, pleasurable abyss that sucked every care and worry from her mind.

Kissing her rescuer had thrust her from a half-formed notion of showing Collin she'd found someone else, into an encounter with a man who had her more aroused than she could ever remember being. Either that, or the act of kissing a stranger with her ex bearing down on her, had given her an unbelievable adrenaline rush. Because, for the first time in her life, she lost sight of where she was or who was around her. The feel of the tall, dark, and devastatingly handsome man against her had short-circuited—everything.

Being the boss over a crew of construction workers had made her draw a hard line of propriety a long time ago. She'd never let that line lax and had never let any of the men get anywhere near it. Ever. They gave her respect with a bold, capital R.

Most of the crew was at Sally's celebrating Mack's birthday and were likely getting an eyeful, but she didn't care enough to stop the moment.

Had some latent need for revenge against Collin suddenly unleashed itself?

She didn't think so. What had captured her and fueled her desire for more was the stranger kissing her. Not only did he smell and feel like heaven, but the man was a master of the kiss. The right amount of pressure. The right amount of tongue. The right amount of give, take, and tangle. He took charge enough to lead her, but then relaxed into her every move to match her. Simple sexual synergy.

Or she was so parched that anything would have been amazing. She didn't think so and she didn't get any more time to decide either. A hard hand bit into her shoulder, jerking her back.

"What the hell are you doing, bitch?" Collin yelled, his voice slurred from booze. "You're my woman!" He stood over them, face purple-red and twisted with rage.

Rocky wasn't exactly sure how, but the stranger she'd been kissing, who was still half beneath her managed to plant a boot in Collin's crotch, sending him flying backward. He hit a table before landing on the ground. Beer mugs flew.

"She's her own woman, asshole. And her name isn't bitch," the stranger said, easing her back enough to rise to a fighting crouch, planting himself between her and Collin. The stranger's devilishly blue eyes had turned deadly.

Mack and two men from her crew ran up and pulled her to her feet and away from the fight. "Rory would kill us for getting you into this. We're getting you out of here."

Rocky shook her head. Her gaze was glued to the stranger and Collin, her stomach in her throat. Everything in her wanted to shout at the stranger and tell him to be careful. Collin didn't fight fair...ever. But she couldn't get a word out.

Collin gained his feet and roared. He came at the stranger with both fists raised.

The stranger stepped cool-as-ice to the side, grabbed Collin's right fist in mid-air and forced it down. Then using her ex's rushing rage against him, he sent him careening into the wall.

Collin bounced hard. Angrier than ever, he turned. Instead of going after the stranger, he came right at her.

Mack and the guys hauled her up and dragged her away.

"No!" Rocky cried out in protest as the stranger moved to intercept Collin. She didn't want to abandon her stranger. Collin was capable of anything. But her crew shoved her out the door and into the dim parking lot where it seemed to her a lot a bad things could happen if caught out here alone.

"Wait!" she said, pulling back. She really should warn the stranger that Collin…

Mack shook his head. "No way. You're getting the hell out of here before someone gets killed. Riley, you and Zeke make sure Collin can't find his keys until he settles down. I'm following her home."

"I can take care of myself." Rocky pulled away after they reached her truck.

"I know that boss, but a man's got to be a man or he ain't nothing. For us that means getting you the hell out of harm's way. Who is that guy taking on Collin anyway?"

Rocky shrugged. There was no way in hell she'd let her crew know she'd been kissing a total stranger. "Just a friend."

"Well next time you get friendly with your friend. Don't do it with Collin around."

"What I do or don't do is none of Collin's business. Not anymore."

"You don't need to convince me. In my book he lost that right long before you left him. Problem is he hasn't figured that out yet." Mack looked back at Sally's. "Just might be your friend there is the one to drive that point home. He looked as if he could handle himself very well, but having you anywhere around is just adding fuel to the fire right now."

"Yeah, he can handle himself," Rocky whispered. *And her, too. Real well. Too well.* Her lips and body still burned. She didn't know who he was or what his name was, but maybe that was a good thing at the moment considering how she reacted to him. She needed to do some major thinking. "I'll go home, but you don't need to follow me."

Mack lifted a brow. "I promised Rory I'd take care of you."

Rocky's breath caught. "When? Did he say something before his stroke?"

"No. I told him that when I saw him in the hospital. Don't know if he could hear or not, but if he could, I thought it would make him rest easier."

She exhaled. "He was worried about something before his stroke. Did he say anything to you?"

Mack shook his head. "Rory and I mostly talked about the jobs. He did ask me if I thought you were happy a few months back and I told him that ditching Collin's shadow had done you a world of good."

"Do the words *unforgivable, stop,* and *pray* in reference to my mother mean anything to you?"

"No. Why?"

"Because Da said them to me today."

Mack grabbed her shoulders. "Really! Was he able to do anything else?"

"No. He spoke and then lapsed back into a blank vacuum."

"Still. It's a good sign, right?"

"Yeah."

Gravel crunching beneath a boot made Rocky shiver. It was too dark to see far and the thought of someone purposely lurking in the shadows made her skin crawl. She forced a smile at Mack, glad to have his support. He was somewhere in his forties and looked as if he'd weathered of few of life's storms and hadn't always come out on top.

Mack looked around. "Let's get you home before they bring the fight outside. I'll be right behind you, okay?"

Rocky nodded and climbed into her truck. As she drove home, the feeling that her life had spun around and was careening blindly into the unknown overshadowed her. Implausible events had happened. Collin's rage had reared an ugly head after staying on the sidelines long enough for her to almost forget him. Her parents' had death secrets that remained beyond her grasp. And she'd been in the arms of a stranger whose kiss she didn't want to forget—ever.

Jared knew to his core that only a fool, a dead fool, took his eyes off his opponent in a fight. No matter what. Still, when he heard the woman cry out, he glanced her way and it cost him. If it hadn't been for the mirror over the bar and James's warning shout from the crowd, the woman's bruiser of an ex would have nailed Jared at the base of his skull with a bar stool. Instead, Jared took the brunt of the blow on his shoulder and ended up getting a bloody nose, before knocking his opponent out.

It was a good ten minutes before Jared reached James on the sidelines.

Two well-endowed blondes clung to him for protection. He looked like the perfect knight in shining armor. "I told Chloe and Ginger we'd walk them to their car."

Jared nodded and headed for the front door. Just maybe they'd get out before the cops arrived. He'd yet to be able to let go of his nose and seriously wondered if he hadn't broken the damn thing. That's what he got for sticking it into someone else's mess. He didn't know the woman's name, much less her number.

And while the kiss had been out of this world hot, the more he thought about it, the more wretched he became. She was obviously a woman in a very bad situation and part of him felt as if he'd taken advantage of her. He could have just as well busted her ex's chops without having coerced her into an all-out public kiss-fest on a barroom floor. Some class. Some style. Some hero. It didn't help that he hadn't meant to carry the kiss that far. The fact is he did.

He needed to find her and apologize and hope beyond hope that she'd want to see him again. Because for the first time in a long damn time, maybe even ever, he really, *really* wanted to see her again.

James pocketed both Chloe and Ginger's number before seeing the blondes off—in a green mini-van. Jared didn't have to ask to know James would not be calling. Mini-van meant kids and James had a rule that he didn't date a woman with baggage. Kids were complications he wanted to add on *his* timetable and not one already pre-set.

"You okay to drive?" James asked.

Jared tossed James the keys and headed for the passenger's seat. "Better safe than sorry."

"You're damn lucky not to be leaving in an ambulance. That guy was bent on dealing you a lethal blow. Was she worth it? Did you get her number?"

Jared groaned and rested his head back as he nursed his nose. "I didn't even get her name."

"Thought so or you'd be a lot more pissed right now." James shifted gears fast and pulled out onto the highway, nearly pushing the Porsche to ninety in mere seconds.

"What do you mean by that? And for Christ's sake slow down. We can't afford the ticket or the hospital bill."

James downshifted and settled close to the speed limit. "While you were kissy-facing the woman and bouncing her man, I asked a few questions."

"He's not her man. He's her ex."

"With a lot more of a bone to pick with her than who gets custody of Fluffy."

"Huh? Are you saying she's got kids with that jackass?"

"No."

Jared cracked an eye at James. "Then what?"

"Her name is Rocky McKenna. She is currently the R. McKenna running McKenna Construction since her father fell ill last month. *The very company putting us out of business.* And her ex is Collin Brady, the son of her father's business partner. She ousted Collin from the company after their divorce three years ago. He'd apparently been working for the company as long as she has, but she and her father have controlling interest. According to gossip, she is one hard Irish woman and it isn't because she wears a hard hat."

Jared pinched his nose as he felt another rush of blood. "What a clusterfuck."

"Actually no," James said. "It's freaking perfect. Today you were her hero. And tomorrow, you're going to waltz into her office and check things out. You're going to discover what illegal corners McKenna Construction is cutting."

Jared's denial died in his throat. He would go see her tomorrow to apologize, but that was it. Anything else they discovered would have to be done differently.

Nursing a gourmet hot chocolate, Rocky nearly scalded her cleavage when someone pounded on the door. She had the lights off, curtains drawn and taped shut, her doors locked, and her truck parked in the garage. She had 911 pre-dialed on her cell phone. All she had to do was press *send*. She even had her car keys in her pocket, just in case she needed a quick escape. She had her shotgun loaded, but it was hidden and would stay hidden. Shooting was the last measure she didn't want to ever have to take.

It wasn't until after Mack left and Rocky got to reliving what happened in the bar that she realized just how pissed off and drunk Collin had been. She had no doubt that he'd come after her. Her heart pounded hard and her hand shook so bad she barely got the cup to the coffee table.

Another pounding knock was followed by a bark.

"Rocky? It's Dessie? You okay?"

Shuddering with relief, Rocky rushed to the door. "You two are a sight for sore eyes," she said, giving Dessie *and* Pebbles a huge hug.

"Can't say the same about you. You look like hell. What's going on?" Dessie pressed her palm to Rocky's forehead. "Last time your house was dark at nine at night you had the flu, a fever of one-hundred-and-four and needed the hospital."

"I wish it was the flu." Rocky locked and dead-bolted the door as soon as Dessie and Pebbles were inside— actions that had Dessie raising both brows.

"Better dish out the whole story fast, girl. I'm not liking any of this."

Rocky spilled it all, starting from her father's cryptic words, to Collin's rage and to the stranger's searing kiss.

"First thing, there is no point in worrying and wrangling about your parents' stuff. Time enough for that when you get your hands on something concrete. God only knows what drives parents to leave confessions from the grave. In my opinion if it wasn't worth saying while alive then they should keep it that way. Nothing you can do about it tonight, right?"

Rocky found herself nodding agreement. Leave it to Dessie to put a mountain into anthill perspective.

"Second thing you're going to do is spend the night with me and have a drink or two. Any argument there?"

"Or three," Rocky added, finding her voice amid the grateful rush of emotion. If it wasn't for Dessie, Rocky realized that she would really be alone, just as Uncle Pat had worried.

"The third thing is you're going to tell me the last part of that story all over again. The man-kiss part. Damn. He must be something. To get you to do in seconds what I've been pushing you to do for years is beyond believable."

Rocky laughed.

"The fourth thing we are going to do is figure out what you've got to do to be comfortable in your house and do it. I know one sexy-as-hell bouncer you'd just love having around for a while and he'd make mincemeat of your ex."

"Have I told you lately that I love you?" Rocky smiled through her threatening tears. She hated herself for this weakness. She wished like hell she could march right up to Collin, plaster his ass to the ground and walk away, leaving him to cower in fear.

"Not nearly enough, dear. Now let's get the PJ party on the road, but don't forget your shotgun. My Bessie hasn't been oiled in a while, so no telling what she'd do in a pinch."

"I'll bring my kit and clean her up for you." Rocky left the room, thinking what a difference a friend makes.

Everything from the day's events and the past that had been crashing down on her moments ago had been pulverized to dust. By the time she walked into Dessie's house and cleaned her friend's shotgun, she was almost wishing Collin did show up just so she could show him that she wasn't afraid of him.

"You do that like an expert," Dessie said.

"What?"

"Handle that gun."

"With what goes on in today's world, a woman needs to know the business ends of her weapons."

"Oh, I know the business end of a gun, doesn't mean I can handle it like a, pro."

Rocky shrugged. "I'll take you to the shooting range. It won't take you long to learn." She set the unloaded weapons on the counter and washed the gun oil off her hands.

"Deal," Dessie said moving into the living room. "Speaking of hot guns. What's his name? This miracle man who managed to kiss your socks off?" She plopped down on her zebra print couch and sank deep into a sea of pink satin pillows.

Sighing, Rocky joined her. "I don't know."

"What do you mean?"

"I've never seen him before. He just showed up in the middle of the bar fight and took on Collin."

"This is great. I'll call Sally tomorrow. She'll be able to playback surveillance and we can ID your mystery man in a jiffy."

"You sound like one of those high-tech spy shows. You going to run his picture through a computer or something?"

"Honey, nothing so complicated as that. If he was in that bar, he had to have had a drink, which means he had a waitress and these days he likely used plastic. Just leave it to Dessie. I will find your man. What you have to decide is what you're going to do with him when I do."

That was one question she did not what to answer at the moment. *Would. Should.* And *Could,* were often worlds apart. "What did you decide to do with yours?" Rocky asked, turning the tables.

"My what?" Dessie blinked.

"Your Redford hunk. What did you decide to do with him? And what is his name. You've never said."

"He goes by the name of Saint. Don't ask me why because there is nothing saintly to what his bedroom eyes incite. But fantasy is as far as it will ever go. The young man has a whole life to live in front of him. I've lived most of mine already. And even though I can be talked into gratuitous sex on occasion, wisdom demands that I draw the line. He's too young."

"We'll see," Rocky said.

Dessie's eyes went wide open then narrowed with suspicion. "That's exactly what he said."

"Great minds," she replied.

Dessie shook her head. "More like insane minds. Speaking of which, let's go ahead and open the can of worms though there's no place for them to crawl. What's this with your parents' after death deliveries? And what exactly did your father try and say?"

Rocky retold the story.

"Hmm. So both your mom and your dad felt the need to leave you something to see after they've moved on to the Blue Sky Mansion."

"Yes, according to Pat they have. He's got the box from my mother and supposedly the lawyer has stuff from Da."

"You know this doesn't sound like it's going to be good, especially from your mom. If it was just love-letters an ill-parent writes to their child, your father would have given them to you by now. You also realize that the lawyer isn't going to let you have any of your father's things. He'll be bound by ethics and law to only deliver them after your father's death."

"I can only try. I have power of attorney for my father, so maybe that will make a difference. I am more worried about the effect on my father's current health. He's trying to tell me something important. Maybe knowing their secrets will help. Something needs to help me figure out what my father meant. He loved my mother."

"Close your eyes and think about her for a few minutes. What comes to mind?"

Rocky followed Dessie's lead. "Quiet, gentle, creative. She had dark hair like me, but her eyes were china blue and she had *fragile, handle with care* stamped all over her. Whereas I'm like the Dodge truck commercials—ram tough." Rocky laughed. "She was petite and into fashion. Growing up I was the ultimate tomboy and I was huge. She'd put me in white lace for church and I'd end up wrestling in the grass with the boys. She wrote in her spare time, whenever she wasn't running the construction office or taking care of Da or me. Poems and short stories."

"What were they like?"

"Tidbits about Ireland, her childhood. She didn't have an easy time of it. Her stories were often sad," Rocky whispered and drew a deep breath, realizing now that her mother had been a solitary, melancholy person. "It's been a while since I've read any of her work. Even when she was sick, she kept writing and self-published collections of her poems and short stories. I have her books on my shelf."

"Seems to me that one way to understand what your father might be trying to say about your mom, is to go back and remember the person your mother was."

"Good idea. When I get home tomorrow night, I'll pull out her books. Tomorrow is a big day. We start the Drake Hotel renovations. I want to be onsite by seven."

Dessie crossed her eyes. "You might have mentioned that *before* I invited you for a PJ party. Pebbles, you're in charge of breakfast and seeing our guest off."

Rocky laughed. "What is she going to serve me? A dog biscuit?"

"Yes. They are gourmet. All natural, organic, and teeth-sinking good. Bacon, egg, and cheese *is* her favorite flavor. She had one for dessert tonight."

"I think I got a whiff of that when I kissed her earlier."

"Speaking of kisses. On a scale of one to ten, how does your stranger rate?"

"Twenty." Rocky sighed.

"Really? Twenty?" Dessie practically fell off the couch. "Oh, honey! I'm having a hot flash just thinking about it. You need to get him bedroom bound ASAP. Do not waste a minute of talent like that."

Rocky rolled her eyes. "Let's watch a movie."

Dessie arched a brow. "I'll let it go for now, but you can't hide from yourself forever. What do you want to watch?"

"*Flirting with Forty*," Rocky said with a grin. They'd both read the book based on author Jane Porter's real life experience about finding love with a younger man.

"You play dirty girlfriend. We'll watch it, but then you've got homework tonight."

"What?"

"You'll see." Dessie smiled.

Two hours later, movie finished, couch made into a bed, and several Bailey's Irish Creams a piece down the hatch, Dessie tossed a small book in Rocky's lap as she said goodnight.

"What's this?" Rocky picked it up.

"Your homework."

"*Pocket Guide to Kama Sutra*. Seriously?"

Dessie grinned, using Rocky's earlier tone of voice. "In today's world, a woman needs to know how to handle big guns on and off the shooting range. Just because you know your way around the bedroom doesn't mean you can't become an expert at the art of love. Night, night." Dessie made a bee-line for her bedroom.

Rocky stared at the book a minute. Hours later she concluded, it was more than curiosity that killed the cat. Intimate images filled her mind and her body was on fire.

Chapter Five

James slammed the truck door and headed for their office in Weldon Estates' model home. Jared winced as he followed his twin. He half expected the rusty hinges to break on the old Ford they'd borrowed from their dad earlier.

Nine o'clock in the morning and reality already had them by the short hairs with no Starbucks to soften the pain. His Porsche and James's Jaguar were back at the leasing company, and they were reduced to their Shamrock Construction work truck and the beat-up pick-up they'd shared in high school. Degrees in business, architecture, and award-winning house designs had done zip to insulate them from a sagging economy.

Besides the money issue, James was still on edge about his "premonition" of Jesse and Jackson. He'd spoken to both brothers this morning...at six AM. Jared was pretty sure James hadn't slept all night and wasn't taking Jared's news well.

"I can't believe you. Our asses are on the line and you have the perfect opportunity to find out what underhanded crap is going on with McKenna Construction that's putting us out of business. But instead of checking things out, you're going to go apologize for kissing her?"

"Yeah, I am. I shouldn't have coerced her into it."

James pressed his palms to his temples. "A Weldon kiss gave that girl the best five seconds of her life and you're going to apologize and walk away? Either her ex knocked a screw loose in your brain or she castrated you. If McKenna Construction was being run by a man you'd have no qualms about checking things out."

Jared frowned. Considering Rocky's response to his kiss, he couldn't argue about it being a damn good five seconds. Hell, it might even be the best five seconds of *his* life as well. He didn't want to "walk away" from her, but given who he was, and what he wanted, it was the only honorable thing to do. He wasn't going to use her, or their kiss, as a way to spy on her company.

"You're right. But then if a man was running McKenna Construction, I wouldn't have kissed him. We'll find out what we want without me screwing her over. She's got enough assholes in her life as it is. I refuse to add to it."

"I don't get how looking around screws her over. But since it eats at your conscience, why don't I take your place? I'll go see her, pretend to be you for a day or two and find out how they are consistently underbidding us."

It had been a long time since Jared wanted to plant his fist in James's face. He sucked in air, and glared.

James raised his hands in surrender and backed off. "Damn, bro. Forget I mentioned it. You're screwed, blued, tattooed, and delusional. Good luck and send me an invite."

"What the hell does that mean?"

"It means I hope our shared DNA doesn't mean a shared fate."

The phone rang and James answered. He hung up after a short conversation and shook his head. "Weird."

"What?"

"The couple from L.A. coming to see the spec house. They sound as if they've already bought it."

"Isn't that a good thing?"

James shrugged. "I guess. Unusual, given the economy. They'll be here in fifteen."

"My cue to head out. I've an apology to deliver."

"I bet you my last dollar that your noble-ass is incapable of walking away from her," James muttered.

Jared pretended he didn't hear. Walking away from her was just until he could settle his professional bone with McKenna Construction. It didn't mean he wasn't going to pick up where their kiss left off ASAP.

He drove all the way to McKenna Construction's main office thirty minutes into South Carolina only to discover that Roxanne McKenna wasn't there. Folks had to have recognized him from the bar fight last night, because he practically had to pull teeth to find out where Roxanne McKenna was. She was back in Savannah at the Drake Hotel, already setting up her crew for the job. The woman apparently didn't waste a minute.

Jared spent the return trip rehearsing what to say without sounding like an idiot, but ended up empty handed. Frustrated, he turned his thoughts to the job McKenna Construction had just outbid them on. During the turn of the century, Anderson Drake had had all of George Washington Biltmore's vision of creating an unforgettable estate, but only half the money and acreage. Word was, to finish his dream, he'd made a deal with Chicago crime bosses during Prohibition and ran liquor through tunnels leading from the estate to the Savannah River.

The association had cost him, though. Five years later, Anderson Drake had been murdered, gunned down in the middle of the night, staining the foyer of his dream with his blood. The murder went unsolved and the Drake Hotel joined several other Savannah landmarks as being "haunted." Over the years a couple of owners had met tragic ends at the hotel and two women guests

had disappeared in the last decade. It was whispered that
Anderson Drake's ghost was responsible.

Jared chalked it up to bad luck and tourists wandering off into
the surrounding marsh lands. Gators lurked in the brackish water
and were known to snatch an unsuspecting bystander if they got
too close. Recently, the hotel had been part of a bitter divorce
battle between a philandering husband, Brian Bentley and his
philanthropist wife, Tiffany Parker Bentley. The wife won and she
was gutting the place like only a woman scorned could. News
reports had the husband currently stewing in jail for assault.

Jared pulled into the parking lot, surprised at the bustle of
activity already surrounding the hotel. McKenna Construction
office trailers had been set up. Industrial dumpsters were in place
and delivery trucks with supplies lined the parking area.

As he exited his truck, searching for the woman who'd snagged
his attention even before she'd appeared on scene, he felt as if he'd
been blown to Oz. The site looked as if it had been underway for a
week rather than a day.

The hotel's four wings and six floors were ringed by balconies
sporting massive white columns and urns of bright flowers. Inside,
twenty-foot high ceilings, intricately carved molding, Italian
Marble, and Byzantine glass mosaics dominated the first floor.
Jared's hands and guts ached that he and James didn't get the job.
Being able to renovate such a treasure would have been an
experience of a lifetime. Not finding Roxanne in the large lobby
area, he decided to check the perimeter before braving the envy the
upper floors of the hotel would deliver.

Giving one last look at the drool-worth artistry surrounding
him, he plowed into someone rushing into the hotel as he was
exiting.

The woman's hard hat hit him mid-chest and she stepped back with a gasp.

"Bloody hell, I need coffee." The buxom redhead wrestled with the clipboard in her hand then frowned at him. "You had better get a hard hat before the boss lady chews your ass."

Jared raised a brow. It would seem Roxanne McKenna was a force to be feared. "I'll do that," he said and stepped to the side. She went on about her business and he snatched a hard hat from a nearby truck then headed around the hotel's perimeter.

Sprawling live oaks, lush gardens, fountains, and cobblestone paths surrounded the hotel. Absolutely beautiful and would need extra care not to damage during the renovation process. He heard Roxanne's voice as he turned the corner. She and a man were standing with their backs to the hotel facing another man who had his gaze fixed to the ground.

"We clear on this, Riley Scott? I'm a fair woman, but I will not be disrespected on the job. You have an issue with me or one of my decisions, then you make an appointment and the management will review your complaint."

A standard hard hat sat easy on her head. She wore work jeans rather than the causal, form hugging ones she'd had on before, but the over-sized T-shirt was a familiar look. This one was powerhouse red and barely gave a hint at the full curves he'd felt pressed to his chest last night.

Now that Jared finally had eyes on her, he froze. He knew who she was, but she didn't know him from Adam and he was beginning to wonder if the whole apology thing was a bit over the top. What if he was attaching more importance to the incident than she was? Maybe he needed to feel her out about things first, and that wasn't going to happen on a job site.

He almost turned around to leave for now, but then decided to at least introduce himself and ask if she'd had trouble from her ex. Jared had spent a restless night thinking about that jerk unleashing his rage on her. His only consolation had been that the crew men hustling her out the door had seemed very protective of her.

Three long strides into the twenty feet separating them, he heard concrete scrape then saw in horrifying slow motion a huge planter falling from the top floor's balcony headed right at the group below.

"Watch out!" Jared sprinted and spread his arms as Roxanne and the man beside her looked over their shoulder at him, clueless. The man facing them looked up and stumbled back. Rather than take time he didn't have to explain, he dove at the two in danger, hoping he had enough momentum to knock them to safety. He hit them low, knowing from his football days that would send them farther out.

Even before they slammed into the ground, pain shot up Jared's left leg as a heavy weight pinned his boot to the ground. Roxanne had been in the center of his tackle, which meant his face was now planted between her legs, just inches away from her delectable ass. He didn't have a clue as to where his hard hat had flown. He just knew there was nothing to insulate him from her softness.

She'd landed on her stomach hard and lay gasping for air, trapped beneath his weight. Blue forget-me-nots and dirt surrounded them.

The men recovered first, one scrambling to his knees, the other rushing forward.

"Son of a bitch!"

"What the hell happened?"

"A planter fell," Jared muttered.

Roxanne squirmed, trying to twist around to see him. "You again!" She glanced at her men. "Don't just stare. Help me up."

Sweat beading his brow, Jared planted his hands on each side of Roxanne's hips and lifted his body up from hers. He moaned as pain shot up his left leg. "Hurry."

She scrambled free and gained her knees as she faced him. "You're hurt."

"Maybe. Might just be pinned. Boots are reinforced with steel."

"Dear God. This is unbelievable. Mack, on the count of three, you and Riley lift the planter and I'll help him slide free," Roxanne directed. She slid in front of him and hooked her arms under his. This left his head rooted against her breasts and he inhaled, letting her citrus and coconut scent imbue him with a sense of the tropics—steamy sun and bare skin.

She counted. The men lifted, and Jared, using his right leg, helped Roxanne to free him from the planter. He flipped onto his back. The pain in his leg worsened and he sucked in air.

Positioning herself at his side, she slid her hands down his legs. "Can you feel me?"

His gaze met hers. She was a picture of raw beauty, crisp green eyes brimming with worry, tanned skin, full bottom lip trapped beneath pearly white teeth. Christ. "Yeah, I can feel you," he whispered, his voice scraping over the jagged lump of need she evoked.

"Call an ambulance," she said, likely mistaking his want of her for overwhelming pain. He hurt, but it wasn't killing him, not like having her all over him was.

"No. No ambulance." He laughed. "You make it sound as if I'm dying. My name's Jared Weldon. In case you need to write it on my tombstone."

She glared at him. "Not funny, Jared. This is my job site. Any man goes down for any reason he gets cleared by the hospital. No exceptions. So don't argue."

"Fine. I'll get checked. My brother's a doctor, so save the ambulance for someone having a heart attack. I can drive myself."

"Wrong. If anything, I'll be taking you." She set her hand on his chest as if to settle the issue.

Jared slid his hand over hers and lowered his voice. "It isn't me you need to worry about."

Her clover eyes widened and her pupils darkened with desire before she slid her hand away. "What do you mean?"

Jared took heart. She was just as responsive to his touch as his kiss. "You need a bodyguard. That planter had help finding its way to the ground. I heard a scrape just before it fell."

He sucked in another breath and shivered. *Dear God. What would have happened to her if he hadn't shown up?*

The men cursed and Roxanne raised a brow. "Mack, go check out where this sucker came from and find out from Maggie who's on today's work list for that area."

"Yes, ma'am." Mack hurried off.

"I heard this place was haunted," Riley muttered, looking around as if a knife was inches from his throat.

Roxanne rolled her eyes. "You men have been muttering about ghosts and curses all day. It's all nonsense, Riley. Now make yourself useful. Bring the first aid kit and move my truck as close to this side of the building as you can."

Riley walked away with a frown.

Jared shook his head. "No truck. I don't need you to take me—"

"You don't get to decide. Around here, I'm the boss. Your job is to listen and comply unless you've got a damn good reason not to. Then I'm all ears."

Jared's jaw dropped a moment before he could snap it shut. Roxanne McKenna ran a tight-assed ship and didn't put up with shit. Hell, if he heard right, she even had lists delineating who was to be where when.

"Right now. We need to focus on getting your boot off before your foot becomes too swollen to get it off. That's one experience you do not want to go through. I know."

"Okay." Jared leaned up on his elbows to watch her unlace his boot. He was surprised to see how bent the boot was. As if the metal support had buckled. Her movements were gentle and precise. She seemed to know what she was doing, and Jared found himself relaxing and letting her take charge. Since she was determined to have him checked out, he might as well enjoy the ride. And in all honestly, he didn't have a good reason why she shouldn't accompany him.

In fact, there were several damn good reasons why she should, besides the bonus of getting to spend some alone time with her. If she was with him then no more planters could mysteriously fall and no asshole ex could abuse her.

The more he thought about it, the more convinced he became that she needed to take his bodyguard comment seriously. He would call Jesse at Sheridan-Weldon Solutions ASAP to see about doing just that.

Something sinister was up. It was likely rooted in her ex's rage. The man didn't necessarily have to be on the jobsite to be behind the planter incident. The man had worked for the company for a number of years and odds that one of the crew might be more loyal to the ex than to their current lady boss were good.

Roxanne completely removed the lace from his boot then eased the tongue as loose as possible.

"Wiggle your toes and tell me what you feel."

"My sock." He winced. A wet one at that. She was about to get a face full of work-boot BO.

"No time for smart ass remarks."

"If you're asking if I can move my toes then the answer is yes. If you're asking if it feels good, the answer is no. I don't think they're broken though."

"Good. I'm going to pull now. Let me know if I need to stop." She inched his boot off. It was already much tighter than usual. The pain shooting up his leg had him fisting his hands. He sighed once free of the boot, but then gasped as he looked down. The blood soaking his sock gave him a shock. Maybe he was more injured than he thought.

Riley returned with a tackle-box-sized first-aid kit and with him a crowd of men and the clipboard carrying woman Jared had run into earlier.

"What in the bloody hell happened?" The woman knelt beside Roxanne.

"Planter fell." Roxanne pulled some supplies from the kit. "Maggie, help me by holding his heel up off the ground."

The Maggie woman eased her hand under his heel. "Damn. These old places are a hazard."

"Or haunted," Riley added, causing a stir among the gathering crowd.

Jared would have argued with them both but was in too much pain at the moment.

Roxanne didn't respond as she peeled the leg of his jeans up. Blood had completely saturated his sock. Her complexion had paled and Jared couldn't blame her. It wasn't the simple little scratch he'd first thought. "I'm leaving your sock on and going to wrap your calf and foot in gauze and an ace bandage, which should stop the bleeding until we get you to the ER."

He nodded. With adept efficiency, Roxanne had him wrapped in minutes then stood and glared at everyone. "There're no ghosts and the show is now over. Everyone needs to get back to work. We can't afford to lose a day on this job," she said. "Mack you're in charge. Maggie, give him the assignment list and call me if there are any problems."

Everyone hopped to work. Before Jared could think much less say Jack Rabbit, he found himself loaded into the backseat of her truck and Roxanne climbed into the driver's seat. The sharp edge of his pain had eased some with the bandaging and Jared welcomed the respite.

Mack came up to her and whispered into her ear as she put the truck into gear. She nodded then hit the gas as Mack backed away. A deep frown creased her brow. "I'm thinking you need to go to the hospital."

Jared shook his head. "Jackson specialized in Emergency Medicine just out of med school, so I'm sure he can handle this." He gave her directions to the Midtown Clinic then waited until she was on the road before he brought up the subject of the planter fall and his concerns for her safety.

"What did he find?"

"Mack?"

"Yeah."

"An empty sixth floor. None of the crew had made it to that floor yet. On the balcony he found the base cementing the planter in place was cracked in half. All it needed was a hefty push."

"A crime of convenience or was it preplanned?"

"Preplanned?"

"Yes, as in someone cracked the base before you were onsite."

She shook her head. "On the off chance that I'd just happen to stand underneath it?"

"You did."

"I wasn't alone."

"You would have taken the full force of the blow, though. As far as I can tell, you're the only one wearing a red shirt on the site. I'm betting whoever pushed that planter knew you were there."

The bodyguard idea wouldn't stop knocking on his brain. Jesse provided security. One phone call would have her taken care of. Jared had two problems though. One, he wondered if he was overreacting. And two, he didn't want some other guy at her side, spending time with her. If a guy was going to do that, he wanted to be that man.

"Maybe," she said. "Mind telling me how you found me and why you hunted me down at work?"

"You think I'm responsible?"

"Good Lord, no. But you're the last person I expected to see today."

Jared sucked in air. Truth time. Only he couldn't bring himself to it. Revealing he was a competitor might break the tenuous thread forming between them. He had no idea what devil snatched his soul, but it happened fast. "I work with my brother. And you need Sheridan-Weldon Solutions. It's a security company that helps folks in need. I worried all night that your ex would hunt you down and finish that fight he started. I wanted to make sure you were all right and maybe offer my services until your ex got a grip or the law does it for him." Jared narrowed his gaze at her. "Did he show up last night?"

"Not that I know of." Relief filled her expression. Her fear of her ex was real. "I stayed at my neighbor's house."

"Damn."

"What?"

"It just pisses me off. That man has no right to make you fear being in your own home. If you don't mind my asking, what did he do to you?"

Roxanne didn't say anything for a long moment then she changed the subject. "Collin's rage last night doesn't correlate to what happened with the planter today. He wasn't even on site."

Jared let the subject of finding out what her ex did go for now and gave her the loyal-to-her-ex crewman theory. "Any man on the job could have pushed that planter."

"Good point." She narrowed his gaze. "How is it you know so damn much about my life?"

"I ask questions and people talk. It's what security guys do." He swallowed hard, wondering if the lump in his throat was the beginning of a noose around his neck. "So, after I get patched up here, I want you to give serious thought to letting me hang around for a bit."

"Provided you'll be functional, are you asking me to hire you as my bodyguard?"

"No. Not hire. This one's on me."

"Why?"

"Let's just say I take issue with abusive assholes, and I want this to be on a personal level, not a professional one. I'll apologize for coercing a kiss from you last night, but I am not in the least bit sorry that I did. And I'm very interested in repeating it, which makes this situation a very personal one." He gave her his best salesman smile." Besides with my leg injured, I'll be officially off the job for a few days until I'm back to full speed so I might as well be useful while I recuperate."

He swore her lips twitched with a suppressed smile. "You're serious?"

"Dead serious. If you have any questions about my character, I can give you references to check." He crossed his fingers, hoping she'd forgo that step. Considering the way he and James had been bacheloring-it-up lately, his reputation might not be so sterling. And there was the matter of his leading her into a lie. He did work with his brother. His brother James not Jesse. And she did need Sheridan-Weldon Solutions.

"Let's see what the doctor has to say first. You might end up in the hospital instead."

Jared hoped not. If Jackson wanted to hospitalize him, Jared just might have to go AMA. The thought of him not being around to stop anything bad happening to Roxanne was unacceptable. Then again, unless he figured out a way to keep all his misleading white-lies secret when they saw Jackson, his plan was completely screwed.

Roxanne pulled into the parking lot of Jackson's clinic and Jared braced himself. His shit was about to hit the Weldon brothers' fan of abuse and fly everywhere for years to come. Even if they let him get away with his deception right now, he'd never

live it down. He was sure that once he knew Roxanne was safe
and told her the truth that she'd understand why he'd had to do it.

But as he hopped into the clinic with Roxanne's help, pain
jarring his every move, he heard in his mind his twin James
laughing. *Screwed, blued, tattooed and delusional.*

CHAPTER SIX

Rocky had to blink twice and pinch herself as she helped Jared into his brother's clinic. Last night's kiss amid the bar fight happened so fast that she really hadn't trusted her impression of the devastating stranger who'd come to her rescue. She'd thought her addled mind had blown him out of proportion. That his eyes weren't quite that blue or his hair quite that silky black. That he wasn't quite that tall or quite that perfectly sculpted. That the cleft in his chin and the dimples when he smiled weren't that sexy, or that the spark of humor and desire in his eyes weren't that captivating…well, that the entire package didn't just send her off the deep end of desire.

She'd been sure her imagination had filled in the blanks because she could not have possibly absorbed all that she had in their short encounter.

As for the perfect kiss and his mastery of tongue and senses, by morning she'd decided her experience with him had been a combination of starvation and adrenalin. If the book Dessie had given her could make her burn as badly as she had, then any drink would have likely been a life saver to a woman parched as she. Over three years in a barren desert was a long damn time.

Well, maybe not any drink. She'd rather die than partake of her ex.

Unfortunately, everything she'd imagined Jared Weldon to be, she was finding he was. Twice in a row he'd knocked her off her feet, literally and figuratively. She'd followed him into a kiss last night, and as she walked in with him to the clinic, she found herself seriously entertaining the idea of letting him stick around for a little while.

Only as a bodyguard, of course. Jared made a good Collin deterrent and Dessie had advised that Collin would be forced to realize the past was completely over if Rocky moved on into another relationship. It had nothing to do with getting him bedroom-bound.

Liar. Liar. Pants on...

Damn. Her pants had definitely been on fire last night. Images from the book Dessie had given her kept playing in her mind, only she and this stranger at her side took center stage. *Don't go... there.*

How could she not? He more than intrigued her. *Good Lord get a grip, woman. You sound like a sappy teenager.*

The fact that he was a stranger to her was becoming less and less a factor, minute by minute.

The Midtown Clinic was simple, clean, and functional, but not overdone. The elderly receptionist greeted him with familiarity and concern. "Good heavenly day, boy. What have you gone and done?"

"Not sure, Mary. Jackson in?"

"Yeah. Come on with me." Rocky felt the woman's scrutiny as she helped Jared to an exam room. "Where's James? He okay?"

"James is fine," Jared told the woman, then met Rocky's gaze. "There are four of us. Jackson, Jesse, James, and me."

"And all of you are devils with more on the way," the receptionist said. "Jake and Jason are following in the Weldon's wild footsteps, for sure."

"Hey, my nephews are both under two."

"And they already have that lady killer gleam in their eyes. You sit back and let me get Jackson. The nurse had to leave early today, so we're on our own."

The receptionist left and Jared slumped on the exam table a little too quickly. Rocky had taken his light banter with the woman as a sign that he was less injured than she thought, but maybe not. He looked pale and sweat beaded his brow. She took charge. "Let's get you comfortable."

Slipping her arms beneath his legs, she helped him lay back on the table. When she'd bandaged his leg at the job, she had rolled his jeans to the knee, which enabled her to see. Just moving from the car to the clinic had caused blood to seep through the bandage. She hoped the clinic had everything an ER had. If it didn't, she was prepared to fight Jared and take his ass to the hospital.

Quick and efficient, she removed his other boot and undid the top buttons of his shirt to cool him off. But no matter how much she tried to dismiss it, the supple, heated feel of him was like an addictive drug. She wanted to touch and feel more. He watched her every move. It was nerve-racking.

Looking for a breather, she went in search of something else to help. She located paper towels and nabbed some water from the sink. Jared had his eyes shut when she returned. He opened them the moment she placed the cool cloth on his forehead. Their gazes met and her stomach clenched at the intensity in his blue eyes. He may be injured, but there was no mistaking the sensual hunger that reached out and grabbed her.

I want this to be on a personal level and not a professional one.

Damn, why was her pulse racing? The exam room door opened and she turned with relief, albeit, a short lived respite. Jared sat up and placed an unsteady hand around her waist, urging her closer to him.

"Jackson, bro. Meet Roxanne McKenna of McKenna Construction Company. I need you to call Jesse and tell him I'm going to be out of work for a few days. I'm going to see to her security while recuperating from this." He motioned to his foot.

Jackson frowned. "Did you say Jesse?"

"Yup. Jesse."

During the exchange, Rocky eased from Jared's hold and held her hand out to Jackson. He shook it with a hard, firm grip. There was no mistaking they were brothers. They'd been cut from the same deadly tall-dark-and-handsome cloth. "Call me Rocky. And we'll see about him playing hero after we find out how bad he's hurt."

"Playing? Thought I did more than that." Jared groaned.

Jackson who'd seemed frozen in place for a moment released her hand and focused on Jared. "What happened?"

"A cement planter fell six stories and pinned his boot to the ground," Rocky answered.

"A cement planter that was *pushed* from a sixth floor balcony and *aimed* at your head," Jared said, glaring at her. "And you're welcome for saving you."

Rocky bit her lip. She'd been so stunned, busy, and worried that she hadn't said anything about his rescue. "Thank you," she whispered.

Jared grinned as if he'd won a prize. "You're welcome."

"Well, let's see the damage." Jackson sanitized his hands and slipped on a pair of exam gloves. "Nice work," he said as he unbandaged Jared's leg.

"She is," Jared muttered.

Rocky would have elbowed him except she noticed the strain of pain on Jared's face and guessed he was grasping at straws to distract himself.

Jackson laughed. "You must not be too bad if you're thinking that."

Jared rolled his eyes. "I'm a Weldon."

"Good point," Jackson said as he slid the sock off Jared's foot. Bloodied and already bruised, he had a large, jagged, gash on the back of his calf. "We're going to need x-rays and you're going to need stitches. There was so much force behind the blow that it split your tissue open. We'll know more after the x-ray and I sew you up."

"Joy," Jared said.

"Not yet. First we need to clean you up and ditch the jeans."

The receptionist popped her head in the door. "How long do you want Tinker on the nebulizer? And the pharmacy is on line one. Something about Mrs. Cooper's prescription."

Seeing help was needed, Rocky stepped forward. "Give me the supplies and I'll get Jared cleaned up for x-ray."

Jackson looked relieved. "You sure?"

"Positive."

He opened two cabinets and instructed as he pulled things down. "Mix a little Betadine with normal saline in this basin. Then use the gauze and the solution to clean off his leg. Press a clean gauze pad to the wound when you're done. Most of the bleeding has stopped but the wound is still oozing. I'll be back in five."

"Don't forget to call Jesse and tell him the situation, okay? I'll explain anything else later."

"Got it," Jackson said then left.

Rocky hoped the doctor's worried frown wasn't because Jared was more injured than he was letting on. She got the supplies ready then forced a smile as she faced Jared. "Let's get your jeans off first."

"Thought you'd never ask," Jared said, unbuckling his belt and loosening the button and zipper.

"That was a command born from professional necessity, not a voluntary request," she quipped back. She knew that line or something similar was coming, but she still chuckled. Or maybe it was just pent up energy escaping. She could look at the situation as objectively as possible but to deny that seeing him shuck down his jeans didn't hit her hot button would have been a lie. Calvin Klein's never looked so good.

"I love a woman who takes charge."

Some take charge *Kama Sutra* flashed. Rocky decided she was going to shoot Dessie. "I'm beginning to think you love any and all women." She laughed again at his responding frown. He apparently had issues about being called a player. By the time she finished pulling his jeans over his injured leg, neither of them were laughing. His pain was too real—for both of them.

"I'm sorry." She set her hand over his fist.

He drew several breaths. "Let's get this over with."

She cleaned him off as gently as she could and was ready by the time his brother returned with a wheelchair and a patient gown.

Jared frowned as Jackson handed it to him. "You can't be serious. You want me to wear this ass flasher?"

"Yeah, over your underwear, bro. No need to strip bare. While I don't mind you going around in your underwear, other patients might take issue with it." Jackson met her gaze. "Be best for you to wait here, okay?"

Rocky nodded. She'd been the x-ray route with a broken limb before and sometimes positioning for it could get really painful. They left and she called Mack.

"How are things on the job? Any other mishaps? Any strangers seen?"

"Things are moving fast. No other incidents but rumors about ghosts and curses are running rampant. The men are on edge."

"Seriously?"

"Yeah, but I'm nipping that crap in the bud. There's no mob-related ghost trying to oust us from his hotel."

"Crazy. I'm not sure how long this is going to take. I might not be back in today."

"We've got it covered."

"Call me if you have questions."

"Just one. I tried to call Patrick but he didn't answer. Do you know where he is?"

"He's supposed to come to the jobsite this afternoon. He was meeting with the concrete suppliers this morning." Mack's question reminded Rocky that Uncle Pat would be bringing her the box from her mother. "Tell him to call when he arrives."

"Will do. And boss, this friend—he keeps showing up at just the right time. What's up with that? You trust him?"

Rocky glanced around the clinic, considered her interaction with Jared and couldn't see why or how Jared wasn't on the up and up. Maybe it was fate, destiny, karma…whatever. He was the right man at the right place at the right time. "Yeah, I trust him."

"Good. Then don't hurry back. I can't remember the last time you've taken any time off, if ever. Nothing big happening here."

The only time she'd taken off recently was to be with her father when he'd first fallen ill with a stroke.

"We'll see." Rocky hung up. A knock on the door had her turning.

The door opened and a man stood there, assessing her from head to toe with a sharp eye. He wasn't as tall as Jared and Jackson, but he was a little broader in the shoulders, and had the unmistakable "Weldon brand" on him—tall, dark, devastation that just didn't let up.

"You're either Jesse or James," Rocky said, holding out her hand. "I'm Rocky McKenna." He moved into the room, immediately filling it up.

"Jesse," he said, shaking her hand. His grip was firm and comfortable. "You'll know James when you see him. I take it you haven't known Jared long?"

Rocky smiled. "Jared sort of introduced himself last night. He took issue with the trouble my ex seemed bent on causing. Didn't he mention it?"

"Likely. It's been a busy day."

"So you run a security company with him?"

"We do business together. Where's he at?"

"Getting x-rayed."

"Good. I'll be back in a minute." He glanced back from the door. "Great to meet you. Amazing in fact."

He left and Rocky exhaled, feeling as if a storm to be reckoned with had just blown by her.

It was ten minutes before all three men returned to the room. Jared looked pale. Jackson concerned. And Jesse, well he looked stormier.

"Is it bad?"

Jared didn't say anything. He glared at Jesse.

"Not too bad," Jackson said. "I'll get a radiologist to confirm, but no major break. A possible hairline fracture low on the tibia. We'll sew him up, strap on a boot, and he should be good to go."

"Okay. That's good then."

"Is it?" Jesse narrowed his gaze at her.

"Leave her out of this," Jared said.

Jesse ignored his brother. "Your ex ever tried to kill you before?"

Shocked at his directness, Rocky took a step back. "No."

"But he or someone meant to cause serious harm today."

Jared clearly resented Jesse's presence. "I told you I suspect that's what happened. Why the third degree?"

Jesse wasn't happy either. "Because, it's my duty as your older brother to make sure I'm not letting you get in over your head."

"This isn't an official job and having a boot on my foot isn't going to hinder my aim."

"But if you get into anything hand-to-hand you'll be at a disadvantage. I want you to check in every six hours and call for back-up at the first sign of trouble." Jesse narrowed his gaze at her. "I'm going to count on you to remind him to do it."

"I can do that," she found herself saying. Meeting Jared's brothers and getting a sense of the bond between them, had been better than any paper recommendation or character referral. That

Jared had put himself in danger twice on her account also went a long way in his favor, but she hadn't quite made a final decision about bringing him to her house, yet she found herself somehow sealing her fate.

By the time Jared got a tetanus shot, stitches, an immobilizing boot strapped on, and pain meds, she'd yet to figure out exactly how it all happened, but it had. Dessie had said for Rocky to do whatever she had to do to be comfortable in her own home. Rocky wasn't sure just how comfortable she was going to be with Jared lounging around. The man defined excitement with every line of his lean, hard body and she had quite a number of ideas on what to do with him.

That damn book Dessie had thrown at her last night was causing her problems. Having Collin bang on her door seemed to be the least of her worries.

From the passenger's seat of Rocky's red truck, Jared thought his life couldn't get any lower. Jesse had pushed him so far under he didn't think he'd surface for a decade or two. That's if he didn't die from embarrassment before then.

Check in every six hours. Call at the least sign of trouble. It's my duty as your older brother to make sure I'm not letting you get in over your head.

Jared nearly snorted out loud with disdain. He'd gotten his wish to be the man assuring Rocky's safety, but some hero he was turning out to be. Not only did he have a lame foot, but his big brother had to show up and make a production of wiping his baby brother's ass.

His only consolation was that Jesse had come bearing a bag of
goodies. Everything a man going on bodyguard assignment
needed, including a well-oiled, fully-automatic Glock 18—a gun
that not every Joe Blow on the street could have. Jared had been to
the shooting range with Jesse and his brothers enough to know that
Jared was more than comfortable with the way the Glock handled.

Rocky had neighbors, but she wasn't exactly in a bustling area
of suburbia. In fact, he'd label the old subdivision carved from
South Carolina's coastal marsh as fairly remote. Instead of a
traditional pitched roof to her salt-boxed style house, someone had
cut the top off and put in a captain's walk to overlook the
undeveloped marshy area behind her property. From where he
stood, he thought he saw some greenery up there, but wasn't sure.
White siding and picket fencing with a plethora of flowers made
for a quaint almost-old-fashioned house. The complete opposite of
his and James's upscale condo.

He'd always felt that property made a statement about the
owner. It was one of the founding tenets in developing Weldon
Estates. Following that truth, Jared determined that Rocky
McKenna liked things simple, gravitated to the old-fashioned, and
was isolated as hell. Whereas the pink-stucco, two-story eye-sore
of her nearest neighbor with the wooden flamingos planted around
a palm-tree oasis in the yard as well as a pink 57 Chevy mailbox,
screamed of flamboyance that had missed the Hollywood turn-
off—three decades ago. Maybe five.

Rocky rounded the front of her pick-up and headed his way.
"Let me help," she said as he pulled out the clothes-filled overnight
bag Jackson had given him, along with a pair of crutches. He wore
a polo shirt and cargo shorts that he borrowed from Jackson, his
jeans and shirt too bloodied and stained to wear.

"I got it," Jared muttered. Even though he had an
immobilizing boot strapped to his foot, Jackson still wanted Jared

to keep weight off his foot until a radiologist read the x-ray—which wouldn't happen until sometime tomorrow. It had been the final coffin-nail in Jared's hero to the rescue illusions. Now he was an invalid on her doorstep.

Still, he wasn't willing to call it quits. He knew if push came to shove there wasn't anything he couldn't do to assure her safety. It was the whole image thing that left him floundering.

"We have a problem." Her hand on his stopped him in his stubborn-tracks. He shifted his balance, leaning back against the truck frame to stop and face her. Less than a foot away from him and just a few inches shy of his six-three, she nearly met him eye-level. The thought a making love to a woman who matched him so nicely physically, hit his hot button.

"What?" He didn't pull his hand away, but forced himself to stay still and enjoy the heat of her touch despite the irritation in her gaze.

"If you can't put common sense ahead of ego, then we're going to go more than just toe-to-toe. Ask yourself, if the roles were reversed what would make sense. You carrying my bag up a few steps while I maneuvered on crutches, or I—"

"Be as stubborn as a blue-nosed mule and insist on doing it yourself." A reluctant grin tugged on Jared's lips. He liked the idea of going toe to toe, leg to leg, hip to hip, chest to chest, mouth to mouth, and everything else possible to her everything. In every way.

"Are you calling me a blue-nosed mule?" Rocky arched a brow, humor making her clover-green eyes even brighter.

Jared smiled and slid his gaze slowly over her. "Not at all. Myself."

She took the bag from him and focused on his nose. "If the ring fits…"

"Ouch!" He tried to pretend outrage but ended up laughing. She did too, chasing the last bit of shadows that had been lingering in her expression since he'd met her. She glowed. It was a beautiful thing. The only look he could imagine as being better was ecstasy.

He shook his head. "You're a hard Irish woman, Roxanne McKenna."

Her laughter died instantly and she turned quickly away, heading toward her house.

He shut the truck door and followed. "What is it?"

She shook her head. "Nothing. Let's get you inside and pack some ice on your leg."

He stood beside her as she unlocked and opened her front door. But before she could march inside, he slid his arm across the doorway, balancing himself against the jamb. Forced to face him, she turned, her brow knitted.

"If I can't be a blue-nosed mule then you can't be a corncob."

"A what?"

"A corncob. The dried up husk that's left after all the juicy—"

"I know what a corncob is," she said, bristling. "I am not being a corncob."

He looked her over a little closer than she had him. "You're right. There's still a lot of juicy left on your husk. Then you're not allowed to be an over-thorned rose. If I said something wrong, then you need to explain so I don't rain on your laughter again."

She sighed. "It wasn't you pissing on me. Just baggage from the past. It has a way of hitting me upside the head when I'm not looking."

"From the divorce?"

"Yeah." She looked into her house and shrugged. "It's a knee jerk reaction. Collin coined that phrase 'hard Irish woman' and everybody bought into it, job and family, until I finally aired some of his dirty laundry. I am long over it all."

"Maybe, and maybe everyone should have had faith in you," he said, soft, his voice rumbling deep from the gut-reaction inside him that wanted to kiss her. He slid his thumb along her cheek, bringing her gaze to his. "Three years is a long time. Maybe you need someone to chase those ghosts away."

Her lips parted and he almost leaned in and kissed her hard. But somehow, he felt as if he were coercing her in a vulnerable moment again, just like he had last night. Instead, he brushed his thumb over her bottom lip, feeling the lush softness of her flesh, feeling the heat of her breath.

His jockeys shrunk in a heartbeat. He dropped his hand while he still had the control to do so. "You let me know when you're ready to go ghost hunting. Meanwhile, what's the story behind this odd bit of architecture? Can't say I've ever seen a chopped off salt-box before. What's on the roof?"

She exhaled hard and looked confused then took a half step back. "What?"

Just damn. She seemed almost disappointed. Maybe he should have kissed her anyway. "The roof," he repeated, calling himself a complete fool. "I thought I saw some greenery. Is there anything up there besides the lattice-fenced railing?"

"Sun deck and a garden." She moved inside.

He followed, curious. He expected old-fashioned lace and frills. The solid colors, the perfectly placed plants and subtle lighting, the sparse but simple elegance of the inside of her home surprised him. "A Feng Shui fan, I see."

Eyes wide, she set his bag on the floor and stared at him. "Most men I know think Feng Shui is a martial art move." She looked at him as if he'd suddenly been imported from another planet.

An architect had to know the ins and outs of every philosophy of design and the energy it produced. Was it not something a security guy would know? He thought about Jesse, and nearly cursed aloud. Jesse would be checking out the vulnerability of her situation and what safety issues needed to be address. He shrugged. "Maybe you don't know the right men. It's not unusual to know the difference between a life philosophy and takedown and submission techniques."

"Take down and what?"

He grinned. "Submission. The foundation for success in Mixed Martial Art fighting is a solid foundation in takedown and submission techniques. You know, determining your opponent's vulnerability, getting him down and keeping him there. Speaking of which, it's the first thing we need to do."

Her jaw dropped. "Takedown and submission? I think you've gotten the wrong—"

Jared roared with laughter. She just stood there glaring at him.

"No, that's not where I was going, but I can show you a few moves if you ask me nice," he gasped when he could speak. Putting her into the equation gave a whole new meaning to takedown and submission moves. "We need to determine what our safety vulnerabilities are. How many exits are there? Do they have deadbolt locks? Do you have your windows locked? And I didn't see an alarm system so I am assuming you don't have one."

"I don't have an alarm. Yes, on the deadbolt locks and window locks. And there are five entry/exits. But all of that can wait. You need to get ice on your leg and take a pain pill."

"No. This is one thing that you can count on me being a blue-nosed mule on. I'm here for a reason. Safety first, after that I'll let you take charge."

She arched a brow and her lips twitched. "You'll submit?"

His breath caught and he nearly lost his balance on the crutches. The interested gleam in her gaze had him feeling as if she'd just taken him down and he couldn't wait to lose this match.

CHAPTER SEVEN

Rocky marched into the living room where she finally got a pale-faced Jared to lay down on the couch and prop his leg up on pillows. She may go Feng Shui in her décor but the brown-leather, over-sized, over-stuffed L-shaped sectional had been a must even though it was a bit too large and didn't quite match the sleek, simplicity of the room. A woman had to have some indulgences.

Jared had been throughout the house, upstairs and down and on the roof. He'd checked every window, found two of them where the latches needed their screws tightened, and secured every door. He'd even traipsed around the backyard and pool, checking the fence and gate, the natural gas tank, and generally made sure everything was locked and secure.

All of this over a dive-bombing planter seemed a bit over the top. She still didn't think it was connected to Collin's rage last night. Her ex was more of a stampeding bull than a shadow lurker. So by separating the incidents, Rocky was left with doubts that the planter had been a deliberate attempt on her life.

Her cowering in the dark last night almost seemed silly by the light of the day. Collin had left her alone for three years.

What had he been doing all that time though? Had he been moving on? Or had he been stewing in his anger just waiting to—

Don't go there. Not now. Rocky closed her eyes and sucked in air, forcing her memory back down a dark tunnel. Maybe Jared's ghost assessment wasn't off base.

The one major vulnerability he'd found was that all of her deadbolts weren't keyed on the inside. And all of her doors had glass panels. Anyone could break the glass, reach in, turn the knobs and unlock the doors before she could even dial 911. She vowed to change them first thing in the morning, then had to practically drag Jared to the couch to rest.

Now she was armed with pain meds and ice.

Jared eyed the pill bottle. "I need to stay on my game. Just give me some Tylenol."

"It's four in the afternoon. Collin doesn't get a good drunk going until about eight or nine at night. By the time dark hits, you'll be fine. You promised me that you'd follow my directions now." He did not look happy, but the lines of pain etching his face told him she was dead on. "Macho only goes so far before it crosses over into stupid. You've a fractured leg and thirty stiches keeping your calf together."

Jared rolled his eyes. "Hairline fracture. I've had worse."

She held out the pills. "You promised."

"Fine. I'll take the pills under one condition. You give me your word that you'll stay inside until I am firing on all cylinders. No roof top meditation. No pool. No gardening. Read a book. Watch TV. Bake cookies. Whatever. Just stay inside. Okay? I guess it wasn't so out of line for Jesse to stick his nose into the situation and demand I check in."

"I thought your big brother being all big-brotherly was…incredibly cool. You can tell how much you all care about each other. Being an only child, I always wanted to have a brother or sister. Wished for it every day up until…well for a long time."

"Guess I don't appreciate what I have. My brothers are all blue-nosed mules. You avoided the promise."

"I promise I'll stay inside." He took the pills from her. She packed ice around his leg, too aware of his scorching gaze burning her senseless. The bar incident, the planter thing, and taking him to the doctor had plowed through barriers she'd had up since her divorce. Barriers that Dessie's outrageous-get-him-bedroom-bound comments and her pocket *Kama Sutra* had weakened.

Sex aside. There was an intimacy involved in taking care of Jared and even more so in the fierce protectiveness he had of her. It was more intimate than she'd been with any man in a long time. It seduced that part of her that had kept a man at arm's length. Did that mean she was weak, or did that mean that Jared was *right guy* material?

She went back to the kitchen to make more ice packs, wondering where this unexpected twist in life was going to lead. Well, hell, she knew where it was going unless she derailed it. To the bedroom—and moving like a runaway freight train at that.

Thank you Ms. Desmond Langford.

When Rocky returned to Jared, he'd shut his eyes and she held off adding any more ice. He needed some rest and she took the opportunity to grab her mother's books off the shelf. Before reading, she realized that she should have heard from Uncle Pat by now. She stepped into the other room and called his cell. Getting voice mail, she left a message for him to call her. That she could either come get her mother's box from him at his house or that he could drop it by hers. Her second call to the nursing home for the day, informed her that there'd been no developments in her father's condition and he'd made no more attempts to talk. After calling her father's attorney again, and getting the same out-of-town message, she left her number and then she curled up on the other end of the couch and read.

Rocky didn't know if she was just older, or if she'd been through more of the pain that life dished out than before, or if having lost her mother made everything different, but Rocky found herself more drawn into her mother's words than ever.

One poem, titled "Unforgiven" stood out, prompting her to read it several times. It wasn't just because the title of it was so close to *unforgivable*, the word her father had spoken yesterday, but the power and the rawness of the poem gripped her, along with the fact that her mother *had* at least felt unforgiven for a sin. *What?*

I know the depths of sin.
The wretchedness of the depraved.
I know the darkness within
I'll never escape it, even in the grave.
Though I know it is wrong
And I'll pay with my soul
I could not turn away from
The love that made me whole.
So I stole every moment of time
And lived in the shadows
To love this child of mine
Before facing heaven's gallows
I was part of the unforgivable
Blood stains my hands
Still I pray for the impossible
That in the end mercy will stand.

A knock at the door startled Rocky. She set the book down and hurried to see who it was. Jared was still asleep. Peeking through the curtain, she saw Dessie and Pebbles. She unlocked the door to let them both in. Pebbles went on a sniffing-the-floor hunt and

Dessie clutched her chest. "God, Rocky. I don't know what I am going to do."

Rocky grabbed Dessie's arm. "What is it? What happened?"

"His tongue sucked my 'no' right away in less than five seconds. I was in my dressing room getting dressed for the show. Someone knocked on the door and I answered. After all, wearing a bra and panties is overdressed for the Golden Bunny."

"Uh, Dessie—"

"No. Let me finish. He was there. He marched right in, fell to his knees and planted his mouth on me. I came right there through the silk. Best orgasm I've had in years, maybe ever. He may go by the name of Saint, but that man is no saint. What am I going to do? What he did with his tongue should be—"

"You must be the pink-house neighbor."

At the sound of Jared's voice, Rocky winced and Dessie grabbed her chest again, this time in true distress.

"I tried to tell you—"she whispered then swung around to Jared. He was sitting up on the couch looking a little woozy. "How did you know that?"

"Uh...I just guessed. She's got pink flamingos on her pants and there're a slew of them planted in the yard."

"Woof. Woof." Pebbles bounded across the room.

"Watch out!" Rocky ran for Jared, but saw she wasn't going to make it before Pebbles pulled her flying lapdog routine. "No, Pebbles. Sit, Pebbles. Hell, stand up, Jared!"

Jared didn't stand up but held out his hand. "Hey, girl. You're a big one aren't you?"

Pebbles reached Jared and...sat, preening so he could pet her. Rocky's jaw dropped open.

"*He* might be a saint, though," Dessie said, staring at Jared. "That was a miracle if I've ever seen one. I insist on knowing the name of men I share my orgasms with. What's yours?"

Rocky felt as if her cheeks had incinerated. She loved Dessie to no end and knew when the woman was boxed into a corner she'd come out fighting more outrageous than ever.

"Jared Weldon. And since we're on intimate terms, what's yours?"

The man took both Dessie and Pebbles in stride and didn't even blink an eye.

Dessie walked closer, looking Jared over. "Desmond Langford. Were you at Sally's Roadhouse last night?"

"You heard about that?" Jared lifted a brow.

"I told her about the fight," Rocky said. "Dessie's the neighbor I spent the night with."

Dessie crossed the room. "Well, it is a pleasure to meet a man who can definitely perform miracles."

Jared levered to his feet and shook Dessie's hand.

"What happened to you?"

Rocky hurried over. The last thing she needed was adding Dessie's worry to the list of complications piling up on her. "Just a mishap at the job site. I'm looking after him…tonight."

"Then I'll just mosey back home and won't worry about you then. Pebbles and I will go watch *Lady and the Tramp*, before I have to be back for the late night session."

"The dog watches TV?"

"Every minute of a movie. Even barks and whines depending on what's happening. And growls at Cruella De Vil every chance she gets."

"I'll have to see that sometime." Jared said.

"Count on it. I'll have you and Rocky over for dinner. Let's go Pebbles." Dessie headed for the door and Rocky followed, feeling as if life had become a surreal odyssey. Last night Jared had been a stranger and tonight, well, he was way beyond that status.

Dessie was at the door when Jared spoke up. "I'd return the favor," he said.

"Dinner and a doggie move?" Dessie asked.

"No. You wanted to know what to do with the man who gave you the best five seconds of your life. I'd return the favor."

"Did I say they were the best?" Dessie stumbled and Rocky caught her friend's arm, unsure if she should be amused or flabbergasted that Jared had just out-did her outrageous neighbor.

"You wouldn't be so conflicted if they'd been your worst," Jared replied.

Dessie shut her eyes and exhaled hard. "They *were* the best."

Rocky decided to join Jared's campaign. "You heard the miracle man, Dessie. Return the favor. Put the fire out and maybe you'll both be able to think straight."

"Hell," Dessie muttered as she walked out the door with Pebbles in tow. "I'm going to burn in hell." She looked back. "You'd better put that pocket guide to use."

Rocky shut the door and leaned back on it for support, half-laughing, half-stunned.

"Why does she think she'll burn for it? Is the guy married?"

"No. He's thirty-something. She's fifty-something and she's been saying 'no' to his every move."

Jared grinned. "Looks like he found one…she couldn't say 'no' to."

Rocky suddenly got the feeling that Jared's mind wasn't on Dessie's orgasm confession, but on something else entirely. Surely he wasn't considering making a similar move? Her heart kicked into overdrive and her mouth went dry.

"What pocket guide was she talking about?"

God help her! Sex was swamping her from all sides. She scrambled for a lifeline. "Pizza. We need some real food and you need to check in with your brother."

"Saved by the check-in?" Jared said softly. "I knew there was a reason I didn't like Jesse's idea. This conversation isn't over."

"I'll get the pizza menu while you call," Rocky tried to hurry from the room before the situation could slide back into that moment of the utterly outrageous made seemingly possible. Jared. Sex. And the pocket guide all happening right that moment. She'd never admit it, but she wanted it *bad*.

"Rocky," Jared said, his voice soft and deep.

She stopped and glanced back.

"You can relax. I won't be storming your citadel." She nodded and turned away, but still heard his whispered, "*Yet*." Her stomach clenched and heat flushed her every nerve. She tingled…everywhere, telling her that storming wasn't going to be necessary. A hot breath would knock her over in a heartbeat.

Jared nearly collapsed back onto the couch. At the moment he couldn't even storm an anthill. He didn't know what in the hell was wrong with him. He slid the Glock he'd pulled out at the sound of a stranger's voice back into his overnight bag on the floor next to him.   Then sweaty and shaky, he re-elevated his foot and drew in several deep breaths until the about-to-pass-out feeling dissipated.

As sharp as Jesse was, the man would pick up on the least note of anything in Jared's voice. Jared wanted to blame his rapid pulse and weak knees on the image of him falling to his knees and sucking Rocky's "no" away, but was afraid the weakness stemmed from his leg.

Either he'd passed his spring-chicken prime, or the damage from the planter was taking a greater toll on his system than he realized it would. Once steady, he dialed Jesse, hating the feeling that his big brother had had any right on his side. Jared had to admit that if Rocky was under assault at that very moment and he had to go balls to the wall to save her; there was a slight possibility his body wouldn't hold up in the fight.

That fact galled his gut and he wondered if he should bow out and let Jared send a "real" bodyguard. He thought about Rocky's appeal and her vulnerable state and realized that the only men he'd trust to watch over her, would be one of his brothers. Maybe just Jesse or Jackson, one of his *married* brothers, considering the identical twin factor he shared with James, and hell, Rocky was one powerful temptation.

That meant he had to get his shit together. No more narcotics. He'd take Tylenol to take the edge off and suffer. Pumped and ready, he called Jesse.

"I didn't think you'd call," Jesse said as he answered his cell.

"Didn't want to, but you're right. It makes sense and makes her safer, which is all that matters. Though you didn't have to wipe my ass so thoroughly in front of her."

"Ha. Considering what you're pulling, you need to have your ass reamed. Not wiped. Why the charade?"

Jared glanced in the direction Rocky disappeared. "It's complicated."

"Best keep the deceit rope short, it has a way of hanging a man really fast."

"I hear ya."

"So what's the situation there?"

Jared explained the security set up and the deadbolt situation.

"I'll send a man out in the morning to set up a perimeter alarm and change the locks. It's on the house."

"It's her house, so let me run it by her and let you know in the morning."

"All right. You need anything else? How are you feeling?"

"Good. Not one hundred percent, but enough to handle the situation. I think we're set for the night though. I'll text you for the midnight check."

"That works. Have you spoken to James?"

Jared winced. Considering the gist of their last conversation, Jared had been putting of getting in touch with his twin. "Not yet."

"I have. He said to tell you that last dollar bet was not only binding but he'd multiplied it exponentially. Care to explain?"

"No. Damn, but he's going to be a bitch to live with."

"That anything new?" Jesse laughed. "Don't know what it is about twin-karma, but James called me this afternoon and hired us, too."

"For what?"

"Seems as if a couple came bearing cash for your spec house. All great, but he got a strange vibe. They're in such a rush that he wants to know why. I'm running a background check on them before any formal papers are signed."

"Can't hurt. Maybe we need to do that on Rocky's ex."

"Do I look as if I just fell off a turnip truck? This is my business. That's already in the works, along with the man's father, Roxanne's business partner. We should have a report by midday tomorrow. Do you know her father suffered a stroke about a month ago and is coma-bound in a nursing home? She's been officially in charge of the company since, but from what we've uncovered, she took charge about eight months ago when they were skirting bankruptcy. Seems she turned the company around."

"Christ. I didn't know about her dad. But after seeing her in action on the jobsite, I have no trouble believing the company's turnaround. Thanks for the heads up."

"I'm not done yet. She also runs a free summer camp for kids to teach them about construction. She won the Savannah Women's Society humanitarian award last year."

Jared swallowed hard. Jesse's tone of voice was as hard-assed as he'd been at church yesterday. "So what are you saying?"

"You'd better be there because you care and not because you're looking for a fuck."

Jared gripped the phone; sure the damn thing would crack in two. "I'm not sure if I want to plaster your face or buy you a drink. Maybe both. Who the fuck do you think I am?"

"A Weldon who just might have woken up and seen the light. We've all been in no-man's land, bro. Let me know if you run up against anyone we need to look at."

Jared drew several deep breaths. Not sure he liked all of the shit swimming around inside his gut and his head. "I didn't say it earlier so I'm saying it now. Thanks."

"You're welcome. Try and avoid being a landing pad for concrete missiles, okay?"

"I plan on it. Meanwhile how's that matter that had James so wrung out yesterday?"

"Still in the stratosphere of implausible. But I've taken and will take every precaution. Just so you know, I'm taking dad out fishing this weekend and had planned on asking you to join us, but that's out of the picture now."

"We'll do it when I'm back on my feet." Rocky came back into the room. She had a menu, a bottle of Tylenol, and a drink in her hands. Gifts from the gods. Jared mouthed a thank you in her direction. "For now I'll text you at midnight and talk to you tomorrow."

"Right. Good night." He disconnected and smiled, taking the drink and the Tylenol from her. He took two extra-strength tabs and downed half of the Gatorade. "Jesse offered to set up a perimeter alarm and change your deadbolt locks for free in the morning. Is that all right, or would you prefer he doesn't?"

Her expression became puzzled. "For free? Why would he do that? I mean, I'm not even a paying client and he doesn't know me at all."

Jared shrugged. "That's Jesse and his wife Alexi. If there's a need, they're going to fill it."

"Like you?" she said, moving closer and sitting on the sectional so she could face him.

"Me?" He frowned. Philanthropy was so not a part of his living-it-up-bachelor life.

"Yeah. You. Last night. Today. You keep stepping up to the plate. Why?"

Talk about laying things on the table, but that was how she played her cards. Direct and honest. That last thought clogged his throat. He took a long drink then met her curious gaze. "You," he said softly. "Do with it what you want, but I looked across the bar last night, saw you and couldn't look away. I'm hoping I am here with you now because you feel it too. The attraction that goes beyond a second glance but dives immediately into a hungry want, but there's time to sort that out when exes and planters aren't dive-bombing you. Right now, I am starving for food. I think all I've had today was a cup of coffee early this morning. So what kind of pizza do you want? If it has sauce and cheese, I'm good with anything."

"Anchovies?"

Jared held back a flinch. He'd never had anchovies and imagined they'd be similar to salty sardines with a crunch. Something he'd eat if he were on a desert island and starving, but to mix fishy with his cheese didn't sit right.

She laughed. "You should see your expression."

"What? I didn't express." Surely he had a better poker face than that.

She lifted a brow, adding to the mischievous gleam in her green eyes. "You look like a kid facing spinach flavored ice cream."

He narrowed his gaze. "Do you like anchovies on your pizza?"

"No."

Hell. "Then why bring them up?"

"Just testing. You did say anything. I'm flexible on the pizza, pepperoni, supreme, spicy BBQ. My one must is garlic bread with extra, extra, extra cheese."

"You're a triple-X woman then."

"What?" Her voice rose several octaves, almost as if she were guilty, and it was his turn to laugh.

"When you like something then you don't just want extra. You want extra, extra, extra. Wanna wager a bet that I can guess what else you like triple-X of?" He lowered his voice to a deep rumble.

She swallowed as if parched and her pupils dilated. She might play life close to the vest, but a little gamble flipped her switch.

"What?" she whispered.

"You asking what I want to wager or what do you like?"

"Both."

"Wager first. At a time of my choosing, I'll bet you a repeat of last night's kiss that I can name some things you like extra, extra, extra of."

"Hmm…make it a time of *my* choosing and you've got a bet."

He frowned. Now what? She could wait three months and he had a good night kiss in mind for tonight. Still, a guarantee on a kiss at some point was better than no guarantee. And a wager didn't mean he couldn't talk her into one on his timetable. "You're on."

"Okay. Mr. Anything-but-anchovies, what do I like?"

He studied her a minute, thinking. "You like your salsa extra hot, your beer extra cold."

"Anyone could guess that," she cried, rolling her eyes.

"Not finished yet. You like extra whipped cream, extra fudge topping and just a pat of butter won't do. There's more but…" He raked his gaze down her body and back up. He had a feeling her sensual side had a few extras to it, too. "Am I wrong?"

"I decide when," she muttered and marched out of the room.

"Hey. What about the pizza?"

"Read my mind."

"Sa-weet."

An hour later he wondered how he'd missed the thin and crispy crust option. It wasn't bad, but on a scale of one to ten he'd rate it a four. He liked crust he could sink his teeth into, not something that disintegrated the moment he put it in his mouth. After five pieces he hadn't even scratched the surface of his hunger. Next time he'd have to proceed with caution on the pizza front.

As for the triple-X cheese bread, it was thick and chewy, and definitely not a first date food. What she was doing with her tongue and all of that stringy cheese had him on his knees. Well, practically on his knees. At the moment he didn't dare stand or kneel. They sat side-by-side on her soft-as-a-bed couch. He could feel the heat of her body, smell her citrusy coconut scent, and imagine licking every inch of her honey tanned skin. All it took was a heartbeat for her to transport him from an invalid on the couch to steamy-sex-in-the-sun.

Hell, he shifted his good leg to ease the pressure of his fly. With his injured leg, straight out and propped on a pillow at the far side of an over-stuffed ottoman, he didn't have a lot of spare room for a hard on. And it was embarrassing as hell in some respects. You'd think he was a teenager watching his first X-rated movie. Spread out on the rest of the ottoman was the pizza and cheese bread boxes along with glasses of icy Coke on a metal tray. He snagged his glass and took a long, thirsty drink. Something had to cool his ass down.

"So what is your brother James like?"

Jared coughed and Coke fizzed up his nose. Not the cool down he had in mind. A napkin and several gasping breaths later he finally wheezed a response. "What...do you...mean?"

"Just curious. I've met Jackson and Jesse. So wondered where James fit into the mix. Is he older or younger?" She grabbed a piece of cheese bread and paused for his answer.

Damn, how had James popped up already? He sucked in air and prayed that this conversation didn't go far. He didn't want his misleading white lies to keep growing. "James is a lot like me. Honestly, he is exactly like me. We're identical twins."

She almost dropped the cheese bread she was about to bite into. "Seriously? That's...just so cool. Here I envied you your older brothers and you have one closer to you than anybody. Do you like the same things? I've heard that twins separated at birth end up following the same career paths and having the same likes and dislikes." She bit into the cheese bread.

He shrugged, trying to unknot his tongue from telling any lies. He and James *had* followed the same career path—in construction. The one topic he did not want to get near. "Some things are the same, but I'd like to think—"

A long string of cheese hung between her moist lips and the gooey bread in her hand. She opened her mouth to nab more of the cheese and he lost his restraint. He wrapped his finger around the far end of the cheese string, pulling it from the bread.

Her gaze shot to his. He smiled a challenge as he leaned forward and slowly slid the tip of his finger into his mouth, catching the cheese string with his tongue. Then he ate his way toward her mouth. At the last inch, she stuck her tongue out and stole the last bit of cheese away and smiled like the cat that ate the canary, but was facing a bulldog. He got the feeling she was seconds away from bolting. What sort of number had her ex pulled on her?

He didn't want her wary. He wanted her eager and hungry. But for the life of him he couldn't gather the will to back off without at least tasting her lush mouth. He closed the inches separating them and pressed his mouth to hers, easing his tongue across her partially opened lips. Sweetness spiced with pizza.

That was it. All he could consciously steal at the moment. He eased back and took a bite out of her cheese bread then retreated to his space.

She blinked at him. "That was my cheese and my bread."

"Yep. And your hot mouth, too. Mighty fine if I may say."

Her cheeks flushed. "I thought we had a deal. I got to choose when we kiss."

"You do. If you remember I specified a kiss like we had last night. That means you on top of me. My arms wrapped around you. My hands in your silky hair. And every inch of your hot body pressed hard to me. Everything else is fair game in my book. And next time we order pizza we don't get thin and crispy. I like having something to sink my teeth into." He let her know with a look that he wasn't necessarily talking about pizza.

"You do? I can call, Dessie. I'm sure she wouldn't mind running over quick." She bit into her bread and stood up.

He sank back against the couch. Dessie? Why the hell would—"

"Pebbles has a jar of 'teeth sinking' gourmet dog biscuits, if you need—"

"A dog biscuit?" Laughing, he snagged the waistband of Rocky's jeans and tugged. He couldn't remember that last time he'd been so thoroughly put in his place. It felt…great. Off balance, she fell back into his lap. He winced as he jarred his injured leg and her bottom pressed against his unmistakable erection. "Seriously though, all joking aside. You can feel my interest, so there is no point in denying that I want to get to know you a whole lot better than I do, but I don't want you to be uncomfortable either. So, tell me now. Am I pushing too hard, too fast?"

She burst out laughing, a real heart-free laughter that came from a spirit unhampered by ghosts. The naughty gleam in her eye made him realize what he had said.

He actually felt heat flush his cheeks. He wasn't about to examine if he was blushing or having a hot flash at the idea of pushing hard and fast into her soft heaven. "Let me rephrase that. Am I making you uncomfortable? Before you answer, let me just say that I'd eat a dog biscuit if it means you'll laugh like this again."

She stopped laughing and looked at him seriously for a moment. "I think that might be the-"

"Funniest thing," he interjected. "The funniest thing anyone has ever said to you, right?" He interrupted because he had to. If she had said "the most romantic" or "the sweetest" or "the anything" besides funny, he would have likely kissed her again.

"Yeah," she said. "Funniest. I so needed to laugh."

Jared took heart. She didn't ask him to cease and desist as she levered up from his lap. He leaned back into the couch and relaxed a little, having skirted the sensual edge of things enough for now.

"My mom has been known to say that love and laughter can heal all ills. That and wringing her dishrag."

"Just exactly how does a dishrag help?" Rather than bolt from the room as he suspected she was warring over, Rocky sat back down on the couch, albeit a little further away than before. He picked up on the fact that talking put her at ease and he started talking, likely saying more about his mother to Rocky than he'd ever said to another woman. "Maybe it would be better to call it her prayer rag. Taking care of four growing boys, she spent a lot of time in the kitchen and given we were all hell on wheels. Literally. I don't think there hasn't been a bike, a skate board, a tractor, a motorcycle, a car, a truck or you name it that one of the four of us hasn't crashed. So she also spent a lot of time praying while in the kitchen and over the years the dishrag became her rosary of sorts. That's not to say that she couldn't snap a mean wet towel at our bare legs when we got out of line." He laughed. "But in general, to this day, whenever we see her with a dishtowel in her hands we know she's praying for one of us."

"You are so blessed. My mom was different. Very loving, but different. She—" Rocky shifted her gaze to the end of the sofa, bringing to his attention an open book. The name McKenna jumped out at him.

"Your mother's a writer?"

Rocky nodded. "Was. Cancer took her from us about five years ago."

Jared reached out and claimed Rocky's hand from where it rested on her lap. Her father in a coma. Her mother gone. Her ex an asshole. Damn. Life had thrown her some nasty curve balls. Made him wonder what the fuck was his and James's problem. They'd had it relatively good, so why weren't they out there passing it on, doing shit for kids, and helping others out? The sick in his gut went soul deep. He clasped Rocky's hand like it was a lifeline. "I'm sorry. Tell me about your mom. How was she different?"

She released his hand and retrieved the book. Then she sat closer to him and held the book open for him to read. "This might give you an idea. She was passionate. She loved deeply, but she didn't laugh often. Sometimes melancholy and solitary went hand in hand with her. While you slept, I was reading through some of her work to see if I could figure out what my father is trying to tell me. He had a stroke last month and spoke his first words yesterday."

"What did he say?"

"My mother's name, Keira, then the words *unforgivable, stop, pray*. Given how much my father loved my mother until the day she died, I can't imagine there was anything unforgiven between them, anything he would say was beyond prayer. The incident did prompt a startling revelation from our business partner, Patrick Brady. Just before his stroke, my father gave him a box that my mother left for me to be opened on my father's death. Da made Patrick swear he wouldn't give it to me before then, but the cat is out of the bag now. Patrick was supposed to bring it to me today at the job site, but I left early with you."

A spider crawled over Jared's nerve endings. He didn't like the sound of secret boxes to be delivered after death. Rocky was looking down at her mother's book frowning. Jared slid his thumb under her chin and lifted her gaze to his. "Maybe that falling planter wasn't the accident you think it was. What if someone doesn't want you to get that box?"

Her green eyes widened and her brow creased. For the first time, she didn't argue with him about the incident. "Double that.

Pat also let me know that my father has 'deliverable on his death' papers for me at the attorney's office, too."

Jared was glad Jesse had his back on this one. There was a lot more beneath the surface than Rocky first indicated. He wondered what else was out there lurking in the dark.

Chapter Eight

*W*ith *a disgusted sigh at having* failed, Rocky unfolded from a full Lotus, wondering if *another* cold shower would even help. Yoga had failed. Again. Her senses were on fire. Again.

She ached from the tips of her breasts to the soles of her feet. Her long denied, simmering desire had bubbled into a full boil and it was all Dessie…and Jared's fault. The pocket guide had her imagining her back in his lap with his erection pressing not just against her bottom, but deep inside where she burned the most. They were naked and she was riding him side-saddle, her back resting on the sofa's armrest, her legs stretched out, and his tongue and fingers working magic with her mouth and her breasts. Then before she could blink, she was straddling him, then before she could gasp, her back was to his chest, her head was on his shoulder and…

Dear God. She was a mess.

She could be down there and they could be having the time of their lives.

But when all of his hot maleness came at her, only part of her wanted to meet him head-on and match him lick for lick. The 99.9% part of her. But another part of her, the damaged-by-the-past proceed-with-caution part of her, wanted to run.

It wouldn't have hurt to have kissed him again. He'd opened the door wide three hours ago when he'd stolen her cheese. She could still feel his tongue brushing over her lips. She fisted her hands and shut her eyes as the memory sent another tingle burning through her. She wanted his tongue—everywhere. She wanted to taste him—everywhere.

So why had she escaped upstairs to read more of her mother's work? Yes, it was important to read it but it wasn't like she was going to solve the problem right that minute. She'd needed the information her parents hadn't want her to have until they were gone.

Still, she was ashamed to admit that she hadn't been able to concentrate at all. She'd known that before she'd made the excuse and left Jared. She'd left him for a cold shower. What kind of stupidity was that?

She'd left a hot man alone downstairs with water, pain medicine, Tylenol, pillows and sheets, so she could wallow alone in her room.

What was her problem? Opportunity had more than knocked and she'd sat frozen on her ass, then ran fast the other way.

One kiss did not make a marriage commitment.

The world wouldn't end if he kissed her again. Tonight. All she had to do was walk down the stairs…

Rocky didn't give herself time to question. She put her feet in motion and tip-toed downstairs, though marching would have fit her mood better. She was still sane enough to consider that he might have taken pain medication and might be asleep. Rounding the corner into the living room, she found the couch empty and searched the shadows for Jared, then gasped.

He stood at the French doors, looking at the backyard. He wore only a pair of form fitting boxer briefs and the hard-shelled boot strapped to his leg. His crutches were back at the couch, so he'd already gone against his brother's advice to keep weight off of his injury. Somehow that didn't surprise her.

What did take her breath away was the sight of him. Every lean inch of him was honed and tanned to perfection. He dropped the curtain and turned to face her. His broad shoulders and rippled abs made her weak in the knees, but it was the want in his gaze that did her in. It was as raw and edgy as her need, only sharper. The hungry predator had found his juicy prey.

Had she actually thought she could share another roll-on-the-floor rock-her-world kiss and escape unscathed? Rethink time. "I came to see if you're all right." She moved over to the couch and picked up his crutches, planning to take them to him. "You should be using these."

He didn't wait, but moved her way—faster than she thought possible.

He reached her. "They'd only be in the way of this."

She didn't have a chance to breathe before he caught her in his arms and planted his mouth on hers, instantly hot and demanding.

She opened to him, meeting the thrust of his tongue with hers, groaning deep from within as her starving senses found succor for her every want. His tongue tangled with hers, leading her in a seductive dance unlike any other.

He wrapped his arms around her, pulling her tight against his supple heat and burning erection. She pressed her palms to his chest, half thinking to stem the flooding tide, but then went crazy in a quest to feel and know his every contour. His muscles rippled as he shuddered at her touch.

His driving kiss eased only a moment then he swept her into deeper waters as he trailed his lips and tongue down her neck before latching onto nipple through the cotton of her tank top. Pleasure shot to her core.

Scorching.

Intense.

Completely mind-absorbing.

She grabbed his shoulders, needing to anchor herself to this universe as her body went wild for more. She arched her back and shifted her hips, pressing her sex against his urgent arousal.

He made a deep guttural sound of pleasure-pain and jerked her shirt up. His mouth went to one nipple, sucking her deep. His hand went to her other breast, catching her nipple between his thumb and forefinger, tweaking the hardened peak in rhythm to the rub of his erection against her sex.

A fever of quench-me-or-die desire raged through her. Her blood rushed. Her heart thundered. Every pore dampened. Her sex wept.

"Jared," she cried out, begging for help, her body completely lost in him even though her heart and mind were so distant, still captive to her past.

He released her breast and met her gaze. Sexual need burned like a live wire in his blue eyes, electrifying and dangerous, but she saw concern there too. As if he knew and understood her need and confusion.

His breaths came in deep gulps. His body shook as if ravaged by something beyond his control. "God help us both," he whispered and pulled her shirt completely off.

He eased her back onto the couch. But instead of following her down to continue kissing her, he knelt between her legs, grabbed the waistbands of her cotton shorts and underwear and pulled them down and off.

She lay there naked, her breasts rising up and down with every gasping breath, her nipples peaked and begging, and her damp sex exposed and aching. She was shocked.

She wasn't shocked that he had her like this, but by just how much she wanted to be consumed by him in every way, no matter what the consequence.

"You've a golden tan all over. I can just see you up on your roof, hot, needy, and ready to sacrifice your body to the sun, to pleasure. Do you know what I would do if I found you up there naked?"

"What?" she whispered, her gaze glued to the passion in his.

"This," he grabbed her knees and spread her legs wide and looked at her sex, his eyes widening with hungry surprise. "Damn oh, damn. What is this?" He ran a finger across the soft skin of her smooth sex. Except for a thin strip of clipped hair at the cleft of her clitoris, she was waxed bare.

His excitement upped hers. "Blame Dessie, she—"

"Blame? More like *thank*." His voice rasped harshly. She didn't get a chance to answer. He spread her legs even wider than before and brought his mouth to her sex, his passion-dark gaze watched her expression as his tongue slid over her exposed and hardened clitoris then flicked repeatedly with determined strokes.

Intense pleasure ripped through her. Her hips flexed for more and her knees fell even wider as she succumbed to the tide engulfing her from the inside out. She let herself go completely.

After holding such a tight reign over her needs for years, after surviving the hurt and disappointment of her marriage, after being alone for so long, she was incapable of doing anything else.

Sliding his hands up to cup her breasts and tease her nipples, he licked and sucked her sex until a mind blowing orgasm had her shuddering in his arms and crying out his name.

"Delicious," he whispered as he shifted to kiss her mouth. She tasted herself on his lips and tongue. Sweet and musky. She clasped her legs around his hips and urged him until she felt his silk-covered erection hard against her still aching sex. It was as if once loosened, her need knew no bounds.

Jared's heart raced and his dick throbbed. Somewhere between the two, his mind floundered and his injured leg disappeared from his conscious radar. Nothing was going to interfere with the moment.

He had Rocky exactly where he'd wanted her since he'd first set his gaze on her—naked and wanting in his arms. She was a surprise. Sun bathing in the nude and smooth as silk sex. Gliding his tongue over her, seeing every nuance of her wet and wanting flesh had him so hard, he thought he was going to die. She was like a powerful drug that had him on the most intense high of his life and he refused to tag it with any sappy phrase.

Whatever it was, whatever had happened to him, it was real and was whipping his ass, but in a good way. He'd had one night stands. He'd had good sex. He'd had bad sex—if there was such a thing. Sex had always just been sex—a damn easy way to feel good.

But this fever of want for Rocky was a pleasure-ache he couldn't seem to satisfy. He wanted to drown in her. He wanted to OD on her. He wanted her with a neediness that shocked him.

It wasn't that she was more sensually beautiful than he imagined—long, lean legs, firm, full breasts, honey tanned-all-over skin and silky dark hair. It wasn't that her haunted vulnerability had grabbed him by the short hairs either. He couldn't explain it. It was one of those things that just was.

He'd tasted her citrusy-coconut self, saw her come and wanted to see her come again. Wanted her eyes to glaze. Wanted her lush lips to open with need. Wanted to be driving deep and wild into her hot core.

The distant notion that he couldn't hear an assailant if his thoughts were consumed with fucking her crossed his mind, and the fact that he'd stormed her citadel even though he told her he wouldn't, didn't escape his notice. Those two things kept him from grabbing a condom and taking them on a magic carpet ride.

His thoughts didn't stop him from re-storming her citadel though. "More please," he said as he left her lips and moved to her breasts.

"More?" Her green eyes, now misty with desire and sexual satisfaction, widened. "I don't think—"

"Sure you do. You like extra, remember." He sucked a nipple into his mouth.

"Yeah, but I've never been a multip—"

He slid his hand up her leg and eased two fingers into her wet channel. Her hips jerked and the hot walls of her vagina squeezed his fingers. He released her nipple and blew its hardened tip.

"No buts. You can come again. Just let yourself go and trust me. Watch me make it happen for you. Feel me." He thrust his fingers deeper and gave a little twist as his thumb found her clit.

She cried out, her pleasure and surprise more than evident. He grinned as he slid his fingers out. She moaned as if she wasn't ready for him to stop and he wasn't. Not by a long shot.

This was going to be so good. Leaning down, he scooped her legs over his shoulders and straightened so that her hips were up in the air and her head pressed back into the softness of her sofa. With her smooth sex placed just right, he slid his fingers back inside her. This time, he used three and stroked her crevice with his thumb as he indulged himself in the scent and taste of her. He didn't stop until they were both shuddering from the force of her orgasm.

When he released her and moved up to brush her mouth with a kiss, he noticed the sheen of tears in her eyes. He wasn't sure what had brought them to the surface, but knew from the pleasure shining in her gaze that it was a good thing, even though the shadow of her ghosts had returned. It was all the satisfaction *he* needed for now.

Without a word, he settled on the couch with her and wrapped her in his arms to enjoy the feel of spooning. He'd planned to just hold her and brush his fingers through the silk of her hair as they relaxed.

But she didn't just lie still. After a few moments, she pressed her bottom back against his still throbbing dick and wiggled. Hell. He exhaled as if sucker punched. "Rocky. Uh. We need to…um."

She arched her back and pressed hard. He groaned.

"We need to get your Calvin's off is what we need." She turned to face him and slid her hand inside the waistband of his underwear and jerked down. His dick popped free, engorged and burning hot. "Then we can move on to bigger and better things." She clasped a hand around his shaft and gently squeezed as she pulled up.

His hips jerked in response, nearly knocking her off the sofa. Damn. In one touch she had him about to explode.

His mind warred with his body and he finally decided that having her deep and hard and fast, with his Glock within reach, would make him a better bodyguard than lying in the dark alone, burning for her and trying to hear an intruder above his clamoring dick.

Lifting her, he brought her on top and shifted beneath her. She straddled him and braced her hands against his chest, her fingers flexing into his pecs, then caressing his nipples and exploring his chest. He watched her enjoying herself for a bit while his dick stood straight and hard, rubbing against her stomach, just aching to glide home into her silky sex.

He didn't know about other men, but for him tit-for-tat was a turn on. He went for her nipples, filling both of his hands. Her eyes closed and she arched, rising higher on her knees and thrusting her breasts harder against his palms. He squeezed her full breasts and shifted his thumbs to flick the points of her nipples. She brought her hand to his erection and pressed him against the smooth skin of her bare sex as she rocked to the rhythm of his thumbs. She was wet and slippery from his mouth and her orgasms.

He shuddered, feeling like he could come in a heartbeat. He never would have believed how much a turn on her waxed, clear sex could be. He released her breasts. With one hand he reached for a condom out of the gym bag next to him on the floor. With his other hand he slid a finger to her exposed and swollen clit.

Her gasp and responding hip-jerk told him that he could make her come again if he played things right, which meant he needed to slow down. He wanted the first time inside her to be right. Hard and fast could come later. Would come later.

He tore the condom open with his teeth. She opened her eyes at the sound and watched him slid the sheath over the tip of his dick. She moved in to help then, caressing and squeezing as she smoothed the covering down to the base of his shaft.

She seemed a little unsure, maybe a little lost in the sensual storm they were wrapped up in. Hell, putting himself in her shoes, he would be, too. Meet a guy in a bar one night and have sex with him on the couch the next might be his MO, well, except the guy part. But she didn't operate that way.

For a moment, he wondered if he'd pushed too far, too fast. Things with her were different. She was different and he sure as hell didn't want her to have any *morning after* regrets. He wanted morning after sex! Afternoon after sex. Week after sex. Anything. Which meant she needed to be in the driver's seat and he needed to take a chill pill. All aching dick aside, whatever happened would happen and he'd survive.

He caught her hands with his and threaded his fingers between hers. "I have a confession to make."

Her brow creased as surprise cleared a little of the sensual haze from her eyes. "What?"

"I want you so much that I'm afraid I've pushed you places you're not ready to go. So nothing's going to happen unless you make it happen. I want you to want me but when—"

She released his hands and sat back on her heels, looking upset. "Bloody Hell, Jared Weldon, if you think you're going to go all gentleman on me when I'm naked, on top of you, so ready, and haven't had a man in over three years then—"

"Damn, Rocky. I tried!" He grabbed her hips, adjusted his erection and shoved home. He went deep, arching his back until he'd buried himself to the hilt. She gasped and braced herself, hands on his chest. He was a man possessed, determined to possess. He rocked hard, slamming up into her with enough force to bounce. Her breasts swayed. Her back arched. Her mouth opened in that sexy, oh-so-wanting-to-be-satisfied way. He slid his thumb to her clit and in a relentless frenzy of need didn't stop anything and everything he could do to rocket them both out of the freaking universe.

She collapsed on top of him, crying his name, her sheath convulsing around his dick, ratcheting his orgasm to the point that his whole body spasmed. For a moment, his vision blacked, his ears rang, and he was sure he was going to pass out. All he could do was wrap his arms around her and hold on. Even breathing seemed beyond his capability. Heart thudding in tandem to hers, Jared relaxed and focused on enjoying the feel of her and the pleasure saturating the moment. He knew all too well that life would intrude soon enough.

CHAPTER NINE

*D*awn *had yet to break and* Jared was up, partly because his leg
had been clamoring from abuse and required Tylenol to take the
edge off. After reporting in to Jesse and informing him of the
pending "to be delivered after death" packages, he'd awkwardly
showered, shaved and dressed, armed for the day—three condoms
lined his pocket.

This was one morning after that he wanted to mark
as…different. So, he'd made coffee, toast, and bowls of sliced
fruit. Cream, sugar and jam completed his offering as he carried
the tray into the living room where he'd left Rocky asleep on the
couch.

She wasn't there. Frowning, he set the tray down. "Rocky?"

He headed to the downstairs bathroom. Nothing. Heart
kicking up a notch, he went to the stairs and shouted. "Rocky?"

Nothing. He heard nothing—not even the creak of the
floorboard or the rush of water running through the pipes. In a
surreal panic, he grabbed the Glock and-ditched the boot. In
silence, he re-checked the downstairs and rushed up the stairs. He
found the cotton-pajamas she had on last night in the hamper, but
the shower was dry, and the rooms were empty. Had she gone up
to the roof even though they'd agreed she'd stay inside?

Hoping against hope, he crept up the spiral stairs and reached
the center rotunda of the captain's walk. The sun was a pink-
purple haze in the distance and the day had yet to shift from the
gray shades of the night. Shadows filled her roof-top oasis and
honeysuckle scented the air, but Rocky wasn't there. He moved to

the edges and started scanning the perimeter of her yard. Within seconds, he found her-a dark silhouette swimming beneath the surface of the pool.

He didn't know whether to shout in anger or cry in relief as he went back inside and exited through the downstairs French doors. All he did know is his body shook. He reached the poolside about the time she surfaced for a breath. Going to his knees he got as close to her as he could.

"Bang. Bang. You're dead." His voice was rough and harsh.

She gasped and swung around to look at him. "Jared?"

"No. It's Ted Bundy or whoever the hell it is who's after you. You promised you wouldn't go outside."

"I-I forgot. I'm sorry. But it's not like there's some serial killer after me for heaven's sake. A freaking planter fell."

Reaching out, he grabbed her arms and pulled her to him. Christ. She was swimming naked. "Let me be very clear. The planter had help, which means someone who wanted to cause you harm took the moment of opportunity to do it. They failed. They will try again and the next time they'll be a little more assured of the outcome. They may try and make it look like some random accident. They may not. I do know one thing for sure. It will be a deliberate act and you do not need to be swimming in the dark alone!"

Moving as close as she could, she placed her palms on his shoulders. "I'm really sorry. I honestly forgot. I didn't mean to make you worry."

"I'll get over it. But until we know what in the hell is going on, you can't do this—do you always swim naked?"

"Unless I have company. Considering I swim at least twice a day, do you know how much a pain in the ass wet swimsuits are? It's practical."

"It's provocative as hell and you're going to have to change your MO."

She pulled back, her expression wary and fierce. "You have no right to dictate—"

"Ease up. After we're clear safety-wise, I hope to be skinny dipping with you. Until then, can we go back inside? Your coffee and toast are cold by now." He reached for her.

She grasped his hand and he pulled. "You made me breakfast?"

Jared shrugged. He might have said something romantic but she was standing there all sleek and wet and slippery and all he could say was, "Come on." He pulled her to the house.

"Let me get my robe."

"You don't need it."

"Jared. Would you stop acting so—dictatorial. Nothing bad is going to happen while I get my robe."

He swung around. "You don't need it. I want you wet. He leaned down and sucked a nipple into his mouth and pulled deep. She arched and groaned. He released her and pulled her toward the French doors. "We need to hurry."

Once inside with the door locked, he jerked off his shirt, searching for the nearest landing pad. The only thing within his two-step-radius-capability was the back of the couch. He picked Rocky up and set her on it. He put his Glock and a condom carefully aside, flung off the rest of his clothes and slid between her legs. Spreading her knees, he leaned down and ran his tongue up the cleft of her smooth sex, parting her lips. Finding the nub of her clit, he laved special attention to it and didn't stop until, breathing heavy with her hips squirming, she reached for him.

Standing, he kissed her long and hard, pressing himself against her wetness from erection to chest. He kept the kiss fest going as he slid, reveled, and wiggled all over her slick body until he couldn't wait another second to get inside her. Rolling on a condom, he opened her knees as wide as he could and watched as he pressed his erection into her hot sheath. With her denuded sex, he could see every nuance of her flesh taking in his thick shaft. An erotic thrill shivered up his spine. He pulled back out and shoved in again and again. She arched to him and he shifted his gaze to hers.

She'd braced herself on the couch back, hands gripping the tops of the cushions at her sides. She didn't look comfortable and he wanted to drive into her without worry. Making love to her without the boot on his leg was HEAVEN and hurt less because he wasn't straining against the hard plastic shell. No more boot in bed or out of bed when he was with Rocky and if there was consequences, he'd gladly pay then later.

"Lay back." He urged her to let go and fall backward.

She looked puzzled and unsure. He grabbed her legs and lifted them up to his shoulders, so her ankles rested against his neck. This caused her to fall backward, her back and head supported by the thick couch cushions. She wasn't quite upside down, but close enough that he knew the rush of blood would give her quite an orgasm. He shoved home and his balls slid against her sweet ass, almost making himself dizzy with pleasure. He wrapped his arms on the outside of her legs to hold her in place and pumped into her as he stroked her clit. She moaned with pleasure and he gave himself over to the frenzy consuming him—mind, body, and soul. He couldn't get enough of her.

Rocky reveled in the waves of pleasure rippling from head to toe. The sensations were drowning her in a molten pool that she never wanted to emerge from. Jared's erection filled her to the core. Her lips burned from the power of his kiss. Her breasts ached from his touch and the bouncing force of each deep thrust. And his silky hair brushed the arches of her feet over and over. It drove her crazy. Her hips rocked with every flick of his thumb. Her breathing shuddered, her body shook, but what captured her from the inside out and sent her senses soaring to an unknown level was the look of total need and complete surrender in his gaze. It sent her flying past the moon as a wave of orgasms clenched her insides and shot stars soaring though her mind that, exploded with his every thrust until he stopped, and collapsed upside down on the couch with her.

"I'm dying," he whispered as he caught her hand in his.

"Me too," she gasped. "And I don't want to do anything else…ever." She laughed.

"Give me a minute, and I can arrange that."

She shifted to her side to look at him, almost believing he could continue this wild sensual odyssey forever. "We'd likely starve to death."

Humor, hunger, and satisfaction lit his blue eyes. "What a way to go, though."

"Considering how in shape you are, it would be a while." She ran a hand over his sculpted chest then raked her gaze over his body. It was then she realized he wore only a bandage on his hurt leg. "Where's your boot?"

He looked down, frowning as if he didn't know he didn't have it on. "I took it off when I went searching for you. It's not stealth material."

She rolled to the side and sat upright on the couch. "You need to get it back on right now. What if you've worsened the fracture? How in the world could we explain to your brother that you injured yourself more because you were—"

"Having the best five minutes of my life?" Jared grinned and swung around upright. Before he could say anything more, she heard her cell phone ringing. A glance at the clock across the room revealed that it was already seven o'clock. She was due at the construction office in thirty minutes.

"I'd better get that."

"You do that and I'll get this." He caressed her bottom as she stood. "I'll slide inside from behind while you talk business and pretend nothing at all is going on."

She couldn't believe the catch of excitement in her stomach. "Considering you short circuit my every brain cell, all I'd do is heavy breathing. You need to get dressed so I can think."

"Ditto," Jared said.

Rocky laughed and ran for the phone. It was Mack. She answered.

"You all right? You sound out of breath," he said.

"Uh, just rushing in from a swim. What's up?"

"I'm at the office. Alice left several messages for Pat to call Albright Concrete. He missed the meeting yesterday and they want to reschedule."

"I wonder why? Did he mention it at the jobsite?"

"He never showed up at the Drake Hotel. Did you talk to him yesterday?"

Her heart began to pound. "No. I called his cell and left messages on his voicemail."

"Me too. Just now."

"Did you call Collin?'

"No. Was letting him cool off. Should I?"

"No. Not yet. I'll stop by Pat's on the way into the office and call you. He might just be in bed with the flu or something." She hung up. Jared was there and thankfully dressed. He'd strapped on the boot, but had left the crutches propped up in the corner.

"What's wrong?"

She explained.

"He was supposed to bring you that box your mother left, right?"

"Yes."

Hurry up and get ready. "I'm calling, Jesse. I don't like the sound of this at all."

Rocky didn't either. She was ready to go in minutes and noted with a shiver that Jared carried the Glock with him. They were almost out the door when she remembered his crutches and mentioned them.

"Jackson can shoot me later, but I'm not going to hobble around all day, especially if the situation you are in becomes more serious. I need to be able to move fast."

Rocky only nodded and didn't try and ague with Jared, perhaps because she felt it, too—the ominous cloud hovering over her that made her want to run for her life.

Jared offered to drive and Rocky didn't argue. Her nerves were on edge and the butterflies in her stomach had her feeling ill. He dove adeptly with his booted leg off to the side. They parked behind Pat's green truck in Pat's driveway. If he wasn't at home, then he'd left by some other means. He'd lived in the quiet neighborhood for decades. Though he could have afforded and built a bigger house, he stayed in the two-bedroom bungalow that he and his wife Cissy had bought when starting their life together. Cissy had died giving birth to Collin. So growing up, Pat and Collin had been the bachelors that Rocky and her mother, Keira, had tried to fill in the gap for with occasional home cooked meals and spring cleanings.

A black sedan pulled up and parked on the street. The driver got out as she and Jared exited the truck. It was Jesse. The look on his face was as grim as Jared's.

"I arrived a few minutes ago, parked up the street, and checked the perimeter. It's clear. No one answers the door."

For some reason, Jared groaned.

Jesse only lifted a brow.

"There's a key above the door jamb," Rocky told Jesse.

"I know. I didn't use it. Wanted to wait for you, since you're a close friend of the family. You two stay behind me and follow my lead. No arguments." Jesse led the way. Rocky got the idea that when it came to serious situations Weldon's never shirked from taking the lead.

Rocky had had a strange feeling since speaking to Mack. Now her angst doubled. Just the simple act of checking on a dear friend had become a point of danger.

She didn't like what was happening to her life. Everything had a sinister shadow cast over it and she wanted to blame someone— to yell. She wanted it all to go away and have everything normal again. But somehow as they entered Pat's tiny bungalow, she didn't think her life would ever be the same. The moment she stepped inside Pat's house, she shivered hard. It was almost as cold as she imagined a meat locker would be.

"Does he always keep his house this cold?" Jesse asked.

Rocky shook her head. "Cold made Uncle Pat's bones ache. He liked things warm."

Jared and Jesse exchanged a look that Rocky ignored. She was too busy praying that everything was all right and that the doom churning inside her wasn't real. Jesse moved slowly, she followed and Jared closed in the rear, his plastic boot clanked on the wood floors of the foyer like a death knell.

The kitchen and eating area lay to the left and appeared to be empty. To the right was the great room and fireplace. Bedrooms and bath were in the back. She turned right and saw Pat's hand on the arm rest of his recliner and rushed forward. "Uncle Pat? Everyone's been—"

Jesse blocked her with his arm and Jared pulled her back.

She started to protest, but realized that Pat hadn't responded in any way. Jesse moved across the room and edged around the chair. "Jared, call the police. He's dead. Gunshot wound to the head. Possible suicide?"

"No!" Rocky cried, moving forward. "He'd never do that. Uncle Pat would never do that."

Jesse caught her arm. "You sure you want to go closer? There's some things once seen can never be forgotten."

Rocky stopped and sucked in air, feeling like she was going to be sick or pass out. The sensation of free-falling into a dark abyss was back, only this time it was wrought with horror and pain.

After calling 911, Jared wrapped her in his arms and pulled her close to his heart. "Do you want to go outside?"

"No. I'll be all right." She groaned. "I need to call Collin."

"In a minute," Jesse said. "First, I need you to look around and tell me if anything is out of place from what you remember it being before the police arrive and kick us out."

"It's been years since I was here but…Uncle Pat wasn't one to change anything." Rocky eased from Jared's hold and glanced around the great room. The book shelves, entertainment center, even the sofa, were all the same as they'd always been.. Fearful, but unable to stop, she moved over to where Jesse stood, searching the room. The magazines on the coffee table were the same, just newer issues. Pat liked reading about race cars, motorcycles, and fishing. The TV remote was in its customary place on the end table by the recliner. The curtains and pictures, all aged by sun and time, were the same. She shook her head. "No, everything is as I—wait, I smell something burnt. Like wood in the fireplace." She moved to the hearth. "Uncle Pat never uses the fireplace. Wood smoke sets off his asthma."

Jesse and Jared joined her. Before she could touch the thick iron mesh covering the opening, Jesse stopped her. He used the blade of his pocket knife to ease open the grate.

She gasped. Sitting on the rack, with burn marks curled all around it, was a rose painted box she had no trouble recognizing. "It's my mother's hatbox. She kept notecards and letters in it on her writing desk at home. I haven't seen it…since she died. I even asked my Da about it and he'd just said that he might have packed it up with all of my mother's things. Her death was so painful to him at the time that he put everything in the attic. We went through it all two years ago when he sold the house and moved to an apartment, by then I had forgotten about it." She turned to

Jared. "What if this is the box from my mom that Pat had at the bank?"

"I'd bet on it," Jared said. "He opened it."

"And maybe found something that made him take his life?" Jesse suggested.

Rocky glanced Pat's way then quickly averted her gaze. "I can't imagine what."

"Believe me," Jesse said. "I've seen it all. Although there is never a good reason to throw in the towel because life means hope, sometimes a person takes their life over the stupidest reasons. You do realize that if we touch the box, we'll be tampering with evidence that may or may not be part of a crime scene. I might be able to work a deal with the local police so that—"

"Hell no," Jared interrupted. "You and I both know shit gets tied up in red tape and evidence protocol. It will be days if we're lucky before Rocky could even get a look. The box belonged to her mother." He grabbed a stack of newspaper and spread it on the hearth. "What if this man's death isn't an accident? What if the killer tried to destroy evidence? This puts her in even more danger than before. I'll take the blame and pay the penalty, but we're taking that hat box out to the truck before the police arrive. Don't you have the ability to process evidence at the R&D?"

Jesse exhaled. "Yes. State of the art. Better than anything they'll have here. It's still breaking the law."

"You can't tell me that if Alexi or Jake's safety hung in the balance you wouldn't break the law."

"Done," Jesse said. "I'll take it now, before the police arrive. You two meet me at R&D as soon as you are finished here." After snapping several pictures of the hatbox and hearth, he got a large plastic bag from the kitchen and with gloved hands placed everything in the fireplace inside, even the ashes.

"Jared, until the police arrive, use your cell and take pictures of everything, if you catch my drift. Don't know what might become important as this case develops. Don't touch anything though, okay?"

"You got it," Jared said. Jesse started to leave then turned back. "I'm going to send a man to guard her father until we can figure this situation out."

Jared smacked his own face. "I should have thought of that. Might even be a good idea to contact the attorney holding papers for Rocky, too."

"On it," Jesse said and left.

Was her father in danger? Rocky stood in the center of the room at a complete loss, unable to think, to process the facts. Uncle Pat was dead. And something her mother had left could be the reason why.

Someone had to call Collin, but she didn't want to be here with Jared when her ex showed up. She called Mack and told him Pat was dead. She didn't say anything about the circumstances. That would be for Collin and the police to share. "Can you call Collin and come here? He'll need someone to be with him."

"Taken care of, boss. Man, I am sorry about this. Guess I should send the crew home. Maybe even give them a day or two off until we sort this out."

"Yeah. I'm glad you're thinking." She hung up.

Jared turned to her, crossed the room and placed a kiss in the middle of her forehead.

"What's that for?"

"Nothing. I have a feeling you'd worry about the devil being thirsty in hell if you ever saw him. As far as I can tell, the man has given you nothing but grief, but you're still looking out for him. What did he do to you that put the fear I saw in your eyes that night in the bar?"

Rocky started to turn away from Jared, but then drew a deep breath and met his gaze instead. "It was after we'd separated. He showed up at where I was staying, drunk out of his mind. When I wouldn't let him in, he broke the chain on the door, and…well…tried to force me. I fought back, but he was stronger. He ripped my shirt. I pretended to finally give in and hit him in the groin hard at the first opportunity. He passed out. I dragged him outside, barricaded the door, and called Mack to come pick him up."

"I'll kill the SOB. Why didn't you call the police?"

"If he had succeeded, I would have. But the situation was all already so hard for everyone. Collin and I had grown up together. Uncle Pat and my father are best friends. Up until then Collin was still working in the company. Rather than involve the police, I forced him out of McKenna Construction."

Jared looked as if he wanted to take aim and fire the pistol he carried or slam his fists repeatedly in Collin's face. "Christ. I could kil—"

Rocky pressed her finger to Jared's lip. "No. No more violence. I dealt with it and it's over."

Jared pulled back, gripping her shoulders. "Is it? That's not what I saw in the bar Sunday night. Why are you still defending him?"

She shook her head. "I don't know. I just know in my gut that Collin would never hurt his father."

Jared exhaled sounding exasperated and angry. "I need to finish taking pictures before the police arrive. Why don't you check the rest of the house to see if anything else is out of place and we'll talk more about this later."

"There's not much else to say. It's a part of my life that needs to stay buried," she said then turned away as it hit her again that Pat was dead. Tears welled. Thankful to be able to leave the room, she walked through the small house and let those tears fall. Many memories were attached to the place and a lot of them had ended in broken dreams, but that didn't stop them from being dear to her heart. Collin hadn't always been the angry man he was now. His decline into alcohol abuse had amplified his problems, but there had been some good times amid the turbulent ones.

The police arrived, asked a number of questions and took their information. Then Mack appeared and set up vigil outside of the house. She and Jared were just leaving the subdivision when Rocky saw Collin's black truck speed by them as he raced to his father. No matter what her and Collin's problems had been, she still ached for the pain she knew he would be in, even more so because of the unexpectedness and the violence of his father's death.

Her face was numb, her hands shook and she was still shivering, her insides still as cold as the house despite the near ninety degree temperature outside. Her world was shaken to the core and the only thing steady seemed to be the man at her side, a man she mentally realized that she barely knew, but somehow the connection they'd made had broken the rules. On an inexplicable level, Jared was closer to her than any man had ever been.

CHAPTER TEN

*J*ared knew *Rocky was in hurting*, in shock, and that he needed to do something to help but was at a complete loss. She was pale, her gaze was unfocused, and her body shook. Though they really needed to go directly to Sheridan-Weldon Solution's R&D building and meet with Jesse, she was in no shape to face anything else at the moment. He pulled into the first drive-thru that advertised coffee and breakfast to go. They never did eat the breakfast he'd fixed.

"I can't eat," Rocky said, wiping her red-rimmed eyes.

"I know," he said, remembering having uttered those same words to his mother years ago.

Jared went through the drive-thru and ordered a range of things plus lots of coffee then pulled into a sunny parking spot. He put the truck in park and unbuckled his and Rocky's seatbelt.

"Come here." He drew her into his arms, pulling her close to his chest as she sat sideways in his lap between him and the steering wheel. It was a tight fit, but comfortable, and reminded him of the innocence of his first dates a long damn time ago, when he had to spend time growing a relationship before even kissing a girl. Somehow that had all changed and hooking up had become the norm. A mix of emotions wrapped around his heart as he tightened his hold on Rocky. He rested his cheek against her head, closed his eyes, and just focused on breathing. The Collin situation wasn't over by a longshot, but he put it on the backburner for the moment. Rocky was clearly overwhelmed and Jared knew he needed to stay level headed.

His first instinct was to blame Collin for everything happening especially after hearing what the bastard almost did to Rocky, but he realized that was driven by his emotions. He needed to keep an open mind to be sure he didn't miss another shark lurking beneath the surface of her life.

When she stopped shaking and began to relax against him, he started talking, knowing from last night, it was one thing that helped ease her anxiety. "When James and I were sixteen we were out motorcycle riding with a friend of ours. We were young. We considered ourselves hot stuff, and we thought we were invincible. We weren't exactly being stupid, but we were definitely skirting the edge of danger by pulling a few tricks on the road. David motioned that he was going to move ahead and wanted James and I to watch him power slide a little on an upcoming turn. He pulled it off, waved his hand back at us, and the next moment a car ran a red light and hit him dead on. None of us even saw the car coming. David was killed on impact. The driver was drunk. I'll always wonder that if we'd been more aware of the cars around us rather than in how cool we were, if David would be alive today. James and I were a mess. We were shaking so bad we couldn't even ride our bikes home. The whole family came to rescue us. Jackson and Jesse rode our bikes and we sat in the back seat of my dad's truck. My mother talked the whole way, telling us inane things about I don't even remember what. I just remember the steady sound of her voice. The first thing she did when we got in the house was to sit us down at the kitchen table and make us a cup of tea. I remember thinking at the start that she had screw loose. My gut was wrung so tight I couldn't even breathe and she wanted to serve tea? James looked as if he felt the same way. By the time she finished, put the cup in front of me, and I'd drunk half of it, I was shaking less. She'd made it extra sweet and heavy on the cream. By the time the cup was empty, I could breathe. Sugar, sitting still, the comforting sound of her voice, and the simple act of drinking

something counteracted the shock I was in. James felt better, too."
Jared gave a half laugh. "Especially after the little dollop of
whiskey my dad added to our cups when my mother had her back
turned."

He shifted back and met her teary gaze. His insides went
haywire, a mix of care and fear for her and anger at whoever was
behind this. He gently brushed a light kiss to her lips. "You're in
shock. You need to eat something and drink some coffee. It will
make you feel better and will help you think clearer when we get
to Jesse's, okay?"

She nodded and he helped her ease from his lap to sit next to
him. He laid out the food on the dash. "Pick something. A biscuit
and jam, a piece of fruit, some of the cheese off the egg sandwich
if you can't eat the whole thing. And how do you like your coffee?
Oh, I almost forgot. You're a triple X-gal. Extra cream and extra
sugar, I bet."

She stared at the food then sighed. "I'll take three creams and
four sugars."

"Good. For a moment there, I thought you were going to be a
blue-nosed mule."

She gave a weak grin and took a deep breath as she picked up
the fruit cup and a fork. "That's better than being a corn cob."

He exhaled hard. Apparently that comment was going to haunt
him. "You are not a corn cob, okay. A prickly pear maybe, but
not a corn cob."

She frowned and he laughed, relief flooding through him. She
was going to be okay. By the time they ate, drank coffee, and
made the drive to meet Jesse, color had returned to her cheeks and
though red-rimmed, her gaze was stronger and more focused.

"Uh, this isn't just a little lab attached to an ordinary security company." Rocky said after they'd been cleared by the guard and drove through the gated entrance to Sheridan-Weldon's Research and Development facility.

Jared winced. The place wasn't little. It was huge, like something out of a James Bond movie. He'd help design and build it. To him, it was one of his greatest achievements in commercial architecture, but it wasn't hyped up in any magazine or even listed in development annuals. The dark granite and glass building, surrounded by strategically placed live oaks, almost seemed to be part of the landscape. It had been designed to blend in with its surroundings. In fact, considering Jesse's top-secret contracts and the importance of what he and his people did world-wide, relatively few people knew the place existed. It wasn't because the place itself was top secret. It was just that security-wise, Jesse believed that the fewer people who knew about the place, the better.

"Sheridan-Weldon Solutions is based in Washington D.C. and does business internationally."

"I had no idea how big the company was," she said then glanced at him. "You're part of all of this and you're bothering to handle my minor problem?"

Sweat broke over his brow as he balanced precariously on the point of his deceit. He was a part of it all only in the constructing of it, not the doing, and running of it. "When it comes to a person's safety, no problem is minor," he choked out, emotion clogging his throat. Even were it not for his lie to Rocky, Jared would have found himself upset by coming to the facility.

Jesse had paid Shamrock Construction extremely well for the work, and if he and James had been wise with the money, they wouldn't have had to worry about finances for a while. But they hadn't been, and seeing the success of what he'd produced in comparison to the failure of what he had to show for it now, wrung Jared inside out. It shamed him, and he prayed to God he and James could turn their lives around.

Once entering the facility, they went through a security scanner and a guard escorted them to Jesse's office on the fourth floor. The first three floors were labs for research and development. Offices were on the fourth and the fifth floor, that only a handful of people knew about, which housed top-level clients at high-risk.

Jesse greeted them at the door of his office. "How did it go with the police?"

Jared scoffed. "They didn't even ask if we'd touched anything and immediately seemed to buy into the suicide. I told them several times that Rocky adamantly believed Patrick Brady wouldn't take his life and that they should do a full investigation. They said no one ever does believe, but did call for a team to process the scene. I think it will be up to us to figure out if there is foul play involved."

Jesse motioned them into his office. "You two have a seat, and we'll talk before going down to the lab. I have some information that puts a twist on things."

Unlike the formal desk and straight-backed chairs of his office downtown, this office was more like a slice from a comfortably appointed home—leather sofas, book cases, classic art on the walls, big screen TV, marble chess set with its own table and chairs, a wet bar and of course, the customary large mahogany desk in the corner.

Jared sat on the sofa and Rocky joined him.

Jesse took in a chair across from them. He opened a file and spread some papers over the table then looked at Rocky. "I've put a guard on your father and we are still trying to contact the attorney. It is better to be safe rather than sorry. As I go through this, keep in mind that we're in this to protect you, not to pry unnecessarily into everyone's lives. That being said, this is what we know so far." He pushed one paper forward. "Your ex, Collin Brady, is in a very poor financial shape. He's been in rehab twice since leaving McKenna Construction and hasn't held one job for more than eight to nine months at a time. I'm not sure how you, your father's, and Patrick Brady's wills are set up, but Collin could stand to inherit a third of McKenna Construction now that his father is dead. With your father in a coma and were something happen to you, I don't know where that leaves the other two-thirds of the company."

"Christ," Jared said.

"Collin didn't hurt his father. I know it, no matter what else he's done in life when drunk. He didn't do this." Rocky grabbed Jared's hand and squeezed, hoping he would realize she didn't want what had almost happened to be part of this conversation.

Seeing from his glance her way that Jared understood, she inhaled and released him. Though after the coffee and fruit, she felt better, her hands still shook as she picked up the report. "To answer your question, Da's share of the company goes to me and mine to him unless I have a child. Then my shares and assets are put in a trust for my child. Should I die childless, the business partner has one year to buy my share before it is sold to an outside investor. The money from the sale along with the liquidation of my other assets goes to my Build-A-Future program for kids."

Jared clarified. "So with his father gone, even though Brady doesn't inherit your shares, if something happened to you, he'd get control of the company and a year to buy out your shares. A good deal from where he stands right now."

"Yes, but Collin would never hurt his father."

Jared cursed. "Would you have ever thought when you married him that your relationship would be where it was during the divorce and afterword?"

She shivered. "No."

"Then keep an open mind. When it comes to your safety everyone is guilty until proven innocent."

"Sometimes, that suspicion is the only thing that saves a client," Jesse said then pointed to the next paper. "Patrick Brady checked out. Born in Ireland. Immigrated to the US. Achieved citizenship and married a US citizen. He's lived simply and saved his money. No surprises until this morning. I have a man over at the bank now to ask what state of mind Patrick was in when he picked up the hatbox. That is assuming the hatbox is what was in the safety deposit box. Hopefully we can get the answer to that today."

Jesse continued. "Your father's report pretty much follows along the lines of Patrick's. Born in Ireland. Immigrated to the US. Became a citizen. He then went to Ireland, met and married your mother, and brought her here. It is with your mother that the story takes a twist. Keira Shona Murphy came into existence on the day she married your father. Before that, there is no record."

"What do you mean?" Rocky set down the paper on Collin and took the sheet Jesse handed her.

"We are still checking, but so far can find no information about her. No record of citizenship in the US. No work or birth records in Ireland. Not even school records are turning up."

"But how? She worked here…she—"

"McKenna construction never claimed your mother as an employee. The only tax records at for a McKenna from the company are for you and your father. She has no social security number."

"I don't understand." Rocky shook her head and brought her fingers to press to her temple. She'd paled, looking really lost and confused.

Jared didn't know what to do. He regretted ever thinking she'd hired illegal labor. In fact, in all of his prior-to-meeting-her-assessments of her company, he'd been a pompous ass, and he didn't like the feeling.

Jesse continued to search for answers. "When she was alive, who handled the payroll and tax information for the company?"

"My mother until she became sick, then my father took over. We didn't hire someone else until…after my mother died. I can't believe this. You're saying my mother wasn't a citizen. That she lived here illegally?"

Jared clasped Rocky's hand, wishing he could do more.

Jesse shook his head. "No. The bottom line is we don't know. Do you have family records stored someplace?"

"There is a box in the attic at my house. After my father's stroke, I put his furniture in storage and all of his personal things at my house."

"If it is all right, I'd like my data expert to look through everything of your father's. Maybe we'll find some answers. Meanwhile, let's go down to the lab. Most of the contents of the hatbox are salvageable to some degree. Hopefully you will be able to make sense of them and solve this growing mystery. We've lifted several sets of fingerprints from the hatbox and the contents. We're hoping to find a match in the system."

Rocky's trepidation grew as she followed Jesse. Were it not for Jared's supportive arm at the small of her back, she might have been tempted to run the other way. She didn't believe Collin had a hand in his father's death, but it seemed that the contents of the hatbox had. Either something her mother left caused Uncle Pat to commit suicide, or made someone else kill him. Why else had someone attempted to burn it all, unless they wanted to destroy its existence?

She wished she could turn back the clock. To go back in time where innocence reigned and this web of intrigue and deception encircling her didn't exist. If what Jesse was suggesting was true, then her parents had lied to her all of her life.

Hadn't they? Or had she just assumed her family was just like everyone else's?

Assumptions had a way of turning out completely wrong. She'd assumed that Jesse and Jared's security company was a small local company. The facility she was walking through right now was a multi-million dollar project. It completely daunted her. The builder in her couldn't help but admire the architectural design and little construction details that spoke well of the builder. The lab turned out to be huge and fully staffed.

"Anything new, Ringo?" Jesse asked as he led them to a large plexi-glass box. "We're taking every precaution to protect the evidence."

It looked like something from a sci-fi film. Inside the box, raised on a clear platform was the hatbox. She drew closer to it, seeing its contents placed there, as well. Surrounding the box, were gloved holes and Ringo had his hands in one set of the gloves, working with the evidence. He picked up a necklace to show her. It was tiny, silver, and its charm was of a woman astride a unicorn aiming a bow at an unseen foe.

Gasping, Rocky touched her neck. "It's mine."

She moved closer to the plexi-glass. "My parents gave it to me on my fourth birthday. My mother told me it was a magical necklace that belonged to a warrior princess who saved her kingdom. It was one of my favorite bedtime stories until I outgrew such things. I thought I'd lost it. We moved to a new house when I was twelve and some boxes that I had taped poorly, broke open. It was a mess." She frowned. "I never mentioned it was missing, because I felt bad about it all. My mother must have found it. Hell, I don't know whether to laugh or cry."

"Information like that is just what we need." Jesse said. "When we're done here, you have to write the story down for us."

Rocky shifted her gaze. Both Jared and Jesse were looking at her as if she had the key to the crown jewels. "Why?"

Jared answered. "It's possible that story can help solve the mystery surrounding your mother. Maybe everything in the box is meant to trigger memories and when examined all together, will give us answers."

Rocky turned back to the evidence. "What's the paperback book about?" The edges of the book were charred, as was the cover.

Ringo picked up the book. The cover was too damaged to read. He held the book upright so everyone could see and opened the pages. Bits and pieces of ashes fell and a flash of anger cut through Rocky. Someone had deliberately tried to destroy what her mother left for her. She felt violated. Ringo stopped on the title page and Rocky thought she'd faint.

She wavered on her feet as her vision dimmed.

Jared wrapped his arm around her. "Breathe. Whatever it is, it's okay. What do you remember?"

Mouth dry. Rocky swallowed hard. "Nothing to remember. I've never seen or heard about this book before. But for my mother to leave a book called, *Unforgivable Acts of Crime*, can't be good. I was reading one of her poems yesterday entitled, "*Unforgiven.*" The words of the poem were so raw and real that it left no question my mother had felt as if she'd done something unforgivable. Who wrote that book?"

Ringo turned the page. Each crime was written by a different author. There were about a dozen.

Rocky searched for her mother's name and didn't find it. "I don't recognize any of the authors. Did she commit one of the crimes?" She shuddered. "I think I need to sit down."

Jared stepped behind her and held her tight. "Hell, get a chair, Jesse. And send someone for some cold water. "Rocky, don't jump to conclusions so damn fast. We'll come back to the book. What else is in there, Ringo?"

"We already have a team member researching the book." Ringo set the book down.

Rocky sucked in air and focused on the next item.

"A stack of post cards tied together by a ribbon with tiny rubber ducks attached. The post cards are all written to Mam. The first one reads:

Dear Mam,

I know you would have laughed until you cried tonight. Just three years old and our warrior princess is already slaying dragons. She was in her yellow tutu, the tallest of all the dancers putting on Duck Lake, a toddler's version of Swan Lake. Rory was at the point of nodding off when a rather large spider crawled across the stage. All of the dancers screamed and ran, but not our little one. She grabbed the wand from the evil frog attempting to put a spell on the ducks and proceeded to attack the spider. She slayed her dragon after much ado, using few choice words that Rory will long regret—I will see to that.

Every day I pray.

The blessing of God and Mary on you and all those I love.

Anchora salutis

Rocky turned in Jared's arms and pressed her face hard against his chest. Tears, pain, and confusion, filled her. "As far as I understood, my parents were both only children and all of my grandparents had passed away before I was born. That sounds as if she was writing her mother, or my father's mother and there is other family alive. They've lied to me and not just about Santa Claus and the Tooth Fairy."

Jared pulled her tighter. "Sometimes lies are told for reasons that seem very important at the time. Before you judge, wait until we find the whole truth. Since they were never sent, it could be that your grandmother is in heaven and that was just your mother's way of sharing."

Rocky leaned back and wiped her eyes, smiling a little. "You lie well."

Jesse coughed and Jared frowned.

She continued. "Nice try to make me feel better, though. Truth is I need to suck it up like I did when I was three and slay the spider-dragons invading my life right now. Getting all emotional is only going to hinder everything. What else is in the box?"

Ringo held up one thing at a time for her to see. The rest of the items were a collection of keepsakes that all related to different events in Rocky's life, but none of them seemed as significant as the first few.

They went back to Jesse's office and he gave her a pad and pen and set a paper in front of her. "The contents are listed here. Write down the bedtime story then anything that comes to mind about the other items. Meanwhile, I'm going to show Jared a few things on the computer in the office next door. Just call, if you need us, okay?"

"I will." Rocky picked up the paper, finding it hard that everything in her mind and heart—the hurt and the fear she felt— was reduced to a list.

Jared set his hand on her shoulder and she looked up at him. He seemed as upset as she did. "You sure you're okay?"

"Yeah," she nodded. "I'm doing as you advised, waiting until we have all the facts before jumping to conclusions again, but I also have to accept the fact that my folks, for whatever reason, deceived me in some very big things."

Jesse took hold of Jared's elbow. "Come on, bro. Let her work and let's go talk."

Jared looked strangely pale as he released her shoulder and went with Jesse. Shrugging it off, Rocky set to work, and the bedtime story took shape.

In a faraway land lived a princess, big and strong. She had a wonderful life being beloved by her father the king and her mother the queen. But all had not always been well in the Kingdom of Ire.

The Kingdom was poor and there'd been trouble and unrest among its people. They wanted to have all of the riches that the Dragon-lords from the neighboring kingdom had. Then one day, a great knight had come to them and promised to do wonderful things for the people of the land. He promised that the Kingdom of Ire would be richer and greater than the Dragon-lord's if the people would follow his lead.

The riches came in and the kingdom thrived, but the knight was not who he pretended to be. In truth, this great knight was really an evil lord, and without the people or the king and queen knowing it, he did bad things to the Dragon-lord people. He stole and killed to gain the riches from them. That brought the darkness of the Dragon-lord's army over the land.

When the King and Queen discovered what the false knight had done, they banished him from the kingdom. The riches that had been ill gotten were sealed away and the King and Queen tried to build anew. They had a precious child, a warrior princess, and thought that all would be well, but the shadow of the Dragon-lords still lingered.

As the princess grew big and strong, the King and Queen knew that she would one day be the salvation of them all and remove the darkness blighting the kingdom. The day came that the Dragon-lords wanted justice for all that the evil knight had taken. They stole the heart and soul of the Queen and left her burning in a fire. The King, destroyed by grief, was frozen in place as he watched his worst nightmare come to life. He was unable to save his beloved Queen.

The warrior princess was at first lost and afraid. How could she save her mother? How could she save her father? How could she pay the Dragon-lords their due? She took up her sword and began searching high and low throughout the land for an answer.

*She encountered many on her journey. One little man, a
leprechaun, told her that a pot of gold could be found at the
end of the rainbow, but the journey would not be easy. She
had to travel through the valley of darkness and fight
monsters that would try and steal all the love she held in
her heart. But the warrior princess remained brave. She
made it to the end of the rainbow, found the gold, and
saved the kingdom by returning to the Dragon-lords what
was theirs. Only then was her mother's heart and soul
restored. Her father took his beloved Queen home and they
lived happily ever after.*

Rocky set the tale aside in a miff, annoyed to realize the story
was obviously more than just a story. It was a message her mother
had embedded in her mind as a child. Rocky wasn't sure what sort
of parent would do that and she wasn't sure she wanted to be a
warrior princess. She was thinking that the princess needed to
move to a new kingdom and not worry about being the salvation of
everyone or paying any Dragon-lord their due.

Jared followed Jesse into another office. It had the same layout,
but was smaller and had minimal furnishings. Pure business
straight up and down. Mulligan was engraved in brass on the
desktop. Jared wasn't surprised. He'd met the enigmatic
employee once or twice. Both he and the investigator Paul Hanson
had been with the company for years.

"Two things. You have to go back into my office and tell
Rocky who you are and where are your crutches? Jackson left a
message on my cell that said you should to stay on crutches for the

next few weeks to be on the safe side. You've a hairline fracture and should give it time to heal." Jesse's gaze as hard-assed as hell.

"Forget the crutches. We both know I'll heal just fine and there is no way I'm telling Rocky anything right now. She's dealing with enough shit as it is."

"Do you think it's going to be any better when we get to the bottom of this and she learns you aren't a bodyguard, but a construction competitor?"

"No. But at least when and if she kicks my ass to the curb, I'll know a freaking truck isn't waiting around the corner, ready to run her over. Don't push this, Jesse. I may not know her well, but given what her parents have dumped on her, the last thing she needs at this point is to find out I led her to believe a few things that aren't true."

"You're making a big mistake, bro."

"It's my deal. And as far as I see it, the only mistake is doing something that will alienate her right now."

Jesse shook his head.

Jared prayed that he was making the right choice, right now. Unfortunately, doubt left an uneasy feeling in his gut. Getting to the bottom of this mystery then telling Rocky what he never should have tried to hide in the first place, was going to be hell.

CHAPTER ELEVEN

Rocky left the R&D facility with her head spinning and her emotions careening. She wasn't sure what was real about her life and what wasn't. Who'd been honest with her and who hadn't. Jared had been a rock of support, but it didn't stop her from feeling that everything around her was falling apart. She had missed calls on her cell from Maggie and Alice. Both left a message about Pat's death. Maggie was saddened by the older man's passing. Alice was shocked and wanting to know what had happened. Rocky couldn't call them back. She couldn't talk about it yet, couldn't fathom that he'd take his life. She just saw Pat two days ago in her father's room at the nursing home. Talked to him. He'd been his usual self. She felt as if she were drowning. She couldn't breathe.

"I need to go see my father," she said, grasping for something, anything to set her world back right. Then she remembered the jobsite. How could she have almost forgotten it completely? "I need to check the Drake jobsite, too. Mack said he and Maggie would take care of it, but it's my responsibility." Everything was crashing down on her.

Jared stopped before pulling onto the highway and heading back into town. He put the truck in park and set his hand over her fist. "Look at me, Rocky."

She lifted her gaze from her lap. The care in his eyes wrapped around her, solid and steadying.

"You sound panicked. You need to take a moment to eat and to regroup."

She shook her head. "I don't—"

"You must. All you managed was fruit this morning. I don't care if we do drive-thru again or go to a restaurant, but you have to eat. You're under a lot of stress. Not eating will only make thinking clearly that much harder. You have to remember that you are not alone. I am with you and we'll figure this out together. We'll go anywhere you need to go and see anyone you need to see, but first we are going to take care of you." He brushed a kiss to her temple and squeezed her hand.

She unfisted her hand and clasped his. She was panicking. Sucking in a deep breath, she let it go slowly, much as she did in yoga. "You're right. I would have fainted in the lab if you hadn't made me eat earlier. We both need to eat and take a moment to breathe. With you and your company's resources, I need to realize that everything possible is being done."

Jared exhaled as if she'd punched him or as if he'd just cleared an Olympic high jump.

"Are you all right?" She studied his expression, seeing that he was as worn and worried by the events of the morning as she was.

He gave a half smile and looked out window as if searching for something. "Yeah, Sheridan-Weldon Solutions is a Godsend right now no matter what the circumstances."

She frowned, but before she could ask him what he meant, he changed the subject. "What do you want to eat?" He put the truck in gear and pulled onto the highway.

"Drive-thru sounds like cardboard at the moment, but the thought of people and crowds is worse. I'm too raw inside."

"I'm with you. I know just where to go. It's close, quiet, and not far from the Drake Hotel." "That was easy. I'd thought I'd have to argue more."

"I can be reasonable," she said, already feeling herself relax inside. Just talking to him for a few minutes and reaffirming his solid presence helped.

He arched a skeptical brow at her response.

"On occasion," she added, almost smiling.

"That makes two of us."

"Some more than others," she quipped and surprisingly laughed when he frowned. Teasing him eased some of the heaviness inside her and gave her that close to "normal" feeling she desperately needed at the moment.

Well, what she could call normal. Nothing had been normal since Jared kissed her in the bar. How would their relationship have progressed under "normal" circumstances? Would they have dated a while before making love?

The speed in which their relationship had progressed was as unsettling as it was comforting. In some ways she knew him and was closer to him than anyone else in her life. In other ways, they were still strangers.

When it came to sex there hadn't been a hesitant bone in Jared's body. He'd thrust her into a full sexual arena and made every moment sizzle. Collin had been her first and only. Their first forays into sex had been tentative and after marriage it had become a weekly routine. Somehow she couldn't imagine sex with Jared ever being routine.

Given the force of their attraction, she wouldn't have been able to keep him at arm's length for long even under "normal" circumstances. They would have kissed the first date, gone farther on the second date, and would have likely hit a home run on the third. Still, there were some normal things that it would be nice to have. "Guess this lunch will be our first date."

He sat up straight, blinking with surprise. His foot even fell off the gas pedal, causing the truck to list and jerk as he recovered. "Hell...I...but, just damn, Rocky. It never even occurred to me that we hadn't dated. We just sort of hit it off in the bedroom and I just assumed—but damn. You're right. No, this will not be our first date. Our first date will commence when this situation you are in is resolved. There's more to me than a good f—uh, than being good in the bedroom. I'm a great guy. I can be romantic and fun and adventurous."

"Deal," she said, holding back a laugh. She had no doubt that he was a great guy, but someday she'd make sure he amended his assessment of himself in the bedroom. He wasn't just good. He was great. Amazing. Addictive. And she didn't need to sleep around to figure that out.

There was difference between Jared and Collin when it came to sex. Collin enjoyed sex. He wasn't bad at it, but his focus in the bedroom had been getting off. Where Jared's focus and sexual energy were in getting *her* off. Being the center of that charismatic attention was the most seductive thing in the world. A real turn on.

He took her to a seafood restaurant on the Savannah River and she ordered creamy clam chowder along with a shrimp salad. Exactly what her stomach could handle at the moment. They sat in the outside dining area where the breeze flowed in tandem with the river. Spanish moss swayed in the live oaks lining the water and pelicans provided a show as they fought over a fish and pier-sitting rights on the dock. He didn't talk about any of the day's harrowing events. He told her stories about the exploits he and his brother's had while growing up and made her laugh.

"Being older, Jesse and Jackson were naturally doing forbidden things that only older boys should do, like jumping and racing dirt bikes and rafting down the river. James and I were fit to be tied that they wouldn't let us join them. So we'd threaten to tattle on them and pestered them until they let us. Invariably, something would go wrong, James or I would get hurt and then Jackson and Jesse would get their hides tanned, not only for doing what they weren't supposed to be doing but for letting us do it too. They couldn't win for losing. Guess they decided that they'd rather have the fun and get a whooping than not have the fun at all."

Touched by his sharing, she smiled. There was an appealing, heart-warm honesty about Jared. Whether he'd admit it or not, family meant a lot to him. "I'm sure having brothers had its downside, but to me it sounds like heaven."

The meal was over too soon, but the time had been quiet, peaceful, and relaxing—just what she needed after everything that had happened this morning. They left the restaurant and ten minutes later, pulled into the parking area for the Drake Hotel. Besides the construction equipment and office trailers, there were two trucks in the parking lot—one newer and black the other worn and blue.

"I wonder who's here."

"The blue truck is…mine," Jared said, and shrugged, almost hesitantly as if embarrassed. "A lot of memories are wrapped up in her tail-gate. James and I shared it during high school and college.

Rocky rolled her eyes. She could just imagine what all went on in the back of *that* pick up. She exited her truck. "Maybe one of the other men left their truck here, too," she said as Jared joined her.

They walked toward the Drake Hotel and she sighed beneath a wave of flooding sadness. "I can't believe Uncle Pat is gone."

Jared clasped her hand. There really anything that could be said.

"Once I had the site set up I had planned to look for more men. Pat was going to take charge of one crew and I was going to run the other. I won the bid on this because I promised to complete the job in four weeks and there was no way it would happen with just my men."

Jared stumbled and she steadied him.

"You all right?" She kept forgetting that he wore a boot. That he'd been injured. He really hadn't complained at all.

"Yeah. Uh, just missed my step.

"Your leg hurt?"

"Not much now. It was a bitch yesterday, but better today."

"Good. I feel response—" She sniffed the air. "Do you smell smoke?"

"Yes."

Rocky started to run forward, but Jared grabbed her arm. "Stay behind me," he ordered.

She backed up a step, surprised to see the pistol in his hand. "You're not going to put a fire out with that."

"Until we find out what is going on, just stay behind me. And let's hurry. Those Byzantine mosaics are irreplaceable." He ran ahead and she followed, surprised he was even aware of the hotel's artistry and its imported glass tiles.

The front doors were locked. Jared turned right, hurrying. They were both looking for signs of a fire inside as they passed each window. They reached the planter that had dive-bombed her and kept moving, its broken cement, spilt dirt, and uprooted forget-me-nots were a grim reminder of what almost happened.

At the back of the hotel, smoke billowed from a set of French doors.

"Call 911," Jared said as he ran faster, despite the hobbling boot.

She pulled out her cell and called as she kept up with Jared. The French doors were open. He moved through the opening and she grabbed the waistband of his jeans. She wasn't about to lose him in the smoke. One step inside, she smelled gasoline and alarm bells went off. This fire was deliberate and they were going in blind. Jared must have smelled it too. He stopped and moved backward, but fear that he would charge ahead already had her pulling on him with all of her strength. Off balance, they stumbled back, slamming into the door behind them. The door fell open. Tangled up in each other, they grappled for balance but lost and hit the ground. Her on bottom. Jared on top. The door swung shut.

She gasped for air. He shifted, easing some of his weight off of her.

"Did you smell the gas?"

"Yeah," he said grimly. "This fire is deliberate."

Suddenly a fireball burst from the doorway they'd just been standing in, as an explosion blew the French doors open. Broken glass and searing heat blasted over them. Jared covered her with himself. Once the fire-flash was over, the scent of scorched clothes and hair lingered.

"God, that was close," she whispered. Shocked.

"Too damned close," he said harshly. "Some bodyguard. I almost got you killed."

Emergency sirens blared louder and louder.

"No you didn't. In fact we might be able to rule out someone being after me."

Jared lifted himself off her. He looked at the damage to the hotel and the billowing black smoke then glared at her. "How in the hell can you say that?"

She sat up. The blast had been pretty significant. Had they been on the threshold or even next to the doors they would have been killed, or seriously injured. She shivered, but took heart. "Don't you see? Nobody but you and I knew we were coming here and we'd only decided that and hour and a half ago. It could be that someone is sabotaging the job and I just happened to get in the way."

"Twice?"

Rocky shrugged. "You didn't tell anyone we were stopping here, right?"

"No." Jared stood, his gaze scanning the area around them, gun still in hand.

"Neither did I." The fire truck and ambulance peeled into the parking lot then plowed into the grass, driving along side of the hotel. At least at this point they weren't destroying the gardens.

He slipped the gun into the back of his jeans. "I don't know. I'm still not buying the coincidence angle."

The rescue teams converged on them and they didn't have more time for discussion.

Two EMT reached them first. "Are you hurt?"

Firemen with hoses moved passed and started spraying into the hotel through the doorway.

"No, I'm fine." Rocky said as she winced at the destruction of the surrounding flower beds.

"Check her out anyway," Jared said.

"Him, too," Rocky scowled at him. "The blast hit us both."

One of the firemen turned and yelled. "Anyone inside?"

Rocky started to say no, but then realized there could be. "The person who started the fire, maybe?"

The fireman ran closer, pulling out a radio. "Any idea where? I've got men going in through the front, searching."

Rocky shook her head. "I don't know. I was just guessing."

"There's a black truck in the parking lot and we don't know who it belongs to," Jared explained. "Hers is red and mine is blue."

"There are only the red and blue ones out there, right, Dan?" The fireman looked at the EMT taking care of Rocky.

"That's all I saw," the man said.

"It was here when we arrived," Jared told them.

The fireman turned back to his crew. "Possible victim inside," he said into the radio then told the others beside him.

The EMT urged them back. "Let's move over here. After I check you both out, we can talk."

Ten minutes later, just as the EMT finished, the firemen carried a man from the hotel. With blood, soot, and an oxygen mask covering his face, she couldn't tell who it was. She and Jared followed the EMT over to where the firemen were laying the man down.

The EMT called for a stretcher as he set to work. The man had his eyes shut and was coughing. He tried to talk. "Call...my boss. Call Mack. Someone attacked me. Set the fire."

"Riley?" Rocky leaned forward, finally able to recognized the man.

Riley opened his eyes. "Boss Lady? Why are you here?"

"Who?" Jared demanded, stepping to Rocky's side. "Who attacked you?"

Riley shook his head and moaned. "Don't know. A man. Tall. Dark hair. Like you. He came out of the shadows like a ghost."

Rocky saw Jared shudder and clench his fists. She didn't know what was running through his mind, but she was sure Riley was only saying that whoever attacked him was tall like Jared and had black as sin hair. And of course there were no head-busting, fire-setting ghosts rambling around the hotel.

Dealing with the emergency responders, the police, and the hotel's owner via telephone was no picnic. Tiffany Parker-Bentley was currently in New York and immediately accused McKenna construction of being negligent, blaming them for the damages. Riley went by ambulance to the hospital to check for a concussion and smoke inhalation. Whoever attacked him had hit him on the head, leaving a gash just above his right temple.

Before Rocky could call Mack to let him know, Maggie called. Rocky answered the phone, harried.

"Hey, luv. You okay? I called earlier and left a message."

"I'm still reeling from Pat's death and now someone has set the Drake Hotel on fire. Riley was hurt. He is on his way to the hospital."

"What happened?"

"Not sure. We are still trying to sort things out."

"I'll be right over."

"No. If anything you can go to the hospital to be with Riley. He has a nasty bump on his head. I'll call Mack."

"I'll do that. First Pat, now Riley. Who was it? Who attacked him? How badly is he hurt?"

Rocky frowned; she hadn't meant to reveal someone had tried to kill Riley. The police had asked them not to say anything to the press. "Don't tell anyone, Maggie. Until the police have a chance to investigate. But no, Riley couldn't identify his attacker. He's going to be okay, though. I'll call you later." She hung up.

Jared touched her shoulder. "That frown tells me you're thinking what I'm thinking. If someone attacked Mack and left him to burn, it is possible that person could be afraid Mack might identify them."

She gasped. "You're right. We should tell the police."

Jared shook his head. "Let's leave it to Jesse rather than police red tape. I'll call him."

"And I'll call Mack." He answered, sounding out of breath and harried. She told him about the fire.

"What in the hell is going on?" he asked.

She hesitated a moment, wondering if she should tell him about the hatbox her mother left and that she might not know who her mother is then changed her mind. The planter, the attack on Riley, and the fire might not be related to her mother and Uncle Pat's death—she couldn't quite say suicide or murder. "I don't know. Someone could be trying to sabotage the job. Did you send Riley over here?"

"Not specifically. When I called him this morning, I mentioned that we might need some of the crew who lived closer to the Drake Hotel to run by the place. There were material deliveries scheduled today and we were having trouble contacting the companies. He said he could. But I didn't call back and tell him to go over there as Maggie said she would go if needed."

"Right." Rocky exhaled. With everything going on, she'd forgotten about the deliveries. She had better have her act together by tomorrow. If the Drake job went south, if the owner sued them, it could put McKenna Construction under. She shivered.

"How's Collin taking his father's death?"

Mack was silent a moment too long. "Not well. Pat was taken to the morgue for an autopsy. I brought Collin to the office 'cause I didn't want to leave him alone and there were things that needed to be done. It was a mistake. After about twenty minutes, he lost it completely. Was yelling and rambling around, and throwing things. He...said it was...damn it Rocky...there is no truth to this but you have to know. He said it was your fault that his father killed himself. He made a mess of the Rainbow Room. I tried to calm him, tried to stop him, but finally had to call the cops. Collin left before they arrived and I haven't been able to get in touch with him since."

Rocky sucked in air, her heart pounding and her knees giving out. She sat down where she stood. For Collin to blame her cut deep. Jared, who was just a few feet away, ran over to her. She fought for balance.

"I hate to say this," Mack said. "But could Collin have torched the Drake place?"

"Christ, Mack. His truck is black."

"What does that have to do with anything?"

Rocky explained.

"Out of about twenty-five men on the crew, I'd say eight to ten of them have a black truck. Riley's truck is dark, maybe black even. What's the make and model of the truck you saw?"

"I didn't notice. You say Riley has a black truck?"

"Maybe. It's dark in color, can't swear to it though."

"Okay. Let me know if you hear from, Collin." Rocky hung up, her heart heavy. Jared was kneeling next to her, concerned. She told him about Collin's behavior at the office. "He has a black truck, but Mack said Riley does too. Collin would fit the tall, dark-haired description Riley gave, though. I should tell the police."

"Yes, you should. I can't believe I'm saying this, but a number of men fit the tall, dark-haired description—me, and my brothers included. The black truck situation is a puzzle though. Everything was so crazy with Riley going to the hospital and the firemen rushing around that I don't remember what was said about the black truck. I know we mentioned it, but are the police searching for one? Did the attacker steal Riley's truck? Otherwise there would have been another vehicle here, right?"

"Good point."

"I'll tell the police. But first, what is the Rainbow Room and why would your ex trash it?"

"Because the room is special to me. When I was little my mother would bring me to work with her. I had my own play room at the office that she painted with rainbows and unicorns and princesses. I spent hours having tea parties and making sculptures with caulk and toothpicks. As I grew up and worked for the company that room became my office. The murals are still on the walls."

Jared smiled. "I may have had brothers, but I bet very few little girls grew up with a rainbow room."

"You're right."

He went over to talk to the police and she found herself awash in warm memories of those days with her mother. Now that she looked back, she could see that her mother had gone the extra mile to spend every moment she could with Rocky. It would have been much easier to put her in daycare. Her mother had loved her greatly, but what secret had she harbored?

Hours later, Rocky was still sifting through memories and a killer headache, searching for answers. They'd seen her father after leaving the Drake Hotel. It had been both comforting and surreal to have a guard at his door. Just to be on the safe side, Rocky had cut the approved visitor list to only Sheridan-Weldon Solution employees who had ID. Then she had talked to Maggie. Riley had been released from the hospital with a mild concussion and was doing fine.

She and Jared had returned home and barely had time to shower off the soot and smoke before Ringo from the lab arrived to go through her father's things in the attic. He brought them a stack of information to sift through. Jared started looking at the papers, while she took Ringo to her father's things in the attic. Ringo had made quick work of what it would have taken her days to sort through and in less than an hour, he was on his way back to the lab. He now had not only the box of family documents, but also bank statements, job agendas, and notes her father had scribbled down.

In the space of a day her life had become like an episode off Twenty-four. She sank into the soft couch cushions, hoping the Tylenol she'd taken would kick in soon. Jared looked up from her computer. "Ringo all set?"

"Yeah, if he can sort through my father's papers as quickly as he could through all of the stuff in the attic, we'll have answers tonight. You know, I've been trying to connect the mystery surrounding my mother and the things happening on the job together. But what if they are separate?"

Jared frowned as he carried the computer over to her. "It's possible, but I don't think so. Take a look as this. Jesse has emailed a video clip of Pat going into the bank. He wasn't alone."

"The bank gave him a video?"

"Jesse may have clout, but not that much. No. He got this from a shop owner across the street. It shows Pat arriving at the bank first thing Monday morning. Do you recognize the woman with him?"

Rocky watched the clip three times. The woman wore baggy clothes and an oversized black hoodie. Face hidden in the shadows, she walked beside Uncle Pat, who appeared his usual self. No indication that he was under duress as they entered then exited the bank with the hatbox clearly in Uncle Pat's hands. "I don't know who she is," Rocky said, frustrated. "Are there other videos from a different angle?"

"Not yet. Jesse is working on being able to see the bank's feed."

Rocky rubbed her temple as her headache worsened. "As far as I know Uncle Pat wasn't involved with anyone. The way the woman is dressed makes me think she's really young or—"

"Deliberately concealing her identity which casts more doubt on his death being a suicide."

"Collin might know her if we could find him to ask him." Her ex disappeared after trashing her office. "I've prayed over and over that the investigation would prove Uncle Pat didn't commit suicide, but having the alternative be he was murdered chills me to the bone." She shivered and Jared wrapped his arm around her, pulling her close to his heat.

"Murder scares the hell out of me, too. One of the papers Ringo left is the list of victims and crimes written about in

Unforgivable and the authors. We should go over them to see if anything strikes a chord with you."

"Okay." She rubbed her temple again. Her head was pounding harder. Ringo had said that *Unforgivable,* having been published fifteen years ago in England, was out of print now and had yet to become an e-book. The team working on her case wasn't having much luck scouring the used book markets.

"Tell me if any of these crimes jar your memory." He read through the list, giving her dates of the crimes and places, all of which occurred over seas in the UK.

Murders...bombings...kidnappings... and her mother was a part of this? She pressed her palms to her head, feeling as it would explode. She was exhausted. Pat's death, her mother's secrets, the fire. Her mind was racing with so fast that she couldn't think. Some warrior princess. "No, nothing rings a bell. But I don't even know my own name right now. I just want it all to go away. How awful is that?"

Jared set aside the list and the computer. "Come here." She leaned into him and he eased his fingers along her neck to massage the knots.

"Not awful at all and I think it is exactly what the doctor ordered. Come on," he said after a few minutes and urged her up, steering her to the stairs.

"So you're a doctor now?" She sighed. "Where are you prescribing me to go?"

"Your bedroom. I'm going to give you a massage and you're going to sleep for about thirty minutes, then we'll tackle anything that needs to be done together. You're not alone."

"Sounds like a fantasy I should refuse, but can't at the moment." Just even the few strokes Jared had given her neck had eased some of the pressure in her head. "What if I'm too much of a prickly pear to massage?"

He laughed. "Still prickling over our conversation this morning? How about I amend that assessment? You're a biscuit, kind of crusty on the outside but all soft on the inside."

Rocky thought about it, and decided the description fit. "Biscuit is much better than a corn cob or prickly pear. It works."

"Careful." He leaned down and whispered in her ear. "I might pour honey all over you and eat you."

CHAPTER TWELVE

*R*ocky *shivered.* *"I'm a biscuit.* Definitely a biscuit."

Jared stopped in his tracks at the top of the stairs, looking sucker punched. "Hell. Do you have any honey?"

Heat flushed through her benumbed state and she decided she'd buy a case of honey ASAP. It amazed her how things between them could get explosive in seconds. But as interesting as biscuit eating sounded, she was desperate for more of that massage he'd promised. "No. And unless I get that massage you prescribed, I'm going to become a prickly pear."

"Damn, you have a way of making me forget everything." They entered her bedroom. He was the first guy to cross the threshold into her private domain since her marriage ended and it felt as natural as breathing. "Direct me to the lotion while you strip. If you can swim naked you can massage naked, too."

"Bathroom. Under the sink." He disappeared and she shed her clothes, smiling. He did have a point. Still, as she pulled back her comforter and slid between the sheets onto her stomach, she felt a little bit risqué. Their relationship was new and waiting naked for a man wasn't part of her usual routine. After a minute though, her eyelids grew heavy. The emotional roller coaster she was on had exhausted her.

She felt the bed shift and opened her eyes. He was wearing only a towel and the bandage on his left leg, no clothes and no boot. His chest and abs were a sight for hungry eyes. She arched her brow. "This doesn't look like a massage-then-sleep proposition."

He grinned, sensual mischief dancing in his bedroom blues. "It is. I just decided to be prepared for anything should you not be sleepy when I am done. Either way, I will make the world and your headache go away. That you can count on." He held up her lotion. "Blame the towel on this citrus and coconut scent. From my very first whiff, you won't believe the things it had me imagine doing to you." He squeezed lotion into his hand and inhaled as heaven opened its gates. His salvation rested on that breath.

He smoothed the lotion across her upper back, edging the sheet down as he massaged. He was intoxicating and she couldn't resist drinking more. "So what sort of things did you imagine?"

"First of all, you are naked." He ran his hands across her shoulders and along her neck, easing the knots of tension that had been there for months, if not longer.

"Good," she whispered.

"I am naked, too," he said as he slid his palms down her back, kneading the muscles gently on both sides of her spine. Reaching the curve of her bottom, he swept lower, leaving her bottom tingling as he moved back higher, gliding his fingers along her sides and across the edges of her breasts. The tingling became a burning pleasure.

"You naked is even better," she said.

He repeated his motions over and over in long, slow strokes— down her back, across her bottom, and up her sides. She wanted to squirm but didn't. Just the very act of not doing what her body wanted to do in response to his touch, sent her pulse racing.

She was no longer sleepy, but she wasn't going to let him know that. Not yet. She kept her eyes shut.

He swept the covers completely away and went to work on her legs, turning her every muscle to mush. She moaned when he got to her feet. The man knew what he was doing and he did it extremely well.

"Turn over, Roc, and I'll tell you more about what I want to do to you. What I want you to do to me."

"Hmm," she said, pretending sleepiness.

He ran a finger from the arch of her foot up to the back of her knee, caressed there softly then moved along the inside of her thigh. She couldn't help herself. She shifted, just a tad, letting her legs fall open just a bit, exposing herself more.

She heard him inhale. "You need help turning over?" he asked softly.

"Maybe," she said, her stomach clenching, wondering what he would do.

"Spread your legs."

She opened them a little more.

"Like this," he said, grasping her knees and spreading her wide. He shifted and moved from her side to between her legs.

Her pulse kicked up several notches.

"Still can't see enough. Raise your sweet ass a little."

"Like this," she whispered. She arched her back and cocked her bottom up.

"Hmm. Not good enough." He grabbed her hips and pulled her up and back, so she was now on her knees, her breasts and face pressed into the mattress. His hot hand cupped her sex, rubbing her softness. "Will it take a little of this for you to turn over?" His finger found her clit and flicked back and forth.

She moaned. "Maybe. Might need more, though. Might need for you to tell me more about what you want to do to me."

He removed his hand and she wanted to protest until he slid his fingers into her vagina and found her clit again. "I want to slide my dick into your sweetness a hundred different ways and make you come. I want you like this with your sweet ass hard against me, but later, when you've had plenty of rest, because you won't be resting against the mattress when I do."

"I won't."

"No. You'll be holding onto that headboard or a counter top, or a wall, slamming back against me with as much need as I'll be plunging into you with."

She moaned at the image, almost coming at the thought. And this man had a hundred different ways in mind? Were they all possible? That pocket guide had opened her eyes to a few possibilities but he's the one who made them unbelievably exciting. Sharing with him made it real.

"You ready yet?" He pressed against her bottom, his erection hard. He still wore the towel and she couldn't feel the pulsing heat of his arousal. She wanted to feel it. She wanted to taste him. Two could play this wild game.

"I'm ready now." She thrust back against him, driving his fingers deeper, and had to bite her lip to keep from coming. "But you have to promise me something first."

"What?"

"You have to stay exactly where you are until I say you can move." She shifted forward, making his hand slide from inside of her. Then, she turned over and looked up at him. He was flushed and breathing heavy, so excited from touching her, massaging her, and making love to her in his mind that he looked to be straining against his last tether. She hoped to send him over the edge. "Deal?"

"Deal," he rasped.

She smiled, loosening his towel. It was about time this scorching need between them singed his senses raw, too. His erection sprang free, jutting up from a bed of curly black hair. She clasped his penis in her hands, wrapping them both around his thick, pulsing shaft.

Angling him, she sucked his engorged head into her mouth. He was hot, silky smooth, and tasted salty and musky, almost sweet. She swirled her tongue around his head and then flicked the sensitive cleft. His hips jerked and he exhaled, harshly. His hands settled in her hair, brushing the waves back from her face. She looked up at him. He was watching her and she sucked him deeper, then released to flicker his tip with her tongue again and again.

His body strained.

"Hell, Rocky. Can I move yet?"

She drew back and shook her head. This time as she went down on him, she cupped his testicles, stroking him gently as she swirled her tongue over his pulsing head. His body shuddered as he strained so hard that he had to release her and brace himself with his hands on the bed behind him. She wanted him to lose it even more. She—"

"Rocky, please. Having you suck me, watching you make me come, watching your lips and tongue drive me crazy, having you take control, is a fantasy come true. But after a day like today, I want to be inside you when I come. I want to hold you in my arms and get as deep as I can get. I want to look into your eyes when we come together. I need you with me, babe."

Her heart squeezed hard at the raw need in his eyes. He meant what he said. She kissed the tip of his penis and held her arms up for him as she lay back upon the bed. She needed him too. His hands shook as he opened the condom he had on the bed. She reached up and helped him slide it on.

Taking her knees, he pushed her legs up and out, opening her completely as he eased himself into her. She shifted her legs around his hips and locked her ankles, drawing him deeper inside. He clasped her hands in his and threaded his fingers through hers as he brought them to the bed on each side of her head. Leaning down, he suckled each nipple to a hard point. Then he kissed her long and searching.

When she was squirming for more, he began to slowly thrust and rock in such a way that he slid against her clitoris with each stroke, slow and deep. She clenched in response, tightening the walls of her vagina around him and edging her pleasure higher. With each thrust, he pressed her legs up and out, exposing her more, going deeper than ever before.

The pace and depth of his kisses matched his thrusts. Slow and easy, he drove her higher and higher. He watched her, gaze intent, his body in tune with hers as he drove them relentlessly toward a new pinnacle.

Coming hard and fast was great, but this slow burn was more intense. She shook, aching with a sweet, edgy pleasure that was a whole new experience for her. She arched to him, demanding more. He thrust harder, making her entire body shake, but didn't change his slow, steady pace.

Crazy with desire, she squirmed, rubbing her clitoris harder against him. Wanting. Needing. Her breath caught and perspiration dampened her everywhere. She couldn't open her legs wide enough. She couldn't get enough of him going deep.

Rolls of pleasure rippled through her. Her nipples hardened even more, becoming points of intense pleasure. She was on the verge of—everything.

Her body tightened like bow. She was going to explode. "Take me," she whispered. "Hard. Give me everything."

"Hell," he cried out. His control snapped. The bed shook with his frenzied thrusts, banging the headboard against the wall. She arched and rocked, slamming herself against him. "Come," he demanded. "Come with me."

She clenched hard, squeezing his penis with the muscles of her sex and screamed as a mind-stealing orgasm captured her body and her soul. Her vision dimmed, her heart thundered, and her body shook. Wave after wave of pleasure crashed over her, leaving her quivering, replete.

He released her hands and she wrapped her arms around him. She pulled him tight against her heart. She closed her eyes, safe and secure with him in every way, and fell asleep. The world had disappeared and she had the only thing she needed right there with her. Jared.

Jared woke. He had not survived the day whole. Bits and pieces of him lay scattered all over the place. He could see how hurt Rocky was from her parents' deception and realized he would shortly add to it, didn't help matters either.

Now he knew how she'd won the bid for the Drake Hotel. All of it had cut him off at the knees. No cut corners, no illegal workers, just hardworking nose-to-the-grindstone drive and a little out of the box thinking. He'd regularly bid on jobs and had never once thought to deliver a product in a shorter time than requested by the customer. He'd finished jobs before the deadlines, but that hadn't been by design. It made sense, though. The sooner the job was done then the sooner the customer could be making money, especially on a job like the Drake Hotel.

Rocky had claimed his mind the moment he'd laid eyes on her.

His body had been next. His sexual drive was completely slave to his desire and his need for her. It unsettled him, left him floundering.

But much deeper and more disturbing than anything else were the pieces of his heart and soul that Rocky had stolen. His heart was all tangled into a knot and she was at the core.

He'd never felt this powerless in his life. Powerless to stop his fall into her and powerless to stop whoever the fuck was threatening her. He didn't believe in coincidences and he didn't think that the events at the job site were separate from the mystery of her mother and that of Pat's death. Whether it was her ex, or some other shark lurking beneath the cloudy surface, everything had to be tied together.

Rising, he took care not to wake her as he dressed in the bathroom and headed down the stairs, waiting until he reached the bottom before strapping on the boot. Personally he felt better without the restrictive plastic, but was willing to follow Jackson's advice for at least a day or two more.

Patrick Brady's death and everything else that happened had delayed the deadbolt exchange and the alarm set up, which meant he'd needed to be extra vigilant tonight. He did a quick scan of the house's perimeter then settled on the couch downstairs with paper, pen, and computer to examine in detail her life and anyone in her inner circle.

He made a page for each significant person in her life and wrote any pertinent facts, including the "after death" messages. Then he wrote a page for each place within Rocky's world, both close—her office, Patrick Brady's house, the Drake Hotel. For each place he listed related incidents and the people involved. The break in at the office, Collin's meltdown in the Rainbow Room,

Patrick's possible murder and the stranger woman, the planter incident and the people he remembered being on the jobsite that morning, then and the fire and the attack on Riley. It irked him, but he included the ghost stories about the hotel. Then he wrote Ireland at the top of a page with Patrick Brady's name, her father's, and mother's below and a big question mark. Even on paper Collin's name popped up in association with a number of people and situations. Was he the tying thread to it all? The man looked guilty as hell. Jared had to draw a deep breath and reexamine the facts, because he realized his anger had him focusing on her ex more so than anyone else.

"I thought we were supposed to tackle this beast together?" Rocky, wearing tank top and shorts joined him on the couch.

He drew her closer and showed her the lists. "We are. I was just laying some groundwork. Look at these and add anything you can think of to them. Maybe by putting everything we know about each person and each place will help us see any correlations and possibly slide pieces of the puzzle into place. Start with your mother, your father, and Patrick Brady. They could be the core of what is happening."

Rocky worked on the lists. Jared read as she wrote and asked questions.

"Let's put all of this on a timeline, too," Rocky said. When she finished, she spread the papers on the ottoman, putting the timeline in the center, people at the top, and places at the bottom.

Jared's cell phone rang. It was Jesse. "We finally found Rory McKenna's attorney, Steve Vance."

Jared put on the speaker-phone. "Vance is back in town?"

"Never left. He's been in the hospital. He walked in on his office being burglarized."

"Dear God." Rocky moaned. "This nightmare doesn't end. How is he?"

"Intensive care, but will recover," Jesse said. "He can't ID the burglars."

"Let me guess," Jared interjected. "McKenna's stuff is gone."

"Won't know until Vance can check it out."

Jared looked at the time line. "So Sunday afternoon Rocky learns that two people have things for her to be given to her after her father's death. And within twenty-four hours they are both shot. One during a burglary, the other from an apparent suicide. So who found out about the future "after-death" deliveries?"

Rocky answered. "I left the nursing home and went to Sally's Roadhouse. From there I came home then spent the night over at Dessie's. I told her everything, but there is no way she's behind this. Besides her, only you and Mack know Pat was supposed to bring me the package from my mother, but I didn't tell either of you that until Monday night."

"Who's Dessie?" Jesse asked.

"Desmond Langford," Jared said.

"Neighbor and close friend," Rocky added.

"Wolf in sheep's clothing?" Jesse asked.

"You never know," Jared answered. "Check her out."

"What?" Rocky glared at him and at the phone.

"We'll get back to you," Jared told Jesse.

"Hold up," Jesse said. "One other thing. Because of the fire damage, Ringo is having a hard time scanning *Unforgivable* into word files for everyone. But from reading the preface, he gathers the crimes listed were all acts of violence between the British military and the Provisional Irish Republican Army. The first chapters detail key conflicts events between them dating back for centuries, but the rest are recent and infamous events, which might have some significance. He wants you to get to that list ASAP."

Rocky gripped Jared's arm. He zeroed his gaze on her pale face. "What?" he asked. Had she remembered something? "Were on it," Jared said. He disconnected the call and set his hand on Rocky's. "Do you remember something?"

"No. But I can put two and two together. My mom has no past. My mom came from Ireland in the early eighties when the IRA was one of the premier terrorist organizations in the world. I don't want to know what's in that book."

Jared exhaled. "Me neither, but for your sake we have to."

Rocky was already reaching for the list they'd read earlier. "Since we don't have the book and none of the crimes rang a bell. Why don't we Google each of them and see if other facts or details bring something to mind."

Jared set the computer between them. "What's first?"

Rocky ran her finger down the page. "We can start in 1974. My mother would have been ten then, if she wasn't lying about her age. The event we're looking for is called the M62 bombing."

Jared typed in the information and Rocky leaned in to read. "Off Duty British Soldiers and Their Families Murdered. Several different branches of the military were traveling on a bus with their families when an onboard bomb exploded. Over fifty people were wounded and eleven were killed, including a Corporal Houghton his wife and two sons. The Provisional Irish Republican Army claimed responsibility, which lead to celebrations in Belfast. What victory lies in the death of innocent people? "

"None. Let's keep going."

Rocky drew a deep breath, trying to ease the knot in her stomach. Nothing helped. Not even Jared's supportive presence. The crimes went in chronological order and showed atrocities committed on both sides. "Type in Lord Mountbatten," Rocky said, going to the next name on the list.

Jared did, this time he read the article. "In 1979 Lord Mountbatten, the cousin to Queen Elizabeth II, was assassinated by a bomb on his yacht, *The Shadow V*. Also killed were his fourteen year old grandson, Nicholas Knatchbull, Paul Maxwell, a fifteen year old boy from a nearby village. The Dowager, Lady Barbourne, died the next day from her injuries. Leader of the Provisional IRA said what the IRA did to Mountbatten, Mountbatten had been doing all of his life to other people."

Rocky pointed to a paragraph at the bottom of the article. "Says here that eighteen Bristish soldiers were killed that same day. Ambushed in a guerrilla assault called the Warrenpoint Massacre. To label these times as 'The Troubles' is an understatement. So far, all of these are horrible tragedies that make me sick inside, but doesn't tie into anything that I know about."

Jared moved on to the next crime. "Just a few months later it says here that five Catholic college students in Belfast were murdered, supposedly in revenge for Mountbatten's assassination. The three men and two women were believed to have been involved in the IRA. They were tied to fence posts in a rural area and boiling pitch was poured over their heads before they were set on fire. Protestant, British soldiers were suspected but no charges were ever filed. The victims' names were Liam McNall, Shona O'Loughlin, Deidre Finaggan, Alan Dunlavey, and Sean O'Prey."

Rocky gasped. "Dear God. I think I'm going to be sick to my stomach. How can people do this to each other?"

Jared met her gaze with a troubled expression. "I don't know. It is...unforgivable."

"College age? Two women?" She shuddered. "Shona is my and my mother's middle name."

"Hell yeah." Jared grabbed his cell phone. "Keep on, reading. This just might be the tiny fissure that will break this ball-buster wide open."

Rocky's mind raced and her body tingled as Jared communicated to Jesse her name connection to one of the crime victims.

"Jesse's moving heaven and earth," Jared said. "We should have information shortly.

Rocky kept reading. She finished that article and read several more on the murders. After months of riots and protests from the community the five students were from, the British officer in charge, George Pearson, found his forces innocent of any wrong doing despite some evidence. Pearson blamed a protestant militia in Belfast. That militia adamantly denied its involvement.

She sighed. Her heart burdened by the senseless loss of life and the inhumane cruelty. "You know, insanity doesn't lie in the mentally disturbed, but in the ideologies of men."

"Too true," Jared agreed. "Especially ideologies that gave no quarter, compassion, or acceptance for fellow human being who differ in beliefs or in any other way."

They kept reading.

"George Pearson's name appears again," Rocky pulled up and scanned the article, giving Jared the highlights. "In 1982 Pearson and his wife, a niece to the rich Duke of Westbury were kidnapped by the IRA. Supposedly the ransom of a million pounds' worth in diamonds was paid, but the couple was never found. Rumors were

Pearson was killed for exonerating the British soldiers, but nothing could be proven. Though the brothers of McNall and O'Prey, two of the murdered college students, had been seen in the area of Pearson's abduction, no other evidence surfaced."

Rocky closed her eyes as dread grabbed her insides. "My dad married my mother in 1982. She would have been eighteen then. Is it possible that…"

Jared leaned in close and cupped her chin, locking his gaze to hers. "Maybe she had a connection to what happened to Pearson, if she had a connection to the Shona who was murdered. I'll let Jesse know. Whatever it is that we find, remember two things. It may change the past as you know it, but it doesn't change who you are inside. And you are not alone. I am right here with you, however you need me, behind you as support, beside you as a friend, in front of you as your protector, and" he grinned. "Inside of you as your lover."

She didn't know whether to laugh or give into the tears threatening. She kissed him instead and wrapped her arms around his neck, bringing her mouth to his. In her moment of uncertainty, he seemed to be everything she needed to face her fears and the past. The kiss was light, just a meeting of their lips, a brief taste of heaven, but it went as deep, if not deeper than anything they'd shared before.

She moved back, stunned at the flip her heart made.

Jared let her go. A question lingered in his eyes as he dialed Jesse's number. She hoped he didn't mistake her surprise as rejection. This time, he didn't put on the speaker-phone and he hung up within a minute. "Ringo is already on it. We should know a lot more in just a little while. The international computer banks that Sheridan-Weldon Solutions have access to are amazing."

"The whole company is amazing. How long have you worked for Jesse?"

Jared coughed. "Dry throat," he rasped. "Let's get a drink." He headed for the kitchen and she followed. "I started the R&D facility two and a half years ago." He opened the fridge and snagged two bottled waters. He handed her one. "I don't know about you but, lunch disappeared a while ago."

Rocky shrugged. Just like a man to go from a kiss to grub in sixty seconds. She didn't think she'd be able to eat anything, but fixing him something would help her keep her mind off the horror of *Unforgivable* and what part her mother might have played in the tragedies. "Grill cheese sandwich sound good?"

"Perfect. My mother could never make enough grill cheese sandwiches to feed me and my brothers. We were like a bottomless pit. Same thing with mac and cheese. James and I both lived on those two things during college. I'll check the perimeter and then come help."

"It's a deal." She set to work.

Jared escaped the kitchen sure the hair on his chiny, chin, chin was singed. This was stupid. He should just tell Rocky that he'd lied. That he was in construction and…

Hell. The only person a midnight confession would make feel better was him. She was dealing with enough shit already. He'd made his bed and he had to eat his guilt until this crap was over. Besides, Riley's words describing his attacker still rankled. *Tall, dark, just like you.* While Jared had a solid alibi, it didn't escape his mind that he also had an identical twin. The sabotaging of the job site could easily be blamed on a competitor, which is exactly what he and James were.

It was with a heavy heart and a knotted stomach that he went through the motions of checking the perimeter from the windows.

The moon hung bright and full, bathing the darkness in a silvery glow and he welcomed its light. When he reached the French doors at the back of the house, he caught a shadow moving across yard.

His body tensed as an icy bath of reality hit him. The mystery surrounding Rocky had gone from the almost juvenile pushing of a planter to a possible murder that might have its roots in a terrorist's organization. This shit was real. He went for his Glock.

Had he really thought they were safe in her house with him guarding her?

Sure, it might take ten seconds or ten minutes for the neighbors or the police to arrive, but he was beginning to realize a lot could happen in that span of time.

He heard Rocky gasp and glanced her way. "There's someone in your backyard and I'm not going to wait around like sitting ducks for them to set us on fire or something. I'm going to check it out." He nodded to his cell phone. "Lock the door behind me and call Jesse."

"What? Are you crazy? You can't go—"

Jared slid open the French door and disappeared into the night with a grim determination. Anyone attempting to cause her harm in any way would meet his steely rage. Using his fist or his gun, he'd stop the SOB.

Remaining in the shadows, he let his eyes adjust to the night then scanned the backyard. He didn't see or hear anything, so he stayed put with his back to the house and waited.

The steps leading to the roof-top garden cut away to his left. He was fairly certain that the intruder hadn't had time to make it to the steps yet, but Jared didn't discount the threat. He strained for the slightest sound.

Before him, red tile paved the way to the pool that shone like quicksilver in the moonlight. Surrounding the pool were plenty of tall shrubs and plants for a man to hide behind. Suddenly, a clank of metal rang through the night and Jared shifted his focus to the far right, remembering that Rocky's natural gas tank and the lines that fed gas into the house were in that direction.

Moving a little closer, Jared watched as a shadow separated from the darkness.

Jared aimed the Glock. "Stop or I'll shoot." The man ran towards him.

Cursing, Rocky hit the redial on Jared's phone.

Jesse answered. "Bro?"

"It's Rocky. Jared's gone outside after an intruder. He said to call you."

"Son of a bitch. He's supposed to call BEFORE he does anything. Lock the door and stay put. I'll have a man there in minutes." Jesse hung up, leaving expletives ringing in her ears.

Minutes? That wasn't possible.

She wasn't about to let Jared face an intruder alone. She debated for a heartbeat on going back upstairs for her shotgun or running outside after Jared. She compromised by grabbing the iron poker from her fireplace and following him.

She reached the end of her back porch and heard Jared's shout. "Stop or I'll shoot!"

Jared was limping at a fast pace, chasing a man trying to escape, running toward her back fence. The man didn't even pause at Jared's warning, but ran faster.

Rocky's throat shut down, trapping her scream. While it scared the hell out of her to have a man in her yard, she didn't want to see that man killed, because of it. Jared paused and took aim.

"Oh God! Don't kill him," Rocky yelled and ran toward Jared. He glanced her way and the escaping intruder hit her back fence, vaulting over it.

Jared lowered his gun, cursing. "I wasn't going to kill him. Damn it, now we don't have a clue as to who he was. What are you doing out here? I told you to stay inside. Go back."

She held up the poker. "Not without you. Jesse says he'll have a man here in minutes."

"He probably has a backup man at the end of the street. When I came out, the intruder was over by the natural gas tank. I'm going to check it out first. I don't smell gas, but you had better go back inside." Jared moved toward the tank and she followed. She wasn't going to leave him out here alone.

He looked back irritated. "Go-"

"Don't waste your breath. I'll go in when you do."

Jared bit back a few choice words, thinking he'd needed to set some bodyguard ground rules. "I think your mother's Warrior Princess story brainwashed you. Your safety is more important than anything else, including your ego or my neck."

He'd make sure there was no damage to the natural gas tank then leave the rest up to Jesse's backup. His brother should have told him he had a man close by, but then Jared realized he would have gotten his Jockey's in a wad over it. Which made him realize his ego was the biggest block to her safety after all.

"Ego has nothing to do with it," Rocky said. "Two people facing an intruder are better than one."

"Not when one of them is the target."

Five feet away from the tank, out of the corner of his eye, Jared caught a flash of red digits glowing in the dark up by where the gas pipes attached to Rocky's house.

His blood froze and his body exploded into action.

"Run!" He swung around and grabbed Rocky's hand.

The pool was just yards away to the left. He went left.

Every split second seemed like an eternity. Visions of them being burned alive in a ball of fire filled his mind.

His heart thundered painfully as he pumped harder to run, he couldn't breathe, and he couldn't move fast enough as if he knew deep in his gut they weren't going to make it.

CHAPTER THIRTEEN

*"D*ive!*" Jared yelled when they* were feet from the pool's edge. The blast wave slammed into him just as he hit the water and nearly had him plowing nose first into the cement bottom.

A quick glance at Rocky confirmed she was with him underwater and all right. He had no trouble seeing. The world was cast in red. Above them, fire raged as if they were beneath hell itself.

Still holding his Glock in one hand, Jared grabbed Rocky's hand and led her to the far end of the pool, away from the fire and the house. Maneuvering underwater with the immobilizing boot on his leg was no picnic. His lungs were screaming by the time they cautiously surfaced. He sucked in hot smoky air and coughed.

Flames raged to at least fifty feet in the air, coming from the area of her natural gas tank and the left side of her house. Everything that lay within the blast zone had been blown away or leveled—planters, lounge chairs, trees, the fence. The glass windows and doors on the lower level to the house had been shattered.

He watched Rocky turn a three-sixty, her eyes wide with horrified shock. The fire ball burned out as it consumed the gas from the tank. The fire at the left side of her house still burned. Why was the fire contained, and not house wide? The ground around the pool smoldered with debris, some of it still burning. Most of her privacy fence had been leveled. He reached for her, and drew her shivering body against his, pulling her securely into his arms. He needed to hold her, was incapable of anything else.

"Thank God." He shuddered. "Thank God you are all right."

"You too," she whispered and buried herself into the crook of his neck. "How did you know?"

"I didn't know. I just got glimpse of glowing red digits on the pipes by the house. The rest was instinct and gut reaction."

She looked about clearly in shock. "I lost the cell phones when I dove into the water."

"Forget the phones. You've got a bigger problem. It's official."

"What?"

"Someone wants you out of the picture." He saw a shadow to their right, coming around the non-burning side of Rocky's house. Adrenaline kicked in. He shifted Rocky behind him, aiming the Glock. "Don't move another inch."

"It's Mulligan." The man stepped forward, hands held up. Jared recognized the Sheridan-Weldon Solutions employee whose office at the R&D facility he and Jesse had spoken in just this morning. Jared lowered the 9mm. Born in Ireland, the seasoned bodyguard known as "Black Irish" traveled all over the world into harrowing situations, but looked more rattled than Jared had ever seen him. It was as if the gray at the man's temples had doubled.

"Holy Mother Mary, I'm damn glad to see you two. Jesse went off the deep end with the explosion. Talk about shooting the messenger." He drew out his cell. "They're safe, boss. Will report back shortly." He hung up and moved over to the pool steps. "What in the bloody hell happened? This looks like a war zone. Fire and rescue are on the way."

"Bomb," Jared said.

Mulligan snapped his gaze to Jared's, his expression as lethal as they come. "Game changer. You two are going in. I'm calling Jesse. He called me into this because there might be an old IRA connection, and maybe he was right." Mulligan turned away, speaking low into the phone.

Rocky moved to Jared's side, starring at her house.

He wrapped his arm around her. "Where's the hose?"

"Same side that's on fire," she whispered.

Mulligan turned back. "We're heading to the R&D ASAP and Jesse, putting two guards on your father. One inside and one outside the nursing home."

Rocky shivered. "Thank God you all are here. This is unbelievable."

Jared heard barking and Dessie yelling. "Rocky! Rocky! Dear God! Rocky!"

"I'm fine," Rocky shouted.

"Dessie appeared, stepping cautiously around the pieces of the downed fence. She saw Rocky, bent double and rested her hands on her knees as if she were having trouble standing. "Thank God. What happened?"

Jared assessed the woman's white-faced, teary-eyed shock and concluded Dessie was not a player in this game of intrigue even she was the only one Rocky told about the "after death" deliveries.

"Duck!" Rocky cried. She slipped from Jared's grasp and went underwater.

Gun drawn, Jared looked for an unfriendly threat, seeing Mulligan to do same. It took a second too long for Jared to register the fact that Pebbles, two-hundred pounds of trouble, was headed right at him. Pebbles took a flying leap and landed in the pool not more than two feet from where Jared stood. The belly-flop-like dive sent water flying in tidal wave that plastered Jared.

Rocky surfaced.

"You left me for the wolves," Jared said, blinking water from his eyes. The sound of sirens blared closer and closer. A man appeared from the same direction Dessie had, carrying a fire extinguisher.

"The hose won't reach, but the fire department is almost here," the man said. Wearing just jeans, he ran up and sprayed the area around the pool with the extinguisher, putting out the last of the fires.

Jared, with Rocky's help, escaped from the pool and Pebbles. He had a good idea of who the man was. About six-six and built, his all-American good looks didn't detract from the fact that he appeared more than capable of handling anything thrown his way or in *getting* his way for that matter. No wonder Dessie hadn't been able to say "no". The open button of the man's jeans and bare feet told a story of their own.

"You must be Saint," Jared said, assessing the guy, feeling that every person he now met hat to be suspect in the growing danger to Rocky. Was Saint on the up and up? Could he be a player trying to get closer to Rocky through Dessie. Dessie could have told him about the "after death" deliveries.

Jared shook his head. How could seducing Dessie gain the man anything? Next thing Jared was sure he'd be blaming the UPS man or mailman.

"I'm Saint to my friends. To others Francis Frances." The man frowned. "You've been to the Golden Bunny?"

"Not in years." Jared relaxed. Spurred by his and Rocky's encouragement, Dessie must have been putting her young suitor's fire out. "Thanks for the help," Jared told the man. "Makes us even."

"Meaning?"

Rocky coughed.

Dessie looked as if she was about to sic Pebbles on him. "Meaning the explosion has addled Jared's brain. What happened?"

"A bloody bomb," Mulligan said stiffly. "I hate to rain on this party, but the sooner you two are out of here, the better. If anything else happened, Jesse would really have my head."

"A bomb!" Dessie cried, looking at Rocky with horror and concern. "Your ex is going that far?"

Rocky shook her head.

Saint spoke first. "Want to tell me what in the hell is going on?" He moved to Dessie's side.

Mulligan handed Saint a card. "Gladly, but after we're on the road. Have the fire chief and police call me when they get the fire out. Sheridan-Weldon Solutions security team will arrive afterwards to handle this. They are already on their way."

"You two come with me," Mulligan ordered. Dessie hugged Rocky and Jared silently mouthed a "watch-out-for-her" to Saint. Then they followed Mulligan, moving as cautiously as he did through the shadows. A surveillance van was in the yard.

Mulligan opened the side door. "Get in. There are blankets in the storage boxes under the seats."

Jared helped Rocky, then climbed in. Mulligan shut the door and went around to the driver's side. The van was equipped with what appeared to be every surveillance gadget available. Jared fished out the blankets and wrapped one around Rocky's shoulders as they sat in two captain's chairs. She was shivering, likely from shock and adrenaline than from cold.

Jared had been in the same state just a few moments ago, but this van semi-pissed him off. "It would have been nice to know that we had ears and support moments away. How long have you been out here?"

Surveillance would have picked up his and Rocky's every word. Their every fuck. Jared decided he was going to kill Jesse.

Mulligan shoved the van into gear and pulled onto the street. "I just flew in from D.C. tonight. Arrived about thirty minutes ago to relieve Paul, so you'll have to ask him or Jesse. It's a bloody good thing we're here."

"Maybe," Jared muttered.

Rocky was frowning, she pointed at the high-tech equipment. "Does all of that mean what I think it does?"

"Yeah," Jared said. "Welcome to reality TV."

Mulligan laughed. "There's no video set up. Just audio and nothing's being taped. But in our line of work, we tune everything out except danger to our clients, anyway. We've seen and heard it all. There is nothing new under the sun."

Jared didn't say anything else and searched to change the subject. It was a wonder Rocky hadn't questioned his bodyguard status already. How could he work for Sheridan-Weldon Solutions and not know the van was there? "So Jesse brought you in from D.C.?"

"Yes. As soon as I heard the book, *Unforgivable Acts of Crime* was possibly part of this case and that Miss McKenna's parents were from Ireland, I caught the company jet."

"Mulligan is Sheridan-Weldon Solutions' European expert. If it happened, he knows about it."

"You're familiar with *Unforgivable*?" Rocky asked.

"In a way. I knew the editor who put the book together. It was Brianna's burning mission to see an end to the conflict."

"Knew?" Jared asked.

"Yes. She was killed just after the bloody book came out. A pub bombing in Loughlinisland in 1996. The UVF took credit. Buggers."

"Who are the UVF?" Rocky asked.

"The Ulster Volunteer Force. They were in essence a terrorist group who formed in Northern Ireland to combat the IRA on their turf. They called themselves loyalist, wanting to keep Ireland part of the UK."

She rubbed her temple. You mean it wasn't enough that the Irish and the British were killing each other, but the Irish were killing the Irish, too?"

"You aren't even scratching the surface of the situation. For the UVF I think it was more that the Protestants wanted to kill the Catholics. Brianna was meeting with a reporter doing an exposé about the Shankill Butchers, a mass murdering gang with a number of UVF members when she was killed."

"Why didn't Jesse mention that you have a connection to the case?" Jared demanded. Hell, he was almost…almost feeling like he should have his Glock in hand. But Jared trusted Jesse and he knew Jesse trusted Mulligan with his life.

"Because I asked him to keep silent. I didn't want anything revealed unless it was necessary. The bomb tonight changed that. I can't tell you how I know what I know. I can't tell you who I was working for then either. Before I worked for Sheridan-Weldon Solutions, let's just say I was in my mid-twenties and I was from Ireland. Leave it at that. But let's not lose sight of the point of all of this. I knew the editor. Brianna was thirty-nine years old and her last name was…Finaggan."

Rocky gripped the armrest and leaned forward. "She was related to one of the college students murdered, right? I don't think I will ever forget the names after reading how they were killed. What else do you know about the murders? About Shona?"

"Not much. That was in '79. I was a young boy at the time. I don't have direct answers, but once we learn more, I might know how and where we can find the answers."

"You know Stakeknife?" Jared asked.

Mulligan's smile in the rearview mirror wasn't really a smile, and told Jared he'd better not pry. "Nice try, Weldon."

"Stakeknife?" Rocky looked at Jared.

Jared winced, realizing he shouldn't have brought the man's name up. "A spy the British planted inside the IRA and was part of the organization's core group. No one knew his identity for years until just recently."

"Bet his family didn't either," Rocky said. She fell silent and Jared kicked his own ass. She didn't need any reminders of people not being honest about who they were.

Mulligan spoke up a short while later after talking to Saint and the police on the phone. "Focusing on facts—not feelings will—get you to the truth. I need to examine is why there isn't more damage from the bomb and the natural gas explosion. Assuming the person who set the bomb knew what they were doing."

"I've replaced the stove, dryer, and water heater with electric, so I only use natural gas for heat during the winter. Every year I turn the main valve to the house off and there wasn't much gas left in the tank, either. I wait until late fall to fill it."

"To get as much bang for his bomb the perp had likely cut the gas line, hoping to ignite a cloud of gas. Explosions can sometimes level a house. You're both lucky as hell."

Jared shivered. Yeah, he'd been lucky as hell, but luck didn't last forever.

"Wake up, Roc. We're here."

Rocky jerked upright, despite Jared's gentle tone. The van door was open and Jared had already moved from his seat to hunch next to hers. She couldn't believe she'd fallen asleep. With all that had happened, she didn't think she'd ever sleep again. "Where are we?"

"The R&D building. We are going to be living high on the hog for a few days."

She reached up and pressed her palm to his forehead. "You delirious? Hogs live in muck."

"Not in Sheridan-Weldon Solutions' safe penthouse. There're only a few places safer in the US."

"Fort Knox and the Federal Reserve Bank of New York?"

"Nope. The President's underground bunker and Sheridan & Weldon Solutions'."

"Which you shouldn't be mentioning at all," Jesse said sternly, leaning into van.

Jared held up his hands. "You've never indicated that it was—
"

"Just teasing," Jesse clasped Jared on the shoulder. "For a moment there I thought James's premonition was of the wrong brother."

Rocky sat up straighter. "What premonition, Jared? Is there something you're not telling me?"

Jared answered before Jesse could. "It's a situation about my brother James that I will tell you *after* you've had a hot bath and we find you some clothes." Jared turned his gaze back to Jesse. "I want the bastard that's causing this nightmare. Did Ringo come up with anymore about Pearson's kidnapping? Where did Mulligan go? We need to ask him about that case, too."

Nightmare didn't come close to describing this day's events for Rocky. Hell did. She shivered, pulling the damp blanket closer.

"It's a quarter after one and I'm pulling rank. We all need rest in order to think clearly. With both of you here, there's nothing that can't wait until morning. Mulligan had to hurry inside. He's video conferencing some key people in the UK before they head to work today. Even I can't know who he's contacting. He'll let us know what he finds out in the morning."

Thankful for the delay, Rocky followed Jesse and Jared like a zombie. Jesse left them in the penthouse suite saying there were robes in the bathroom and a collection of new, loose and comfortable clothing in the closets. They could take whatever they needed.

The door shut and she stood with her dirty, bare feet on cold white marble. The plush gold-accented foyer was palace-like and she was drowned rat. She didn't know what to do.

Jared caught her hand. "Come on. Bath, a hot drink, and bed. I can't wait to shed this wet boot and get horizontal."

A short time later, Rocky lay wrapped in Jared's arm on a heavenly bed. He kissed her temple and pulled her closer. His body had relaxed completely against her. And she realized it was the first time he'd done so since she'd met him. His commitment and diligence in keeping her safe touched the very center of her heart. Just as some of his words had. *Whatever it is that we find, remember two things. It may change the past as you know it but it doesn't change who you are inside. And you are not alone.*

CHAPTER FOURTEEN

Rocky woke early to the patter of rain against the windows. Her internal clock rarely let her sleep late, no matter how tired she was. For a brief moment, as yesterday's event flooded her mind, her heart pounded until she realized that everything critical was being taken care of. The house and her belongings were just things and were insured. What was important was that her father was safe, that she was safe, and that Jared was snuggled warm and wonderfully against her back. She drew a deep breath and forced her mind to relax, to rest, knowing that she wasn't alone in this nightmare.

Muted light streamed through the blinds covering the rain-splattered, arched windows. What she'd been too exhausted to absorb last night was now revealed and she found herself speechless. The furnishings and art surrounding her were luxurious enough to accommodate anyone, no matter how rich they were or how important their status.

Jared's very male, very naked body was warm and too tempting to ignore. Either by design or by restless sleep, her robe was completely open, covering only her shoulders.

The world was waiting outside the penthouse doors. She knew it was going to be ugly. But, the hurt and confusion of her parents' having hidden things from her paled in comparison to the losses she'd already had and was currently dealing with—her mother's death to cancer and her father's stroke. She'd gladly take a hundred deceptions to have them back and healthy again. But that was never going to happen. And as much as she wished the script between she and Uncle Pat and the distance between them over the past three years had been different, she couldn't change what happened. She had to move forward and solve the mystery closing in on her.

But the world would not end if she clung to a few minutes more of not knowing everything. For the first time in her life, she didn't want to charge ahead and tackle her problems, as she'd done at three in Duck Lake with the spider. She wanted to turn the other way and bury her nose in Jared's intoxicating, spicy, and fresh scent.

The irony of her situation didn't escape her. She'd been alone for so long and to find a man she wanted to be with when she couldn't just focus on the relationship sucked. It was worse that after no sex for so long, she couldn't just enjoy having sex when she wanted to without a pinch of guilt intruding—like now.

It ticked her off a bit. It wasn't fair. And she wasn't going to let the hell-storm surrounding her steal the heaven within arm's reach. Not right now.

She wiggled against Jared's arousal, feeling the heat of his sex along her butt cheek.

"Mornin'" he said. His hand slid to her hip and up her stomach to cup her breast.

"Rise and shine," she whispered, pressing her bottom back, urging his erection closer to her sex.

"Oh, I'm rising, but you're the one who's going to be shining." He rolled her nipple between his finger and his thumb, sending a dart of pleasure to her core. "You're going to be wet all over by the time I make you come."

He thrust and his erection slid between her legs, teasing the lips and folds of her sex with the hot, smooth tip of his penis. She squeezed her thighs together to grip him closer and rocked her hips to rub him more. He sucked in air and she rocked faster, she loved making him feel it so much that he had to have her that second.

He licked her ear. "Want me inside you?" he whispered.

She nodded.

"Say it."

"Yes, I want you inside me."

"It's a damn good thing this place is stocked with everything or I'd be running bare-assed to the nearest drug store."

She smiled at the image.

He pulled back from her and she heard him tear open a condom. "While I'm getting ready, I want you naked and on your knees."

Shrugging off the robe, she sat up on her knees and faced him. He lounged along her left side. There was nothing soft and romancy about a man's body. They were all hard angles and muscle built for action. She drank in the sight of him, broad shoulders, sculpted chest and abs, lean hips. A thin line of dark hair bisected his stomach and led to a triangle of curly hair from which his thick erection jutted from. Engorged and reddened from his need, the taut skin of his penis seemed to be straining from his want. The image was deeply erotic, stark in contrast, and throbbing with promise.

He handed her the condom. "My hands have something else they need to do." He immediately went for her breasts and worked her nipples to hard points.

"I like that." Pleasure shivered up and down her spine. She leaned down and sucked his silky hot head a moment before she slid the condom on.

"Good. There's lots more." He released her breasts and patted the mattress. "Put one hand here and your other hand here."

She followed his request. That put her on all fours. He moved in behind her. "Remember what I said?"

"That when you take me from behind I'll be pushing as hard against you and you'll be pushing into me."

"You've been thinking about that, huh."

She nodded.

"Say it."

"Yes, I've been thinking about you and me, coming fast and hard."

"I have, too." He chuckled and ran a finger down her spine, along the crevice of her buttocks and sex then pressed on her clitoris with unerring accuracy. Once there, he stilled his touch. "We'll get to head banging sex sometime, but this morning I want pearly gates."

She shifted a little, wanting his finger to slide over her clitoris, but he stayed with her, applying the same maddening pressure. She shifted again, rocking a little, wanting him to press her clit harder. He took his hand away instead.

She moaned. "What's the pearly gates?"

"One step at a time. First I have to get you dewy wet all over. Every pore of you will weep for an orgasm. Spread your legs a little more."

She moved her legs a part. "Like this."

"Perfect. Now close your eyes and stay just like this for me."

She closed her eye, anticipation raced over her senses.

He shifted on the bed and the next thing she felt was his mouth covering her clitoris and sucking her. He'd turned onto his back and eased his head between her legs. She moaned and shivered as she imagined what he was doing and how he was doing it. He spread the lips of her sex wide and thrust his tongue into her vagina, swirling around and around her sensitive opening, making her want to scream.

She arched and strained. Wanting more. Wanting him to go back to her clitoris. Wanting him inside her. Her hips jerked. And he backed away from her, only giving her clit a little flick. She cried out.

"You're starting to get a little pearly," he said, moving to kneel behind her again.

She opened her eyes. "Only a little?" she huffed. "I feel very wet."

"Patience. You'll see." He slipped his fingers into her vagina and she pressed back against him, her breath catching. He pulled his fingers out.

"Come inside," she begged.

"Like this?" He shoved his erection into her, filling her in one thrust.

"Yes!" She cried out arching her back and pushing against him.

He reached around and cupped a breast with each hand, flicking his thumbs over her hardened nipples as he thrust deep into her three times. Then he stilled.

She moaned and pushed back, wanting more.

"Tell me you want me deeper."

"I want you deeper, Jared. Please. Take me hard."

Releasing her breasts, he straightened. He gripped her right hip, holding her steady as he reached down and grasped her left thigh. "Lift this leg for me."

With him anchoring her in place, she balanced on her hands and her right knee, and lifted her left leg.

"Sa-weet." He pulled her leg up, shifted the angle of his thrusts and went deeper than before. His penis stroked the front wall of her vagina. Suddenly a gripping shudder of pleasure rippled through her. Her palms grew damp.

He thrust three more times, each stroke intensifying the shuddering pleasure. Her body strained, arching for the orgasm that wasn't quite within her grasp—just a little more, just a little. "Oh, yes. That's amazing. Don't stop."

Jared pulled out and she shuddered hard as her body ached for what he didn't finish. A sweat broke across her brow, her entire body.

He lay back on the bed and stretched as if he didn't have a care in the world. She reared up and set her hands on her hips. "Jared Weldon. If you think that—"

He ran a finger down the center of her chest all the way to her clit and pressed.

She almost screamed at the shard of pleasure. Her legs shook.

"You're dewy enough get started."

She glared at him. "What if I don't—"

"Trust me. You do. You will. You will want everything." He tugged her arm, making her fall on top of him. Then he caught her shoulders, and turned her until her back rested on his stomach. He bunched a pillow to support her head just above his left shoulder.

Maneuvering his legs inside of hers he spread hers wide and used his hand to position his penis at just right angle to thrust into her.

Once inside, he used his legs to open her legs wider. Then he clasped her nipple between his finger and thumb of his left hand and put the forefinger of his left hand on her clitoris. She was so excited, so ready that she could taste the pleasure. She'd never felt this open and vulnerable. She was splayed wide like a sexual sacrifice just waiting to be devoured. Her already racing heart thumped hard. She ached. She needed. She wanted.

He didn't move though. He just held her like that, whispering softly into her ear. "Feel me squeezing your nipple?"

She nodded.

"Feel my finger on your clit?"

She gasped. "Yes."

"Feel me inside you?"

"Yes. Oh, yes."

"Want to come?"

"Jared, please." She shuddered.

He rocked his hips twice stroking the front wall of her vagina. "Along here is your G-spot. I'm going to find it. The pearly gates will open wide and we'll enter heaven."

Rocky didn't think she had a G-spot, but she couldn't think at the moment. Couldn't do anything but feel. He pressed his palm down on her sex, as he thrust up, an intense, shard of pleasure ripped through her. More intense than before. Her body shook.

"That's it, Roc. Do you feel it?" He stroked again.

"Yes." Her heart pounded. Her vision swirled.

He thrust five more times. "Do you want it?"

"Yes. Hell, yes." She felt feverish. Perspiration covered her.

"Then let's open the pearly gates." He shifted his thighs up and out, forcing her legs as far opened as they could go. In a frenzy of thrusts he gave it to her hard and fast, lifting their hips off the mattress with each stroke. He rubbed her clit and rolled her nipple. The world as she knew it cease to exist. Her body was no longer hers to control. Pleasure exploded inside her and burned a trail over her every nerve. Her vagina clenched over and over. Her mind tingled everywhere. Her lungs spasmed in shuddering breaths that rocked her whole body. Her vision went black and lights burst before her eyes.

"Jared!" she cried out, ecstasy consuming her.

"Heaven," he whispered as his body spasmed beneath hers with his orgasm.

Once her thundering heart slowed and she could breathe again, she turned her head toward Jared. He turned, too, and kissed her softly. At that moment, she felt as if she could face any trouble and weather any storm. And she realized she hadn't run from her problems this morning, to escape mindlessly into sex, but had turned to Jared and bonded with him, so that together they could slay dragons and conquer the world.

Coffee in hand and Jared behind her, Rocky walked into the video conferencing room. It was set up boardroom style, with a massive oval table surrounded by about twenty chairs. Jesse and Mulligan were already there, looking solid, and oozing I-can-solve-anything confidence. Papers and files littered the table and Jesse had a laptop in front of him. Rocky assumed it was his desktop displayed on the massive TV screen at the end of the room.

It was eight in the morning. She'd already spoken to Maggie and Mack. Riley was doing fine, but Collin had yet to be located since he'd lost it in her office yesterday. Last night's bomb had blown her already crumbling world completely apart and the only element keeping her from drowning was Jared and the company he worked for.

"Pick a chair," Jesse said then frowned at Jared. "Jackson is going to shoot you for not wearing that plastic cast."

"He won't know unless *you* tell him. Besides it being cumbersome as hell, after last night, the lining is wet and I hurt worse with it on. So it stays off for now and these Italian leather loafers are staying on." Jared pulled a chair out for her and she sat. He sat next to her.

Jesse shrugged. "It's your leg." He brought his gaze to Rocky. "Good news and bad news. The good is that we know how your UUSUB is getting information, and staying a step ahead. My team located a bug in your house last night when securing it after the fire. Besides smoke and water, the damage is minor compared to what it could have been. They then checked your car and your father's nursing home room for bugs and found listening devices planted in both. Most likely your construction offices are bugged, too."

Rocky set down her coffee cup before she dropped it. "Bugged. As in someone is listening to every word I've said? Good God, how is that good news?"

"Because once we get our facts in order we can use the planted bugs to set a trap for the UNSUB. Hind-sight always bites a man in the ass. The bad news is that when Jared brought us your case on Monday, with only the planter having falling, and no apparent reason for violence immediately visible in your life, I didn't follow the company's usual protocol of thoroughly checking out a victim's environment. I figured having Jared with you was enough. If I had done so on Monday and found the bug, we would have perceived a real threat, which might have led to preventing the fire at the hotel and the bomb attack last night. The bug also broadens the scope of this case to those beyond your inner circle. We need to take a look at everyone you come in contact with or have had contact with over at least a month before the break-in at McKenna Construction's office. Thank God I put you both under surveillance and Mulligan was able to get to you so quickly. It wasn't enough though. You both could have been killed because I didn't follow protocol."

Rocky frowned. Sure she could understand where Jesse was coming from, but she thought he was being too hard on himself.

"No, this is all my fault," Jared said. She glanced at him. He was white as a sheet. "From the very start I should have—"

Rocky held up her hands as if to stop a freight train. "Hold it. Both of you. You two are looking at this all wrong. The fact is I didn't even remotely believe there was a threat to my life until...well until the bomb last night. Call me stubborn or stupid, but I thought someone was sabotaging the jobsite. And I really hadn't processed what happened with Uncle Patrick. Murder was more farfetched than suicide. Both were unbelievable. The truth is that if I hadn't just wanted to be with Jared I would have done exactly what I've always done—rejected help and dealt with things all by myself. You all saved my life. Now I need to find out who is trying to kill me and why."

Jared sighed. She didn't know if it was in relief or not. She couldn't look at him. She'd basically just confessed she brought him home with her because she'd wanted him in her bed.

Mulligan snorted. "Only a Weldon's sex appeal could be strong enough to stop a murder."

Heat flushed her cheeks and Jared groaned. Now she really couldn't look at him.

Jesse rolled his eyes. "More like another example of the twin's dumb luck." He smiled at her. "You'll see. The rest of us mortals struggle and scrape and just maybe have something end up well, but Jared and James, they can get into the damnedest situations and come out on top."

"Can we stop roasting my ass now?" Jared muttered. "It's already going to get a blistering."

"Sooner better than later," Jesse replied.

She finally shifted her gaze toward Jared. He looked worried as if he was facing the gallows. That confused her. Did her confession of wanting him with her upset him? She could hardly think why. She thought the sex had been amazing for them both. And he was the one who'd pursued her into having him with her.

"Meanwhile, let's get to the case," Jesse said, steering the conversation back to the reason they were all there. "First, you should know that we couldn't have stopped Patrick Brady's death even if we'd followed protocol from the second Jared brought you to us. The ME has Brady's time of death as being around nine or ten Monday morning, not long after leaving the bank. The suicide vs. murder question is still being investigated. The police want to question the woman who was with him at the bank. In my book, it's a strong indicator of foul play. Jared's positive it was a man who planted the bomb. Let me ask you this. Is there a person or a new couple in your life that could possibly have a connection to Ireland?"

Rocky sifted through the people she knew but no one stood out in her mind. She shook her head. "No."

"Anyone who gives you an off vibe? Sometimes we *know* something isn't right even though we don't realize it."

"Just Colliin's rage. That's nothing new. But I still don't believe he'd hurt his father and as for building and planting a bomb, that's just not him. He'd get drunk and do something stupid."

"The guy last night was tall, muscular, but not necessarily built. Like Collin, but also like other men you work with. What about Riley?" Jared asked. "I gather from what I overheard on Monday he's giving you some problems?"

Rocky shrugged. "I've encountered the same attitude from other men too many times to count. It's normal male ego stuff in my book. Men don't like women bosses, especially in construction. Besides, he was attacked yesterday at the hotel."

"So he claims," Jared replied.

Jesse nodded. "A criminal playing victim to his own crime is a dynamic to consider here. He could have faked what happened to him once he realized the explosion missed you both."

Rocky frowned. "What about the truck disappearing from the scene of the fire? Or the planter? Riley was with me when the planter fell."

Jared leaned forward. "An accomplice, maybe? One who could have taken off in the truck? One who could have pushed the planter? If you remember, Riley was facing you and Mack that day. All he had to do was step back to avoid harm. Did Riley lure to you that spot? What do you know about him?"

"Lure me?" She rubbed her temple. "It was a hectic morning. I don't remember how or why Mack and I stopped and spoke to Riley and I don't know much about him. My father hired him about four months ago. The office secretaries, Alice or Maggie would know more. They processed his paperwork. I can call them and ask, but it seems to me you two are stretching to make things fit. He went to the hospital for a nice bump on his head."

"Maybe we are," Jesse said. "After last night, the team here will be looking into everyone who was on the jobsite Monday. I'll need a list if possible."

"I'll have once sent."

"Good. You know, instead of causing a rift, it could be someone who goes out of their way to be helpful. Ted Bundy worked at a crisis center and his co-worker's never had a clue."

"Like Mack?" Jared asked. "He goes above and beyond."

She rolled her eyes. "Now you're really stretching. Mack has been around for years and he always goes above and beyond."

"You should read Ann Rule's *The Stranger Beside Me*, maybe then you won't shoot down everyone we bring up."

"I don't..." Rocky stopped her denial. She was dismissing their suggestions. She really had to keep an open mind. After all, her parents, whom she'd lived with and loved all of her life had kept secrets from her. "You're right. Until Sunday, and Uncle Pat's revelation I never would have thought my parents were hiding something either."

"Speaking of which, we've had some interesting interviews from my man on the ground in Belfast, Ian Conelley. He's been tracking down the families of the murdered college students. I'll let you listen to his reports, starting with Shona O'Loughlin's family. As of yet, we've been unable to make a direct connection, but we've found people who knew her family well." Jesse hit a button on his computer and a video popped up on the TV screen.

Rocky fisted her hand, disappointed, but anxious as well. The name Shona was the only apparent connecting dot between her and the book her mother left. But as the interview unfolded, Rocky saw more pieces fall into place. Not only had Ian asked questions during the interviews, but Jesse and Mulligan had as well. What they'd learned was Rose and Seamus O'Loughlin had four children, three daughters, and a son. Shona, the eldest, had been an outspoken young woman studying to be a lawyer who'd had strong views and had fought for them. She'd been pro-woman, anti-British, and anti-religion—both Catholic and Protestant— which were unpopular beliefs for a woman at that time, especially in Northern Ireland. In contrast, her younger sister, Anne, had been quiet and studious, always reading and writing, and wanted to be a teacher. After the murder of Shona, Anne grew bitter, dropped out of school and ran away when she was sixteen. The family never heard from her again. The O'Loughlins left Ireland with their remaining daughter and son and moved to Australia.

"The description of Anne fits my mother's personality perfectly," Rocky whispered after the interview. "She gave me part of her real name and part of her sister's name. Anne…Roxanne Shona. Shona would have been my aunt."

"I've got someone trying to locate the family in Australia," Jesse added. "One other thing Ringo discovered that fits is, in the closing of her note, your mother signed the Gaelic words—"

"*Anchora salutis*," Rocky said. "It means *anchor of salvation*. She always wrote that at the end of her manuscripts."

"What you might not know is that it is the motto for the O'Loughlin family Coat of Arms."

Rocky shook her head, almost speechless. "How many other clues are woven into what I thought was a normal life?"

"Sherlock, rollover. Welcome to the new world of Cyber investigation," Jared said. "No need to globe-trot and pound the pavement when you can do it with your fingertips and a keyboard."

Mulligan frowned. "Don't fool yourself. There are some cyber-less places so dark that a sane man would rather die than go."

Rocky got the idea Mulligan had been to those places. So was the man calling himself insane? "Sitting here and not being out there asking the questions does feel a little odd."

"Safety for our clients is our first priority," Jesse said. "We do the fieldwork."

Rocky held up her hands. "That wasn't a complaint. Seeing Uncle Pat…the bomb…it was more than I want to experience in a lifetime. Were you able to find out more about the other families?"

"We are working on it. First, I think you'll find this interview interesting." Jesse pressed a button on his laptop. A burly faced man with watery eyes and a stiff mustache appeared on the big screen. His Irish accent was thick. "Deputy Chief Inspector of Criminal Justice Inspection, David McNall here and you're going to owe me more than a pint, Mulligan. It's too early in the morn to be digging up me brothers' past. Liam was murdered and Finn was executed for murdering Pearson. Let's leave the ghosts in their graves. It's all bollocks."

Rocky straightened with surprise. She'd thought the murder of Pearson had gone unsolved.

"Maybe not all ghosts are in their graves," came Mulligan's recorded reply.

"Like you? It's been ten years. I thought you——"

The video went black then picked back up a few seconds later with Mulligan speaking. "You said once that a few days before the police hunted him down and shot him, Finn told you a story. One that you didn't quite believe. What was it?"

"Why ask now?"

"Because I need to know. It may be related to a case I am on."

"I might or might not be willing to share. Ya need to tell me more and who is involved. Since Stakeknife's exposure folks are edgy, looking for a reason to cause anyone with close ties to the past trouble. Talking about my brothers might have someone questioning my loyalties."

"I might know where Anne O'Loughlin disappeared to," Mulligan said.

McNall's eyes widened. "Bloody hell. Who have you said that to?"

"Only you."

McNall looked at the watch on his wrist. "Don't tell a soul. I'm coming to you. I'll catch the first flight out. Where am I going?"

The video ended and Rocky drew a breath realizing she had forgotten to breathe. "Why is he coming here? Do you know more?" Her gaze bounced between Mulligan and Jesse.

Mulligan shook his head. "Bugger wouldn't say a word. He'll be here later today."

"You didn't tell him that Anne wasn't alive," Jared said.

Mulligan shrugged his shoulders. "He didn't ask and he didn't volunteer any information. So, I'm not about to *either*. If just the mention of her name can get that kind of reaction from him then regardless if Anne was alive or not, I'd want to see him." Mulligan smiled. "Saved me a trip."

"And me some money," Jesse added, grinning.

These men played hardball even when it came to humor. To come all the way from London, thinking someone was alive...but Rocky had to agree with Mulligan. For someone to have that intense of a reaction upon hearing her mother's name this many years later, Rocky wanted to meet the man face to face and ask some serious questions.

Jesse looked at his watch. "That leaves one last interview for now. Ian should be calling shortly. He's made contact with a relative of Sean O'Prey, which wasn't easy. The O'Prey's were heavily involved with the IRA and aren't easy to find, even in these times. We're still trying to locate any news about Alan Dunlavey's family."

Mulligan grunted. "I have a hunch McNall will know the fate of the Dunlaveys. And you already know Deidre Finaggan's little sister, Brianna, was killed by a bomb in Ninety-six."

Rocky shivered at how close she came to sharing that fate last night. For the first time she realized just how violent of an environment her mother had grown up in. How frightening to never know from one minute to the next if you would live or die. And how fruitlessly hopeless it would be to know that there was nothing that could stop the madness.

Jesse's computer made a sound and he pressed a button. "Ian's right on time."

On the big screen Rocky saw a grim looking man with a gray beard, an odd-looking hat, and somber clothing glaring at them. "I tell ye son, these gadgets are of the divil."

"Yes, sir," Ian said.

"They'll lead to a world of sin. Mark my words."

"Yes, sir. I just need a few statements from you so we can keep track of this ancestry search. All you need to do is answer a few questions, okay?

"Let's get on with it."

"Deacon Diarmuid, you're a relation to Sean O'Prey, right?"

"Not claiming him or his brother as kin. They're my sister Fiona's lot. God rest her soul. Those two boys were bad eggs that met bad ends. Dodgy blokes that'll stab you in the back while smiling at your face. Tried saving one of them's gel, but Mary Magdalene had a divil in her that neither God's rod of discipline nor Father Finney's exorcism could cast out."

"Do you know how I can find any of them?"

"Ye can try the graveyards though none of them deserved to be buried consecrated ground."

"So they are all dead?"

"Sean in 79, murdered by the Brits. Dougal in 87, killed by the premature explosion of a bomb he was on his way to plant for the IRA. I'd already been taken care of his gel, Mary, since he hit trouble with the Brits 82. After Dougal died she up and left in the middle of the night. Last I heard she was on the streets of London. Good riddance."

"Ian, the girl's name was Mary Magdalene O'Prey?" Jesse asked.

Ian repeated the question and the Deacon confirmed it.

Mulligan spoke up. "Ask him if Dougal ever mentioned George Pearson's kidnapping? Or talked about Finn McNall?"

Ian repeated the question.

The man shook his head. "Not to me and nothing about Pearson, but on the few occasions Dougal came to see Mary, he'd piss up and go around yelling that Mary and Finn McNall's brasser ruined the only good chance he had in life."

Jesse turned to Rocky. "Do you have any questions?"

Rocky started to say no. She didn't want to have to talk to the man. Her stomach churned from the condemning, hatefulness emanating from him. If this man was a deacon, a supposed pillar in the community and the church there, what kind of life had any of the youths had? Especially Mary. It made Rocky know deeper in her heart that programs like Build-A-Future were so very important, not just in the US, but worldwide. "How old was Mary when she left?"

Ian relayed the question. The deacon's scowl deepened. "The ungrateful scrubber was fifteen."

Just fifteen. Rocky wondered if the girl had survived. She hoped so.

"Anything else?" Jesse asked. Rocky shook her head.

Jesse concluded the interview. Before he could say anything else, his cell phone, which he had sitting on the desk, vibrated. As he answered, it suddenly hit Rocky that she didn't have her cell phone or any of her personal belongings from driver's license to credit card. She'd lost her and Jared's phone in the pool and had left with only the clothes on her back.

Jesse's gaze shot to her within seconds and she knew something was wrong. He hung up, his expression grim. "There's a major fire at the nursing home. Everyone is being evacuated to different area hospitals."

Rocky jumped to her feet, her vision dimmed as she fought for air and for balance. "My father?"

"Is fine. One of my men is with him. The other is helping with the fire, which appears to have started in the kitchen."

"I've got to go to him." She looked around for her purse and realized she didn't have it. She didn't even have her truck.

"I don't believe in coincidences," Jared said as he stood. "Odds are this fire is meant to draw Rocky into a trap."

"My thoughts exactly," Jesse said.

Worry and a gut clenching rage pumped through Rocky. To have someone come after her was one thing but for him to put the lives of vulnerable, infirm people in danger, chilled her to the bone. "Then let's give this bloody bastard what he wants. Me."

Chapter Fifteen

That Jesse had a plan in place didn't stop fear from tying Jared's gut into a knot. With the explosion last night and having come so close to failing to protect Rocky, he realized the only safe place for her was in the Sherridan-Weldon Solutions' R& D penthouse with just Jesse and Mulligan in the know. Having her be anywhere else was like planting a target on her back, which was exactly what she was determined to do.

Jared fully understood the anger and the guilt she felt over the cowardly low-life putting her father and other completely helpless people at risk, but moving out into the open wasn't going to change what happened and just might get her killed.

This is what Jesse did day in and day out. He gave people protection, which was great when locked in a secure place, but out in the real world it was hell. There were too many variables beyond control. And for the first time on a gut level, Jared understood why his mother wrung holes in her dish cloths. He was praying harder than he'd ever prayed in his life.

The evacuated residents of the nursing home had been split up and transferred to different area hospitals. Roxy's father was now at Memorial Hospital's extended care unit, located on the third floor of the hospital's newest wing—an addition that Shamrock Construction had built and served as another example of excellent work followed by bad decisions. He and James had squandered the proceeds with their born-to-be-wild-bachelor lifestyle on fast cars, women, and parties.

As they drove up to the hospital, it really hit Jared hard that Rocky and McKenna Construction hadn't put Shamrock Construction in jeopardy of bankruptcy by outbidding them job after job. He and James had done it all by themselves. Part of the change in his viewpoint came from seeing his life in hard comparison to hers. But the seriousness of the recent events and the realization of how fragile and fleeting life was also held Jared's feet to the fire.

He was a low dog for even being with her at all. She deserved so much better than who and what he was. He could rationalize it a number of ways, but the real reason he hadn't told her the truth and why he hadn't called his twin since going to see her was because…he didn't want to be Jared Weldon—player and squanderer. He wanted to be the man who Rocky thought he was…someone worthwhile and worthy.

He wanted to be a different man. And the sad truth was that by misleading her about himself, he wasn't improving himself. He was only adding liar to player and squanderer.

What a loser.

Jesse pulled up to the side entrance to the hospital and Jared shoved his thoughts to the back of his mind. He needed to be completely focused on keeping Rocky alive and would have to deal with how to tell her who the real Jared Weldon was later.

The ten second walk from the protection of a bullet proof car to inside the lobby had him sweating bullets. Rocky was sandwiched between he, Jesse, and Mulligan. She also wore a bullet proof vest beneath a light jacket. But none of that eased Jared's angst. There were just too many damn strangers around and every move made by the people around him rocketed his fear higher.

He reached the elevators and stabbed the up button, then scanned the area again with his jaw clenched. Thankfully the elevators opened quickly. They moved inside. He stayed closest to the door and as the doors started to close, he breathed a sigh of relief. Suddenly, at the last moment, a man shoved a briefcase into the opening.

Startled, Jared reacted, seeing all kinds of bomb-in-brief-case horrors flash through his mind. He grabbed the hand and pulled hard, assuring whoever it was couldn't drop the package and run. The doors, already reacting to the intrusion, widened and a man in surgical scrubs cried out in surprise as he flew off balance into the elevator.

Jesse and Mulligan shoved Rocky to the side out of harm's way. The man bounced off the back wall of the elevator and stumbled back cursing.

"Good God. What in the hell is wrong with you?" He shoved a swath of blond hair back from his eyes and glared at Jared. "Have you lost your mind?" The man dropped the briefcase and flexed his hands, clearly assessing their function.

Jared already had a grip on his Glock behind his back, ready to pull Rocky out of the elevator and run when he noticed the embroidered name over the left, breast pocket. *Dr. Brad Swanson, Chief of Neurosurgery.* A vague memory of Jackson saying Nan had dated the man at one time flashed across Jared's mind. He slid the pistol back into his waistband.

"I'm reporting this to security." Swanson said, reaching for the alarm button on the elevator's control panel. Then he made a sudden halt, narrowed his eyes, and bounced his gaze between Jared and Jesse. "Wait a minute. You two are related to Jackson Weldon, aren't you?"

"Maybe," Jared said, coming to the conclusion that he'd over reacted a little and not liking just how hard his heart was pounding in his chest. The elevator doors re-closed and they moved up the shaft.

"Does irrational violence run in the family?" Swanson asked, bristling with irritation. "I didn't think anything could top Jackson's kidnapping me from my office, but assaulting me in the elevator is the height of idiocy." He looked at Jared. "So you're Jesse the security man?" Then he looked at Jesse. "That makes you one of the twins. Jared or James? Hate to say it but your company did an excellent job on building this new wing. Shamrock Construction isn't it?"

"What in the bloody hell is this?" Rocky gasped and Jared's heart sank.

"Something like that, Swanson," Jesse said grimly. The anger in his gaze bore a hole right though Jared. Jesse glanced at Rocky. "I'll explain shortly."

The elevator doors opened.

"No *you* won't." She grabbed Jared's arm and pulled him out of the elevator. "*He* will."

Jared's tongue stuck to the roof of his mouth. Jesse and Mulligan followed, their movements hurrying to assess and secure a perimeter of safety for her.

"Weldons are just weird," Swanson said. The elevator doors closed.

Rocky shoved him up against the wall. Jesse gave him an "I told you so" look. Mulligan seemed amused. Both men turned their backs, shielding him and Rocky from approach. Jared was so disgusted with himself, there wasn't a rock low enough to crawl under.

"You've got ten seconds." Hurt and anger clouded Rocky's green eyes. Lines of tension, worry, and pain creased her brow. This had hit her hard at a vulnerable moment.

Jared opened his mouth. Shut it then opened it again. "I lied," he whispered. "Pure and simple. I led you to believe something that wasn't true. I work with my brother James, not Jesse. We own Shamrock Construction. We were at the bar Sunday night looking for information on how McKenna Construction was consistently outbidding us."

All the color drained from Rocky's face. "You deliberately lied to me? Just like that? You wormed your way into my life...my home...my hear—" Her voice broke. Tears filled her eyes.

Jared knew he was losing her. And considering how betrayed she felt with everything else that had happened, that loss could be forever. He grabbed her shoulders. She was stiff and unyielding. "No. It wasn't like that. You have to believe me. I didn't know who you were at first. Didn't find out until after James and I left Sally's. I came back the next day to apologize. To explain maybe, but then the planter fell...and...and I couldn't walk away...and then things started to happen...and hell."

"Christ, is there anyone in my life who isn't hiding something?" She planted her finger in the center of his chest and pushed him away from her. "The man I thought you were would have never done what you did."

He exhaled. Sucker punched. He wasn't the man he'd been pretending to be. He was a wastrel and a jackass and he didn't deserve her.

"Why should I believe anything you said to me ever?" she choked then wrenched away from him, almost running down the corridor to escape him. Mulligan was on her heels.

"Because…" Jared whispered, floundering for words. *Why should she believe him?* He started to go after her.

"Later." Jesse shoved him back, his disgust evident. "You screwed up royally. So give her some space and get lost. We're lucky she didn't tell all of us to take a hike."

Jared shook his head, unable to wrap his mind around the idea of walking away from Rocky, ever. And especially not now. "Someone is trying to kill—"

"Mulligan and I can handle it," Jesse muttered as he turned away and headed down the corridor. Rocky and Mulligan had disappeared behind double doors at the end of the hall.

With his heart and gut in knotted turmoil, Jared watched Jesse follow after Rocky. He didn't have to get lost. He was already so lost he didn't think he'd ever be able to find his way.

Rocky couldn't see where she was going from the tears flooding her eyes. Every part of her body felt numb except for the ball of pain centered in her chest. There was so much deceit and intrigue whirling around her that she couldn't see anything at all.

She thought Jared was an anchor in the midst of the storm and to find out he wasn't who she thought he was left her free-falling again. If he could lie to her so easily from the start, then he wasn't much different than her ex.

Swiping her eyes, she made a beeline for the nurses' station just ahead. Though the hospital staff moved about in a calm, orderly manner, you could tell they were in rush mode, doing their best to process the evacuated patients. A quick glance behind showed that only Jesse and Mulligan had followed her. She thought she'd be relieved not to face Jared at the moment, but somehow the pain inside her sharpened. It wasn't rational. But then what had been rational ever since Collin came after her in the bar? Nothing. Especially Jared.

Did she have "lie to me" stamped on her forehead?

A nurse in blue scrubs with a floral print lab coat looked up from her clipboard as Rocky approached the desk. "May I help you?"

Rocky straightened her shoulders and gathered her wits. "Yes. I'm Roxanne McKenna. My father, Rory McKenna was transferred from Stonebrook."

"You're his daughter?"

"Yes."

"We've been waiting for you. Your father is fine. No exposure to smoke or trouble during the evacuation. You'll want to see him first, of course. Then we've a few admission papers for you to sign and some information on his medical history we need to get. Your father must be well loved. He already has several visitors. A room full in fact. Room 310."

Rocky expected that only Jesse's guard would be with her father. She hurried down the corridor, shoving anything to do with Jared away from the forefront of her mind. She also ignored Mulligan and Jesse who were shadowing her every step.

Before she could open the door to her father's room, Jesse put his hand on the knob and spoke low. "Let Mulligan check the room out first while we pretend to be having a conversation in the hall."

She nodded and stepped back. Mulligan went into the room. Jesse brushed her hand with his. "I'll always be first in line to kick my brothers' asses when they need it, but before you judge Jared too harshly keep two things in mind. He may have stepped up to the plate with the wrong foot, but he did step up to the plate. And Weldons have a tendency to do stupid things when it comes to women they really care about. If you need references on that, I can name two."

"You're offering to give me stupidity references?"

"Something like that."

Rocky shook her head. She wasn't drinking Jesse's Kool-aid. Deceit and stupidity were two different ballgames.

Mulligan came to the doorway. "Harvard is here. We're good."

She turned away from Jesse and entered her father's room. Mack, Maggie, and Alice were all there. They looked up anxiously and seemed to breathe a collective sigh of relief when they saw her. They all spoke at once, rushing her way.

"I've been trying to call you since the Stonebrook called us! Why haven't you answered your cell?" Mack said.

"What's going on, luv?" Maggie asked.

"Who are these men with Rory and with you?" Alice glared at Jesse and his guards with her hands on her hips. Her fifties style hair and plump figure made her a cross between Betty Crocker and the Pillsbury Dough Boy. One with red rimmed eyes. She'd been crying recently. A lot.

Patrick Brady's death had likely hit Alice hard as it would have it Collin. Rocky had sometimes wondered if the woman was secretly in love with him. Not that Patrick would have noticed. His wife and a pint were the loves of Uncle Pat's life.

Rocky drew a deep breath and tried to ease the pain inside. So much had happened so fast she didn't know what to say. And how much should she say? Was it possible that one of these trusted friends was trying to kill her?

Jesse stepped up. "We're with Sheridan and Weldon Solutions and we're here to provide protection for both Ms. McKenna and her father. Recent events indicate this is necessary."

Mack grunted. "Good. The planter falling. The fire at the hotel. I agree. Something is really rotten in Denmark. Where's your rescuer? He's been glued to your side for days."

"Jared is outside," Jesse said.

Rocky bit down in the inside of her cheek. Her rescuer? Her wolf in sheep's clothing? Well, maybe that was going too far. From the start, Jared had been focused on two things. Keeping her from harm and getting her into the sack. That he'd done both while lying about who he was pissed her off.

She unstuck her tongue and followed Jesse's lead. No reason she needed to give the details about anything. The bomb, her mother's history, or her gullibility. "How is Da doing?" She moved over to her father's bedside, quickly checking him out. His heart rate and level of oxygen saturation appeared on a digital screen above his bed. "Why is he being monitored again? Did anything go wrong?"

Jesse's man, Harvard, cleared his throat. "No. Ma'am. I was told they are monitoring all of the transferred patients for the first twenty-four hours."

"Good." She clasped her father's hand and bent closer to him. "Hear you've had some excitement, Da. Don't worry though. Everything will be all right."

Her father gripped her hand, and like before, looked at her with desperate intensity. This time the monitor registered his racing heart.

"Da? What is it? What are you wanting to tell me?"

He didn't say anything though and soon his grip went slack and his heart rate returned to normal.

Mack, Maggie, and Alice joined her at Rory's side.

"You're right," Mack said. "He's trying to tell you something. And only you. We've been with him for a while and he's done nothing like that. Did you every figure out what he meant the last time?"

"No," Rocky said.

Alice gasped. "Rory spoke before. Why didn't someone tell me? That's great news. When?"

"Sunday afternoon," Rocky answered.

"Patrick will be ecstat-" Alice's voice died and she burst into tears. "I'm sorry. I just can't get over it. Patrick can't be dead. He never would have taken his own life. I just know it. He was catholic to his core and his dearest wish was to be buried next to Cissy in the church cemetery. Once a month we'd have dinner and he'd talk about his Cissy and I'd talk about my Harold. You probably don't understand devoted love these days with everyone hopping in the sack with whoever, never forgiving or working out problems, just moving on to the next. But there are those of us who loved once and will never love again."

Maggie put her arm around Alice's shoulders and hugged her.

Rocky blinked, barely able to draw a breath. She started to go comfort Alice, too, but Mack moved in to help. Though Alice had her face buried in her hands and was too grieved to be chastising anyone, Rocky still felt the sting of her words and a wash of sadness as well. She'd always thought a love that deep and abiding would be hers one day. More than ever before, she believed that Uncle Pat had been killed and the reason lay in her mother's past.

"Rocky," Maggie said leaving Alice for Mack to comfort. "Is there is anything we can do to help you right now?"

Rocky shook her head and squeezed her friend's hand. She was at a loss for words. She didn't know who to trust. Even Jared had easily deceived her in some ways…a sharp ache sucker punched her heart and she scrambled for something to say. Tears stung here eyes. "You've done so much already. All of you have. I don't know what I would do without you."

"Just glad we could come," Maggie said. "We were all at the office when Stonebrook called about the fire. What a nightmare."

Mack's cell rang, but he ignored the call.

After a few moments, Alice brushed at her tears and patted Mack's shoulder. "Thank you, dear."

"It's a hard time for us all," Mack said.

Maggie gasped, drawing everyone's attention. She held up her phone. "With everything that has been happening, I forgot, I had an appointment. I'll reschedule for next week." She stepped from the room.

Rocky felt her pockets for her phone, then realized again that she had zippo. No truck, no license, no money, no phone. She didn't like how vulnerable that left her feeling.

Jesse's plan was to take her and Jared to her house. After Rocky picked up a couple of needed items, she and Jared were supposed to make use of the bug planted in her truck. While driving to Jesse's office in Savannah, they were going to make plans to spend the night at a special place. This is where Jesse would set a trap to catch the person trying to kill her.

She didn't feel as if it was doing what needed to be done fast enough. They'd have to wait until dark and that was hours away. It was a bad as waiting for word on Chief Inspector David McNall's arrival from Ireland.

And would Jesse's plan still work? Could she still pretend well enough? She was livid with Jared for playing her like a fool. All of the hurt from Collin's betrayal and her parents' secrets tangled up with Jared's deceit and mushroomed larger and larger. Where was he? She really needed to give him another piece of her mind.

Jared couldn't bring himself to leave Rocky, but he did need some air. A monstrous emotional vise had him by the throat. He went back downstairs and outside to the parking lot next to the bullet-proof car they'd arrived in. He didn't care if Rocky or Jesse liked it or not. He wasn't going anywhere until they caught the killer after her.

The hot southern sun beat down on him. Sweat trickled along his spine and he shivered as he replayed last night's bombing of her house.

Screeching brakes wiped the memory of the flames from the back of his lids. He snapped his eyes open in time to see the edges of a black sack close over his head and throat. Resisting the urge to grab at the sack, he went for the Glock, but something slammed against the side of his head and his legs buckled. He struggled to stay upright, trying to keep the bag from choking him as he grappled for a foothold. Instead of gaining any edge in the fight, he fell back off the curb and lost the expensive, Italian loafer he was wearing, just before the world went completely black.

Chapter Sixteen

Rocky was just finishing the last of the papers at the hospital's admission office when Jesse stepped away to answer his phone. Mulligan stood reassuring and silent at her other side. She kept her ear tuned to Jesse's conversation, hoping that it was Jared calling. Whether she wanted to or not, she kept wondering where in the hell he was. She wasn't through giving him a piece of her mind.

"Calm down, bro and say that over again. What do you mean something is wrong with Jared?" Jesse moved a step closer to the wall as he switched the phone to his other ear.

Mulligan snapped to ramrod attention and Rocky paused, her fingers tightening painfully on the pen in her hand as her heart began to race. Something was wrong with Jared? She strained to hear as Jesse lowered his voice.

"Christ, James. Don't scare me like that. This premonition crap has me worried that you're on your way to the loony bin." Jesse signaled and Mulligan relaxed. Rocky still felt as if she couldn't breathe.

"No I'm not making fun of you or dissing your worry. But you can't let what you think is happening wig you out like this. All of your angst over Jackson and me and nothing has happened, right? So, you're making a mountain out of a mole hill now, okay?

"Yeah, I get twins have a thing sometimes. But I'm telling you to calm down. I was with Jared not more than an hour ago. Physically he's fine, but otherwise he's up a creek without a paddle by his own doing and he's going to have to face the music for it."

"He can't answer his cell phone because…well, hell, because he doesn't have it. It was destroyed last night. Maybe you're just having a post-premonition here. Last night, Jared had a close call, but all turned out alright."

Jesse turned and looked back at her, and Rocky shifted her gaze back to the paper she hadn't finished. "No. He isn't at the moment. That's part of that creek thing I mentioned. I told him to take a hike and let things cool down a bit. Yes. As soon as I talk to him, I'll have him call. Meanwhile you take a chill pill, bro."

Jesse hung up the phone and Rocky blindly scribbled the last few answers then placed the clipboard on the admission desk. Maybe she'd gotten up on the wrong side of the bed after all because she was now irritated with Jesse.

And maybe wrong side of the bed was the wrong phrase to describe things because all sides of the bed this morning had felt damn good—but she didn't want to think about *that* now. She was too pissed off because who she thought she was with wasn't who she'd been with, right?

Jared wasn't Jared. Jared was a liar. Just like Collin had been…

Rocky stood and narrowed her gaze at Jesse as she crossed her arms. "What right did you have to tell Jared to take a hike?"

Jesse's eyes widened in surprise, something she didn't think happened often. "Because I didn't think you wanted to see him."

"I don't think I do, but I am the one wronged here so it was my right to tell him to take a hike, not yours."

Jesse opened his mouth then shut it, confusion knitting his brow. Mulligan snorted. "She has a point, Weldon. Meanwhile, I have a text from McNall. He just landed in Newark. He'll be at the Savannah/Hilton Head Airport in about two and half hours."

"Good. That gives us just enough time to set things up for tonight."

"How? Without Jared how am I supposed to-"

Jesse held up his phone. "You'll call and I'll answer. The rest is up to you." He looked confident. She wasn't so sure. They headed for the lobby. Mulligan left to bring the car up to the entrance while Jesse stayed with her. Rocky found herself scanning the crowd. She should have been looking for whoever was out to kill her, but she wasn't. She was looking for Jared.

It seemed as if only seconds passed before Mulligan jerked the car to a halt and she and Jesse hurried out and got into the back seat. Jesse shut the door and Mulligan pressed the gas.

Jesse leaned forward. "Something wrong?"

Mulligan held up a leather loafer. An expensive leather loafer that Jared had put on this morning. "On the ground by the car. You might want to call James back."

"Shit. Later. Call Ringo and have him activate the tracer."

Mulligan made the call then hung up. "Ringo's searching with the satellite now."

Rocky grabbed Jared's shoe, her stomach sinking even as fear lodged a knot in her throat. "What's going on? What tracer?"

"My guess is whoever is after you took Jared for leverage. As for the tracer? All of the clothes in the safe penthouse have a tiny tracer placed in them. Added precaution to help us keep track of our clients, especially when, like now, something goes very wrong. Damn, Mulligan, I fucked up bad. From now on you're in charge of this case. I'm thinking like a brother not a bodyguard. If anything happens to Jared, I'll—Dear God…"

"Jared was armed. There wasn't a glaring reason he couldn't be left alone," Mulligan said.

"There was every reason," Jesse said. "Sure he was armed and can shoot the ass off a gnat, but he's not trained for this and I sent him off in mental duress."

Rocky gulped for air. Her whole body was shivering. Jesse wasn't at fault. She was. She found out in a flash that the pain she felt over Jared's lying was nothing compared to the agonizing fear stabbing her now.

Jesse's phone went off. He answered and his expression twisted in anger. "We have our ransom demand. Ringo tried to trace the call, but it was too short," Jesse said as he hung up.

"What? They want me, right?" Rocky was practically ready to give them herself on a silver platter. Anything to save Jared from suffering or dying because of her.

"No. They want the diamonds."

"What diamonds?" Rocky shook her head. This didn't make any sense.

"The million in diamonds that disappeared along with General Pearson and his wife in 1983."

Jared struggled for consciousness. Every muscle in his body shook and pain stabbed his brain with each pounding thud of his heart. The acrid scents of mold and rotten wood burned his nostrils. He managed to crack and eye opened and then wished he hadn't. He no longer had a bag over his head. In fact, he no longer had any clothes on. He was buck naked except for the gauze wrapped around his left leg. He was gagged and his feet, hands and chest were tied to a cheap lawn chair that sagged and creaked. A bad enough situation, but the noose snug on his neck and tied to a beam overhead, told Jared more than anything else that his odds of getting out of there alive were slim to none.

It wasn't until he got it together enough to look around his surroundings that he shit a brick and panic grabbed his guts. He was in an abandoned sawmill, very similar to the one near the family's farm that he and James had had serial killer nightmares about when they were ten. He wasn't alone though. Collin was there and his state sent a chill down Jared's spine.

Eye-bulging desperation came close to describing the look on Collin's face. He too was gagged and tied to a chair, but from his soiled clothes and the stench, he'd been that way for some time. A layer of thick padding appeared to be protecting Collin from getting any rope burns—thus preventing evidence of foul play.

The bottles of whiskey on the ground and a rubber funnel sitting atop one told another story. Someone was forcibly keeping the man's alcohol level high.

The set-up painted a very clear picture to Jared. He was about to become the victim and Collin was being set up to be the perpetrator. What he didn't know was how all of this was related to Rocky's mother's past.

As much as he wanted to smash in Collin's face, he sure as hell wouldn't wish what his saw on his worst enemy.

Jared heard approaching footsteps behind him and braced himself. The gag was shoved painfully down from his mouth.

"The bitch figure out where the diamonds are at yet?" the man whispered.

"What diamonds?" Jared asked, searching his mind. Suddenly his ribs exploded with pain as the man swung what must have been a small wrecking ball. Jared shuddered violently, his whole body breaking out in a sickening sweat of fear and horror. The chair wobbled beneath the force of the blow and the noose tightened around his neck.

Dear God. Dear God. Dear God. Jared could do nothing but pray. He wasn't even sure what he was praying. For help. For a quick death. For Rocky that she be kept from ever knowing this inhuman evil dogging her.

Rocky had her hands clenched so hard her short nails cut into her palms, leaving them bloody. Mulligan was at the wheel. Jesse had moved to the front seat and had his laptop open. From the R&D lab, Ringo had picked up the tracer signal from Jared and had directed them from Savannah toward the rural and muddy swamp lands riddling South Carolina's coast. They were now close enough to pick up the signal on Jesse's computer.

Only Jesse spoke, giving Mulligan directions as the man raced fearlessly down the dirt road. The car bounced over ruts and lumps so hard she was sure it would fall apart at any minute. It had been an hour since they discovered Jared had been taken.

She was still in shock to learn that a million in diamonds was at the root of the death and destruction ruining her life at the moment. Her mother hadn't had money and neither had her father. They'd always struggled and even more so when her mother had been stricken with cancer. There were several times over the years that McKenna Construction had been on the verge of bankruptcy. This was completely insane and heart-sickening.

For someone to come after her for something related to the kidnapping and disappearance of General Pearson and his wife meant that Rocky's mother had been involved in that horror. Her gentle, loving mother had been a criminal, a fugitive, an illegal, a….murderer.

"We're close," Jesse said, looking up from the grid on his computer monitor. "Within half a mile. Park the car here and we'll move in on foot. It's going to be at least half an hour before the backup team arrives."

Rocky scanned the area. They were completely isolated on a dirt road in the middle of the woods with deep canals lining each side of the road. The scent of mud mixed with the brackish smell of stagnant water. Clumps of low lying trees and brush occasionally edged the water. Beyond that, the cypress groves with ghastly moss hanging like long dead skeletons stood sentinel, warning everyone to keep out. It was clear someone had attempted to make a swamp inhabitable and had failed.

Rocky opened the car door and something big splashed somewhere in the green-black water of the canal. It had to be a gator. She shivered and hurried over to where Jesse and Mulligan were on the dirt road. She did not like alligators at all. Some folks ate gator meat in the south. She didn't. Maybe it was the whole karma thing about doing unto others. She was willing to eat a steak or a chicken and face either of those creatures in a dark alley, but a gator was a whole different animal.

By the time she made it around the car, Jesse and Mulligan were both looking at her as if she was a child who'd left her play pen and needed to be put back. Had they expected she would sit in the car? Were they planning on leaving her while they rescued Jared? No way. "If you two think that I'm going to bloody sit here alone like a duck waiting to be slaughtered you've lost your mind. I'm coming with you."

"She's right," Mulligan said. "Even if we leave her armed she'd be easy picking. And if we lock her in the trunk who's to say someone won't push the car into the canal?"

"LOCK ME IN THE TRUNK?"

"He's kidding," Jesse said.

Rocky glared at Mulligan, but couldn't read a damn thing from his expression. "Not funny," she muttered.

He grinned finally. "We were trying to decide if we should let you follow slowly in the car while we move in on foot. That way we'll have our getaway vehicle closer but can still make a fast, but cautious approach."

"Let's stop wasting time and just do it," Rocky said. "Give me a phone and a gun."

They both looked as if she'd lost her mind. "I can shoot. Maybe not a gnat's ass but close."

Jesse shrugged and handed her a pistol he had strapped to his leg.

Rocky took the short barreled 9 mm, pointed it at the ground and checked the chamber. "How many rounds?"

"Fifteen," Jesse said.

"Like the lady said, let's move." Mulligan turned and headed down the road.

Jesse handed her his cell phone. "I'll call you when to follow. Any calls for me, tell them to call Mulligan."

"Got it."

Rather than walk around to the canal side of the car, Rocky got into the passenger's door and scooted over to the driver's side then locked the car doors. As she watched Jesse and Mulligan move down the road, she broke out in a cold sweat. She suddenly realized that if someone did come riding down this road and she was forced to race away from them, she could very well end up in a canal…with the gators.

Diamonds? The word rang over and over in Jared's mind. Dear God. The only diamonds he'd heard about had been the ransom for General Pearson and his wife in 1983. He tried to remember from all he and Rocky had uncovered if there had been any indication that diamonds were a factor. There hadn't been.

The man wanted something they didn't have. With sickening dread, Jared knew that this violence wouldn't stop until the man got what he wanted. This man would torture Rocky or anyone else in her life.

"Know what diamonds now?"

"We don't have any diamonds," Jared said.

"Wrong answer." The monster hit Jared's side again.

A scream burst from Jared's lips. The pain was unbelievable. His whole side felt shattered. He couldn't even breathe. The chair shook and sank a little and the noose clenched tighter. Blood flooded his mouth. He was sure he was going to die. Soon.

His mind left his pain behind and went back to that morning. The pleasure of waking up next to Rocky, of holding her, touching her, and taking her with him to the pearly gates of heaven. He saw the love in her clover eyes and the sexy smile on her face. He felt the silk of her skin, the excitement of her touch, and heard the sigh of her satisfaction as he lost himself in her.

And he'd be damned if this son of a bitch was going to take that all away from him. Jared had found love and he would fight with his last breath to keep it.

Despite the pain, he sucked in air before he passed out and hung himself. He swallowed the blood in his mouth. There had to be a way. He wouldn't let things end like this.

By the time Jesse called five minutes later, Rocky had bitten her nails to the quick and the car widows had fogged over so badly that she had to roll the windows down to see.

"No need to be quiet. We're up around the bend."

"You found Jared?" Rocky cranked the car, her heart pounding and bursting with emotion.

"Just come on," Jesse sounded grim.

"Oh, God. He's dead."

"Damn it! We don't know."

Rocky eased the car onto the road and drove carefully. She found Jesse and Mulligan off on the right. They were both standing, overlooking a swampy pond.

Jesse had Jared's shirt in his hand. Rocky got out of the car, sure she would pass out before her shaky legs carried her to them. Her vision dimmed and her body shuddered, but she kept moving forward. She grabbed Jared's shirt and brought it tight against her chest.

"It's just his shirt," she said. "He's got to be okay. It's just his shirt."

"It's all of his clothes," Jesse whispered, as if he was on the edge of breaking completely.

Rocky looked around and then saw what Jesse meant. Jeans, socks, underwear. It was all there with the gators. Even the other loafer lay in the mud at the water's edge. The jeans had hung up on a cypress stump and had blood on them. She looked down at the shirt and saw blood on it too.

"It's just his clothes," she cried. "It's just his clothes. It's not him. If his clothes are here then they brought him this way. We have to keep looking. We have to find him."

"Look here," Mulligan said. She and Jesse turned to see him closer to the road, studying tire tracks. "They're from a truck and it took off fast heading to the right. I say we keep going. This road has got to go somewhere."

Jesse's phone rang. Rocky had left it in the car. Mulligan sprinted over to the car. Jesse started to follow.

"Wait," Rocky said. "His shoe. Can we get his shoe?"

Jesse looked as if he was about to say no, then sighed. "Sure." He moved over, snapped a branch off a tree, and then carried it in front of him as he approached the water's edge. Rocky was about to ask him what he was doing, when all of a sudden, an alligator shot up from the water, jaws snapping at the branch. Jesse grabbed the shoe and left the branch for the gator to wrestle with.

"Dear God. You knew it was there and you went after the shoe?"

Jesse shrugged. "Growing up we teased the gators all the time."

"Jesus," Rocky clutched Jared shirt to her breast again. "No wonder your mother had holes in her dishtowels."

Jesse stopped dead in his tracks. He gripped her shoulders and studied her face for a good long moment. "I hope to God you can get over Jared's stupidity because I can tell you one thing for sure."

"What?"

"My brother loves you." Jesse released her shoulders and took her hand as if he had a new lease on life. "Let's go find his ass."

"It's James," Mulligan said when they reached the car.

Jesse groaned and took the phone. "Ream my ass six ways to Sunday later. We're out looking for Jared and he is in trouble. What can you tell me?"

"Okay. I'm with you, bro. Stop crying so I can understand you. What? Is that Jackson with you? You're at the clinic? Put him on the phone."

"What is James saying?"

"Fuck. No, he is not losing it. This is for real, Jackson. Jared has been kidnapped. Mulligan and I just found his clothes dumped in the swamp with a bunch of gators. Do not knock James out with drugs. He has to tell me anything and everything he is thinking."

"What? Shit. That's all? Okay. Stay with him. Calm him down and have him focus on Jared. Call me back if he says anything else. And I mean anything, okay?"

Jesse hung up the phone. "All James is seeing is the abandon sawmill he and Jared had nightmares about as kids."

"The one you and Jackson said a serial killer was hiding in?"

Jesse took a step back in shock. "Is there anything Jared hasn't told you? Hell you've only been together a couple of days."

Rocky grabbed Jared's arm. "Don't you see? James will connect any sawmill he's seeing to the one he knew growing up.

What if there is a sawmill down this road somewhere? What if that's where Jared is being held?"

"Hell yeah," Jesse said.

Mulligan rushed to the driver's seat. Rocky piled into the back and Jesse dove into the front.

Through his haze of pain, Jared saw Collin was spasming as if in the midst of a moaning epileptic seizure. It was so bad his chair had flipped to its side and was bouncing up and down like a demon in an exorcism. The monster behind Jared saw it too.

"You sure as hell are not going to fuck up my genius by dying." The killer, who was concealed behind black clothes and a black ski mask went over to Collin. It was then that Jared realized that if Collin was having a real seizure, he wouldn't be moaning like a sick cow.

Jared also found that the arm of the thin aluminum chair had broken free at the back, damaged by the killer's blows. His ribs killing him with every moment, Jared wrenched his hand back and forth enough to loosen the ropes tying down his right hand. Once free, he worked on the noose before he tried to untie himself.

He'd just gotten the noose loosened when the monster caught wind of what he was doing. Jared flung himself sideways as he shoved up on the noose. He'd either slip free or hang. He hit the ground and was breathing, barely though because of the pain in his side.

The hooded killer roared with rage. He ran across the room, grabbed a sledge hammer, and came at Jared swinging. Jared had nothing around that he could use to protect himself from the blow.

And with only one hand free, he couldn't run. He had to do something fast.

Then he saw the small wrecking ball the monster had hit him with. It was lying on the ground near him where the killer had dropped it. Jared grabbed the chain as close to the ball as he could and hurled it at the killer's head.

He nailed him. The man dropped the sledge hammer and staggered back, his hand going to his head where blood poured from a nasty gash. The man keeled over backward.

Jared hurried to free himself before the bastard regained his senses.

Collin was groaning again, and Jared saw the man was urging him to hurry too. Jared had almost loosened the ropes around his feet when the killer sat straight up and roared with rage again. The man was definitely hurt. He wavered as if disoriented, too unsteady to get to his feet. He started crawling across the floor toward the right side of the room and that's when Jared saw the Glock Jesse had given him. It was sitting on top of a crate.

Jesus. Jared ripped free of the ropes. He gained his feet and took one step. The killer reached the Glock, aimed with a shaky hand and pulled the trigger in the space of a heartbeat.

Chapter Seventeen

Mulligan flew down the dirt road. Rocky had her teeth clenched and a death grip on the back of Jesse's seat. Nobody spoke. All eyes were on the road ahead as if Jared would suddenly appear out of thin air. The more they drove, the more Rocky realized the fruitlessness of their search and just how unrealistic her optimism had been. They were taking a wild shot in the dark with barely a whisper of a hope they'd find him.

Sure Jared had to be somewhere, but there were a thousand some-where's in the miles they were speeding through. What they needed was a helicopter, then they would be able to see a large area in a single glance. One was on the way, but that didn't help them now. And it didn't lessen the urgency gripping her gut tighter and tighter. Whoever wanted the diamonds had to have been involved in the kidnapping of General Pearson and his wife.

Once taken, the couple had never been seen or heard from again.

"Hold up!" Jesse yelled.

Mulligan hit the brakes and Rocky slammed into the backside of Jesse's seat, lucky she didn't smash her face into the headrest. "What is it? What did you see?"

"We passed a turn-off to the right. It looked heavily rutted."

Mulligan shoved the car into reverse and hit the gas, driving backward as nearly as fast as he could go forward. Rocky ate her cry of fear, surely they were about to end up in a canal with the gators.

The car flew amazingly straight and halted at the turn. A narrow dirt road went off to the right and disappeared into the dark shadows of heavy palmetto bushes and tangled vines from low lying trees.

"Good eyes," Mulligan said. "The ruts are fresh since the rain this morning."

Rocky held on to the seat and prayed.

Dear God, she wanted to wrap her arms around Jared so badly that second that she could hardly breathe from the pain of not having him with her. She was still pissed at the situation, was still disillusioned with what he had done, but the thought of never holding him again was more than she could bear.

Her rational mind wanted to tell her that what she was feeling for Jared wasn't real. She'd only known him for days. The depth of her involvement with him didn't make sense, especially considering that he'd pretended to be someone he wasn't. Unfortunately her heart wasn't buying it. She wanted him there, despite everything. And it wasn't just because he was in danger. She'd been feeling that way ever since she'd left him in the hospital corridor.

Jared went low. He could have dived to the right or to the left, but chose to go straight ahead toward the killer. His only hope of survival was to take the man down—if he survived the bullet he was sure was speeding his way.

Only the explosion of more pain didn't happen.

The killer missed and was now adjusting his aim. Less than three feet separated them now. Jared knew the next shot would kill him. He hit the ground and rolled himself like a bowling ball at the killer's legs. The man fired.

Jared still did not feel a thing. He swept the man's legs out from under him, grabbed the barrel of the Glock 18 pointed at his head and twisted it downward. He then angled up, a breath away from either shooting the killer with the turning pistol or pinning the SOB to the dusty floor with a rib-crushing slam.

Screaming in frustration, the man flailed wildly, driving his knee into Jared's injured side. Pain hit Jared like a speeding Mack Truck. His vision dimmed, his body spasmed, his lungs froze, and his grip on the gun loosened as he fought for consciousness.

He couldn't believe it was going to end like this. Just as he'd found something in life worth fighting for, he would die in the dust like a dog.

Suddenly Collin, still strapped to the chair but bucking wildly enough to bounce, tipped over onto the killers head. The distraction gave Jared the edge he needed. He shoved the pistol toward the shooter and forced the trigger home. The killer jerked, twitched, shuddered then spasmed, blood spurting from his left breast.

Collin, moaning and fighting against his gag and binding ropes, had landed with his face buried in the killer's now still chest. Pulling the Glock from the killer's slack hand, Jared pushed up, loosened Collin's gag, and shoved him back from the killer's head.

"Thank God," Collin gasped. "Thank God. Thank God. Is he dead?"

Jared ripped off the killer's hood and stared into Riley's lifeless eyes. He checked the man's jugular just to be sure. "Yes. He's dead." Jared glared at Collin, taking in the man's horrible state. Empathy and gratitude mixed with Jared's anger. "You saved my life here, but after your attack on Rocky I am not sure whether I should thank you or shoot you."

Collin paled. "I was drunk Sunday."

"I'm not talking about Sunday. I'm talking about when you tried to rape her during your divorce."

Collin's eyes widened. "You're out of your mind or Rocky is telling lies. I would never force a woman."

Jared wanted to point the muzzle at Collin's face, just to scare the man into telling the truth. Instead, he lowered the gun and hit him with a hard stare. "You didn't go to her house drunk one night, break down her door and tried to force yourself on her? She said she had to nail you hard in the groin to stop you. She had Mack come drag you home. Seems to me that's something a man don't forget."

"Jesus," Collin whispered. "Surely, I didn't do that…but-"

"But what?" Jared's hand shook with the force of his anger.

"One night back then I woke up in the yard with Mack hosing me down until I sobered up enough to yell at him. He then beat the hell out of me with the rubber hose and told me to stay away from Rocky. I hurt everywhere then, but my groin was especially sore. Jesus, I don't even remember having gone to see her. The next day Rocky and her father fired me from McKenna Construction. I'd worked there since I was ten years old."

"And you didn't put two and two together?"

Collin shook his head. "I never could have done that. Even drunk I would never—"

"You did do it. Rocky doesn't lie," Jared's voice caught on his last sentence. How could he slam Collin when Jared was guilty of shit himself? He hurt her too.

Suddenly, Jared heard the sound of an approaching car. He and Collin weren't out of danger yet. Riley had to have an accomplice. Collin heard it, too.

"Untie me!" Collin cried.

Jared loosened one of Collin's hands and as Collin went to work on the other knots, Jared forced his body into motion. Glock in hand, he moved into position, ready to ambush anyone who walked through the barn-like doors.

Scrambling, Collin grabbed the sledge hammer and set himself up on the other side. A split second later, before either of them realized what the sound of the gunning engine meant, the doors splintered inward as a car came through the opening. Both he and Collin stumbled back from harm. Through the flying splinters, Jared saw the muzzle of a big ass semi-automatic 44 appear out the driver's side window and the dark shadow of another man came over the top of the car, sweeping the room with his laser enhanced pistol.

Mulligan and Jesse.

"Don't shoot!" Jared shouted as the red beam from Jesse's muzzle centered on Collin's chest. Collin dropped the sledge hammer and held his hands up.

Jesse didn't alter his aim. "Give me a damn good reason."

Jared had no doubt the two men could have taken out an entire room of Riley's in a heartbeat.

"He was kidnapped, too. How long have I been gone?"

"About two and a half hours." Jesse lowered his pistol, slightly and grunted as if he didn't quite want to. Collin inhaled then sank to the ground and sat with his head between his legs.

Was that all? Not even three hours? Jared felt as days had passed. His vision wavered as he fought against the weakness shaking his knees. Trying to brace his aching side with his arm, he limped forward, noticing for the first time he had blood dripping down from his shoulder and his tongue was swollen from being bit at some point during Riley's torturing Q& A session.

Jesse slid down from the roof of the car and moved toward him. Mulligan shut the car off and exited, heading for Riley's body on the ground.

"Look's like Riley's our man. Ringo get that report back on him yet?" Mulligan asked.

"Negative," Jesse said as he wrapped an arm around Jared's shoulder. "God, it's so damn good to see you."

Jared leaned in to his brother before he fell over. Maybe Jesse wasn't as much of a pain in the ass as he thought. "You knew it was Riley? Since when?"

"No. We started running preliminary background checks on all of McKenna Construction employees after the bomb last night. But with Riley connected to the fire at the Drake we flagged him for a more in-depth check. We did the same with Mack, Alice, and Maggie, as well, since they work the closest to Rocky."

Jared nodded his swimming head. "How in the hell did you find me so fast?"

"We tracked you to within five miles of here with the tracers planted in the clothes you had on. But after finding those swimming with the gators in a road-side swamp, it was Rocky and James who kept the search alive. God did the rest. You look a little worse for the wear, kid. If I'm not mistaken that's a fairly deep bullet trench on your shoulder."

"Just a scratch," Jared said. "Where's Rocky? James?" He twisted to look for her and that tipped the apple cart so to speak. Pain arced up from his side and his vision faded to a narrow tunnel. "Need to sit down. Ribs hurt." Jared shivered.

"You need to lay down, bro. You're in shock."

"Jared?" Rocky called out from somewhere beyond his narrowing field of vision.

"Here," Jared said, but his voice was a whisper. He opened he mouth to speak louder but couldn't seem speak again. He shivered harder.

Jared felt his brother scoop him up like a babe and heard Jesse and Mulligan talk through a long tunnel.

"Mulligan, let's get that helicopter here now. Jared may have some internal bleeding. They can land in the clearing."

"Their ETA is ten minutes."

"A lot of shit can go wrong in ten minutes."

Jared hoped not.

Rocky shoved aside the splintered wood that framed Jesse's car trunk and forced her way into the old saw mill. She'd waited, hidden in the dense foliage lining the dirt road, for as long as she could. But when no gunfire followed Jesse and Mulligan's assault, she couldn't help but think the worse. Jared was either not here or he was...

God. She caught her breath, refusing to even think Jared wasn't alive.

Two black trucks were parked in front. One of them was Collin's. It made her horribly ill inside. If she'd only listened to Jared from the start and hadn't so naively believed Collin incapable of hurting his father, she could have pushed the police to go after Collin. Then maybe Collin wouldn't have had the opportunity to kidnap Jared.

It confused her as to how Collin found out about her mother's past, the Pearson kidnappings, and the missing ransom diamonds.

When her eyes adjusted to the dimness inside the sawmill, she saw Collin sitting on the ground next to a sledge hammer and Jared lifeless in Jesse's arms with blood on him.

She cried out in anguish. Collin looked up, filthy and devastated, as if he was bewildered. "I'm sorry, Rock-a-bye. I am so sorry."

He used the name he used to tease her with when they were kids. Rocky fell to her knees, her eyes flooding with tears. Sorrow and rage warred in her heart. Why hadn't Jesse or Mulligan shot Collin or tied him up or something. "You killed Jared? You killed your father? Why Collin? Why?"

Collin's head snapped up. "What? NO! NO! I didn't."

A strong hand clasped Rocky's shoulder. She looked up into Mulligan's icy eyes and saw a hot core of warmth and compassion that he somehow always kept hidden. "Jared's alive but need's medical attention," he said. "Collin was kidnapped, too. Riley's over there. He's dead."

Rocky sucked in air and jerked her gaze toward Jesse. He was laying Jared in the backseat of the car then stripped off his shirt to cover Jared. Mulligan helped her rise and she rushed to Jesse, knees shaking.

"How bad is he?"

Jesse looked up, his brow creased with worry. "I don't know. He's showing signs of shock. Let's get his feet up and I'll back the car out. There's a trauma kit in the trunk. The helicopter will be here soon and we can get him to the hospital."

Rocky didn't ask. She just climbed into the back with Jared, kneeling in the floorboard. She lifted his legs to rest on the seat back, then took off the t-shirt she had on, folded it and pressed it to the bleeding wound on his shoulder. The bullet proof vests she and Jesse wore were tan in color and so light that Rocky had forgotten she was wearing one. Jared's left side looked bruised and swollen. After seeing her in action, Jesse grunted and hopped into the driver's seat.

He backed the car about five feet, popped the trunk, and then went around and opened the door by Jared's head. He placed a silver thermal blanket over Jared and handed her his shirt. She slipped it over her shoulders for now.

Jesse strapped a blood pressure cuff to Jared's good arm. "Eighty over fifty, low but not critical. His pulse is ninety—a good sign." He hung an IV bag to the hook just above the door, inserted an IV needle in Jared's arm, and within moments had fluids infusing at a fast rate. He then taped her balled shirt to Jared's shoulder, making it a pressure dressing.

Mulligan stuck his head in. "Five more minutes on the helicopter." He held up a nasty, rusted iron ball. It looked like a miniature wrecking ball. "Collin says Riley hit Jared's side with this while Jared was tied helpless to a chair. The bastard's dead but I'm tempted to smash his skull flat. You won't believe the story of the fight Jared put up." Mulligan's eyes were so icy cold Rocky had no doubt that if Riley wasn't dead, Mulligan would have smashed the man's skull.

Jesse cursed. Rocky thought she would either pass out or throw up. Jesse drew the thermal blanket away from Jared's side and studied his brother. "His ribcage rises and falls evenly. If his ribs were severely damaged and detached from the chest wall that part would move opposite from the rest of his chest. He could have some internal bleeding if his spleen or his lungs are contused, though."

"I'm glad you know all of that," Rocky whispered, clasping Jared's hand in hers.

"Assisted an army medic for a few years. You learn hard and fast in the field." Jared looked in bad shape to her, but Rocky could see that Jesse's worry had eased some. He'd have seen a lot worse in combat. She heard the sound of the approaching helicopter and drew a deep breath. It was the first one since discovering Jared had been abducted.

Four hours later, as she paced the hospital waiting room, she had yet to draw a second deep breath. Jared was in surgery to have a minor tear to his spleen repaired. Was there any such thing as a MINOR tear to one's spleen? That minor repair was now almost two hours past the time Jared was supposed to be done.

She shuddered.

Jesse stood sentry not far from her side. She'd given him his shirt back and she now wore a green scrub top with a Property of Memorial Hospital stamp. Another of Jesse's bodyguards was at the entrance to the waiting room. The possibility that Riley had an accomplice still hovered like a dark cloud, though Collin said he never saw anyone except for the black masked man during his ordeal. She, Jesse, and Collin had ridden in the helicopter with Jared to the hospital. Collin was admitted to the hospital for dehydration. Mulligan had gone to collect McNall from the airport and take him to the R& D facility. Jesse's men who'd been in the helicopter had waited with Riley's body for the police.

She was afraid the police would show up soon asking questions that she didn't have many answers to yet. She just prayed she had news that Jared was in the clear by then, because she couldn't think about anything else. She'd been introduced to Jared's family, but their faces passed in a blur. Except for James's. Being Jared's exact double, his only made her ache more. Alexi, Jesse's wife sat on one side of James, and Nan, Jackson's wife sat on the other. They each had a hand on James's shoulder and were whispering comfort to a clearly anguished man. He had his face buried in his hands. She thought she knew exactly how he felt.

It was surreal to see Jared but it not be Jared. The experience made Rocky realize that even though Jared had misrepresented who he was, it didn't change him from the man she'd come to know. Maybe it tarnished his armor a good bit, but didn't change him from being a knight to the rescue so to speak.

Instead of wringing a dishtowel, Emma Weldon sat in the corner furiously knitting what looked like a sweater for a little boy. But Rocky could see her lips moving in a silent prayer with every stitch. Jared's father, John Weldon, paced the opposite side of the room, cracking his knuckles with every turn, making Rocky jump. She wished somebody would hand him a dishtowel to wring. She was so on edge with worry that she was about to explode from it.

Jackson had been there for a while, but then had taken off to the inner bowels of the hospital, hoping his doctor status would get information about Jared.

Though everyone had been polite and nice, Rocky was sure they were all blaming her for what happened to Jared. Even she was blaming herself, so why shouldn't they?

"This is all my fault!" James stood and raked his hands through his hair. He marched across the room and grabbed Jesse's shoulder. "Go ahead a say it. Somehow, I got the premonition wrong. Jared's the one who we needed to be watching out for not you and Jackson."

Everyone froze. Emma stopped knitting mid-stitch. John halted with his foot in the air and wobbled off-balance a moment before he smacked his foot down, cursed, and turned to look at James.

Alexi gasped and glared at Jesse. "That's why you cancelled the trip."

Nan shot to her feet. "What premonition about Jackson?"

"I knew you were hiding something, John Weldon. And I've been waiting for it to come out." Emma set down her knitting and marched over to James. She put her finger in the center of his chest. "Plant your butt in a chair, boy, and breathe. I'll get to you in a minute." She glared at Jesse, but didn't say anything as she breezed by him and went for her husband. John Weldon had stopped pacing and was now busy staring out the window.

"John Donovan Weldon. You've been hiding something since Sunday. Look at me and man up."

All of the men in the room winced.

John turned and sighed. "Remember stories about my grand pappy?"

"Not likely to forget them, as your father relished scaring everyone with the grim-reaper-like tales on regular basis."

"James may have a similar problem."

James groaned. Emma glanced at him then zeroed her gaze back on her husband. "And just exactly how did you reach this conclusion?"

John frowned. "Well, because it was…obvious. He…well…he—"

James stood. "Years ago, the night of my and Jared's graduation. We were all standing together taking pictures and Tyler and Steve just disappeared from my vision. I knew they were right there in front of me. I could hear them talking but I couldn't see them. The next day, they died in a car wreck. Sunday morning in church, during the ceremony, the same thing happened. Jesse and Jackson disappeared from my vision."

"That was thirteen years ago. I have little doubt you and Jared were both sneaking a drink or two then. And I know you were hung-over last Sunday morning, so I'm going to take this story with a grain of salt. You father shouldn't have immediately carried embellished tales that an old man in his cups liked to spew late at night."

She gave John a stern look. "That being said," she moved over and placed her hand on James's chest over his heart. "God gave you and Jared a special connection. You two did not talk until you were five and I put you in different classes at school. The doctors all said it was because you read each other's minds and didn't need to communicate verbally. So you and Jared sharpened a part of your minds at an early age."

"That explains what happened today," James said. I knew Jared was in deep trouble. In pain. And all I could see was a dusty sawmill. All I could fell was the evil shadow of a killer hovering over Jared. All of that is different from having Jesse and Jackson disappear from my vision."

Emma reached up and hugged James. "Son, I believe in instincts and intuitions no matter how the mind communicates them to us. Maybe what happened is really important. Maybe it isn't. I can tell you that you should never ignore what your gut is telling you. Therein lays the extent of your responsibility. You tell who needs to be told, take the precautions your gut is clamoring to take, and after that it is in God's hands not yours. And as much as you men like to think it, you're not God, so don't go taking on his job."

Rocky could almost see the burden and fear rolling off James's shoulders as he drew in a deep breath.

"Well said," Jesse muttered. "Jackson and I did take precautions."

"Then there was no need to play God and keep me, Alexi, and Nan in the dark about it," Emma admonished.

Jesse winced.

"That's right," Nan added. "We are practical, level-headed women, who have every right to be aware of situations as they arise."

"And not learn about them after-the-fact," Alexi said, narrowing her gaze at Jesse. "Or should I say after the fiction? All of those excuses as to why you postponed you're trip this week were lies?"

Jesse cleared his throat. "Uh, not exactly. An important situation did come up that has required me being here."

"And that situation involved Jared and why he's in surgery now?" Emma asked.

"Yes," Jesse said.

Rocky finally spoke up. "Jared was hurt because I didn't take his concerns for my safety more seriously from the start."

"I'm not sure how that could have changed the outcome," Jesse said. "Jared was determined to stay by your side no matter what."

"Yeah," James said. "Jared took one look at you and two things instantly happened. He never looked away and he was determined to put himself between you and anything that threatened you."

"I hate to interrupt this tell all, but I have news on our boy," Jackson said from the doorway.

Rocky whipped around. Once she saw the smile on Jackson's face, she relaxed her cramped hands and breathed deep.

"Jared's in recovery and doing fine. It took longer because there was more damage to the spleen than they thought and they had to do a partial splenectomy. We can see him shortly."

Rocky decided to take the bull by the horns. She turned to Jesse. "The only way Jared is going to rest is if this situation I am in is over and done with."

"If you're suggesting we cut out of here and take care of business then I'm ready. Besides, we just might be able to stop another murder as well."

She gripped Jesse's arm. "What haven't you told me?"

He smiled. "That McNall refuses to tell Mulligan anything until he sees you. They've been in a Mexican standoff for hours now."

James, who was near, leaned their way. "How do you two think Jared will take both of you not being here when he wakes up?"

Jesse grunted. "It will be worse if we stay and then leave. He's down and needs to stay down until everything is healed, including his leg. But the second Jared is aware you can put him into contact with Rocky on live video feed via this phone or the I-pad I will send over."

James took the phone. "Be careful, please."

"Bank on it."

She and Jesse left the hospital after taking a quick peek at her father. Part of her heart was on the third floor with her Da, the rest of it was on the fifth floor with Jared. She had to solve the puzzle before anything else happened.

CHAPTER EIGHTEEN

"*Cagey, bastard. Ye think you* can get away with a move like that?" The man's Irish burr boomed into the hallway. Rocky quickened her step toward Jesse's office with him on her heels. That had to be McNall.

"I did," Mulligan said succinctly. "What are you going to do about it?"

"Pummel your arse. Checkmate!"

"What the hell?" Mulligan sounded outraged and bewildered.

Rocky rounded the corner, expecting to see Mulligan and McNall at each other's throat. Instead, they were at the chess table with Mulligan glaring at the chessboard, and McNall sitting back in his seat with a satisfied smile, as he twirled the edge of his handlebar mustache.

"For real?" Jesse cried from behind her. "You did it? You nailed Mulligan?" He moved into the room, staring at the chessboard. "How?"

"I'll not be givin' away me secrets." McNall looked up and gasped as if he'd been hit between the eyes with a two by four. "As I live and breathe, I'm not believin' me own eyes." He stood and limped across the room, grumbling about gout under his breath. "Let me look at ye, lass. You're the spittin' image of your father."

Rocky blinked. She'd always been told that she favored her mother more, which is what she expected McNall to say, considering he'd come all the way from Ireland at the mention of her mother's name. "You know Rory?"

McNall stopped halfway and narrowed his gaze. He glanced at Jesse, and Mulligan, then sighed. "Perhaps, I should've asked a few more questions before I saw ye. Why don't we sit, and I show ye a picture, and tell you a story."

Everyone settled in the sitting area. Jesse next to her on the couch. Mulligan to the right, in a burgundy wingchair, and McNall opposite, in the matching wingchair. The coffee table separated them in middle. A strange feeling clawed through Rocky that no amount of buttery- soft leather could ease, despite the day's exhaustion and turmoil.

McNall pulled out his wallet, flipped through a thick collection of photographs that nobody these days carried, and slipped a picture from its plastic sleeve. "Here's me brother Finn about a year before Liam was murdered. Ye can say it paints a thousand words."

Rocky's fingers trembled as she reached for the photo. It was frayed on the edges and a little worn from years of being carried, but the young man smiling from the picture had vibrant, clover green eyes and a dimple on his left cheek, just like her. He was in his teens still, but the shape of his strong nose and chin were a slightly masculine version of Rocky's own. She exhaled as if sucker punched.

Rocky had come to grips with the idea that her mother had been Anne O'Loughlin, but she hadn't even questioned that Rory McKenna was her father. Now, she was seeing something that put everything into doubt.

McNall started to speak, his lilt was quiet, gentle, and warming, like a low burning fire. "The murder of Liam and Shona in so brutal a way hit Finn and Anne hard. Up until then Anne had been a studious young girl and Finn had been well on his way to Football stardom. After the murders, they both became obsessed in seeing justice served. Whoever killed Liam and Shona had to pay. They fought hard, petitioned harder, and gathered numerous testimonies that pointed to the guilty soldiers. When General Pearson absolved his men of any wrong doing instead of punishing them, Anne and Finn ran away from home and went underground to get justice. Their grief brought them together and kept them together. I'm not justifying what they did. The Troubles were a horrible time for Belfast, for all of Ireland and for England. I didn't hear from Finn for several years, but just before he was killed in December of '82, he came to me with a story."

Rocky closed her eyes a moment, trying to gather the strength to hear what she knew was coming.

When McNall didn't speak, she opened her eyes. He had his gaze on her, his eyes sad. He sighed then continued his story. "I swore I'd go to me grave before breathing a word of it, but there're some promises that can't be kept. Just isn't right. In early '82 Finn and Anne connected up with the siblings of two of the other murdered students. Dougal O'Prey, Sean's brother, and Riley Dunlavey, Alan's older brother. The man had been with the Shankill Butchers, a notoriously brutal gang who used a political agenda as an excuse to kill. Anyway, Riley had the luck of the devil. He cut himself loose from the Shankills just before the authorities arrested and convicted them in '79. At that time, nobody believed anything the press said about folks. Bloody Hell, back then every Irish man who fought against British rule was evil and a murderer. So Finn and Anne didn't realize what they were getting into until it was too late."

Jesse interrupted. "Riley Dunlavey? Is he the thread that connects Riley Scott to this? I sure as hell don't believe in coincidence. My man Ian has been scouring Ireland for information on Alan Dunlavey's family. This is the first we've heard."

"Won't find much," McNall said. "The Dunlavey's weren't from Belfast. Came from Edinburg. The father regularly beat the mother till she up and killed him and escaped back to Scotland. That wasn't too long after Alan was murdered. Of course Riley had already joined the Shankill gang and the whole family had disowned him. How old is your Riley Scott?"

"Was. How old was he." Jesse said, his voice trembled with suppressed rage. "He kidnapped and tortured my brother today. But it's not the same man. Riley Dunlavey would have to be in his fifties. This Riley was in his thirties at the most."

McNall grunted. "Sometimes mean is in the genes. I'll see if I can have someone check into Dunlavey's trail. An acorn doesn't fall too far from the oak. Riley Scott could be the bastard's son."

"Please," Rocky whispered. "Go back to the story. I can't believe my mother was part of the horror."

"Ye canna judge too harshly, lass. Back then we were all part of the sickness, both us Ulsters and the Brits. Anne and Finn were young and very bitter. The world they lived in had killed all of their dreams, and gave no justice, or mercy. Anne and Finn had left the underground group because the group had moved from writing and printing anti-British propaganda into violent demonstrations."

Rocky felt a wave of relief flood her. She must have exhaled or made a noise, because McNall stopped and nodded. "They hated the violence, lass. Violence had taken what they loved from them. They only wanted the violence to end and freedom for their country. When Anne and Finn met up with the siblings of the students murdered, they thought they were back into printing and distributing material encouraging all of Ireland to stand against

British tyranny. I've no doubt that Anne and Finn loved each other and would have had a different life were it not for the violence."

McNall looked Rocky in the eye and continued the story. "Anne became pregnant in the summer of '82 and Finn took on a local job. Neither of them had been hanging out regularly with the rest of the group for a few months, though Anne did babysit Dougal's ten-year-old daughter often. One day in September, Finn walked into the men's hangout before work to find Riley and Dougal with a man and a woman bound and gagged. The couple had been beaten, but were alive. Dougal handed Finn a club and told him he could take justice for Liam. It was then Finn realized the couple was General Pearson as his wife. As far as the news media and the world knew, the couple was supposed to be vacationing in Scotland."

Rocky closed her eyes and fisted her hands. She didn't want to hear what happened next.

McNall continued. "Finn says he held the club, his whole body shaking. He'd dreamed of revenge. He'd dreamed of justice, but as he looked at the bloodied and beaten couple, he became ill inside. He threw down the club and tried to run. Riley and Dougal came after him, beat him, and tied him to a chair. He told them, he didn't want anything to do with this and that he and Anne would just go back underground. That's when Riley laughed and told Finn it was too late. He and Anne were already involved. It was at that moment that Anne and Dougal's daughter, Mary, were picking up the million in diamonds ransom. Anne thought she was picking up a package of new literature. She and Mary weren't overly surprised when Scotland Yard followed them. Anti-British propaganda wasn't legal, but when the constables started shooting, Anne became worried and suspicious. She and Mary somehow eluded capture. Anne called Dougal to say she had the package and that they'd been followed, but thought they were now safe.

Dougal told them to go to Anne's apartment and stay there. Anne became more suspicious. She opened the package. Amid stacks of paper, she found the diamonds and knew something was very wrong."

"She left Mary and the package at the apartment to go to Finn's work only to find he hadn't shown up for his shift. Returning to the apartment, she collected Mary and the package to go find Mary's father, Dougal. Mary kept asking Anne if they could go shopping first. Anne told Mary they'd have to go later when they had money. Mary said they could use the diamonds and Anne explained that they couldn't because the diamonds weren't theirs. While this was happening, Dougal and Riley made Finn watch as they bludgeoned General Pearson and his wife to death."

Rocky groaned, ill to her stomach. Jesse clasped her hand. "Go on," he told McNall. Finish it." There was a deadly edge to Jesse's voice, as if he wanted to reach into the past and annihilate the evil.

His anger helped to bolster her, Rocky opened her eyes and met McNall's gaze. "Yes, please. I need to know what happened."

"Anne heard Finn's cries for Dougal and Riley to stop before she reached the men's hideout. She left Mary and the diamonds hidden while she crept up to see what was wrong. Got to love a smart woman. Anne went to the closest phone, called Dougal, and told him she and Mary needed help that they were running from Scotland Yard and gave him the name of a street about two miles away. When Riley and Dougal left Finn tied up and rushed to help. Anne went back and freed Finn.

Finn knew they would all be executed for what happened. All he wanted to do was save Anne and the baby. They took Mary to a friend's house and left her there with the package. Finn borrowed a car and took Anne to someone he knew was back in Ireland visiting family, who promised to smuggle Anne out of Ireland. Finn refused to tell me the name of that person. Said if I didn't know, then it couldn't be tortured from me.

"Finn later found out that Mary had taken the diamonds from the package when Anne was out of the apartment, and had put them in Anne's purse so they could go shopping. Finn didn't come see me until three months after everything had happened. He was killed a week later, supposedly by British troops. Personally, I think Dougal and Riley had a tail on me and caught up to Finn because he came out of hiding to see me. It'll haunt me for the rest of me days wonderin' if that's what happened." McNall shook his head sadly. "By the time Finn told me about what happened, a fire, no doubt deliberately set, had burned down the entire block of where Finn said Pearson had been murdered. The General and his wife's bodies have never been found. I had no evidence, but Finn's story. The diamonds were gone. And be it right or wrong, I had to make a choice then. Report a crime there was no evidence of, and send a world-wide manhunt after a young, pregnant woman who'd been a pawn in a nasty game. As well as reveal to a Pearson's bereaved family, who'd already concluded their loved ones were dead, just how horrible those deaths had been. Or let it go. I let it go."

"But what about Dougal and Riley?" Rocky whispered. "They got away with—"

"Ye've got to understand the times, lass. Dougal and Riley were already wanted men for other murders. The authorities were already after them. Back then a man could disappear in the IRA's inner circle and nobody could get to them. I chose to protect you, Finn's child, and I don't have any regrets. Ye can go ahead and tell the world now, if ye think that's best. I'll face whatever consequences there are."

Rocky sat stunned. Part of her ached for what had happened to her mother and the father she never knew. It was tragic. Part of her raged at her mother and Rory, the man she thought was her father, for lying to her. At some point they'd come to love and care for each other, but dear God, she wasn't who she thought she was. Even as all of her emotions were spinning violently like a tornado, there was another part of her that understood what they had done. What choices had they had? And above it all she loved them anyway. And the man across from her was family. Her uncle. By protecting her mother and her, the man had put himself on a chopping block. She didn't quite know what to do with all that she'd learned. Except for one thing...stop the violence.

"Let's cross 'the who or what to tell' bridge later," Jesse said. He squeezed Rocky's hand, then released it to pace away from her as he spoke. "We need to focus on finding the shark beneath the surface of Rocky's life. Now that Riley's dead, that person is going to do one of two things. Get desperate or—"

"Lay low," Mulligan added. "I'd lay low. Reports on Mack, Alice, and Maggie came in while you were at the hospital. All three were not born in the US, but have been here for at least twenty years. Mack is from Australia, Alice from British Columbia, and Maggie from London. So far, no red flags have shown up in their history, and no connection to Riley Scott outside of work. But then, we're having a difficult time chasing down what's fact and what's fiction on Riley's reports. He had several aliases. Looks as if this situation could last a while."

Rocky shook her head. Were Mack or Maggie or Alice involved? There had to be someone else she just wasn't seeing yet. She wanted this to be over with. The thought of living for weeks like she'd been living for the past three days turned her inside out. "The diamonds," she murmured. "My mother ended up with the diamonds. Let's give the shark the diamonds."

All three men looked at her as if she sprouted horns.

"You have them?" Jesse asked.

"No, but the shark doesn't know that. And if he thinks I'm getting ready to skip out on my life here with the goods, I bet you he'll follow me."

"Perfect," Mulligan said.

Jesse shook his head. "No. Too much can go wrong, and not only would Jared kill me if anything happened to you, I'd shoot myself."

"I've a better idea," McNall said. "I'm new on the scene. Whoever is behind this knows the history of the diamonds, and will connect me to Finn. I'll pretend to be helping the lass, but then steal the diamonds from her."

Mulligan frowned. "Who says we can trust you?"

McNall smiled. "You can't." He winked at Rocky. "But the lass can. I've waited a long time to meet my niece and I'm not about to lose her again."

"We have our who and how. Now we just have to decide where?"

"The McKenna construction office." Rocky said. "It's the only property left that my mother spent time in and the only property my father fully owns. Da sold the house they shared a few years after she died and as far as I know there are no safety deposit boxes. Just the safe at the construction office."

"How do you know that diamonds aren't there?" Jesse asked.

"That's just it," Rocky told him. "I think they are. Where they might specifically be, I don't know. In the bedtime story my mother told me, the princess returned the treasure to the Dragonlords to save her mother the queen. My mother painted pictures of a princess in the Rainbow Room. Maybe there is a clue in the murals."

"I'd say that's a sure bet, and even if you are wrong, it sounds perfect," Mulligan said. "There is no way our man will be able to resist acting on it. When?" he asked. "When do you want to put this plan into action?"

"Tomorrow," Jesse said. "Our biggest problem will be convincing the shark that Rocky escaped from me and Mulligan."

"Not a problem," McNall said. "I can just shoot both of you and take the lass in broad daylight."

Jesse frowned at Mulligan. "I thought you said you trusted this guy."

Mulligan shrugged. "I never said that."

Rocky shifted her gaze between each of the men, not a hint of humor showed in their poker-smooth expressions, or their deadpan tones. She pressed her palms to her aching temples. "Can we play mental chicken later? James hasn't called about Jared yet and I am worried."

Jesse winced. "Sorry. We've a morbid sense of humor. Let's go to the conference room and call."

"Please," she said, standing.

McNall stood as well. "You're an answer to prayer, lass, and ye've a slew of relatives who'd be pleased to learn Finn left a part of himself behind, but there's time for all that later. I'll see you in the mornin' for our shark hunt?"

The burly man, whom had likely faced all manner of situations throughout his life, looked as unsteady and unsure as she felt. He didn't have to tell her about the past. He could have pretended he didn't know anything at all, and she would have been left wondering. She moved around the coffee table, and leaned in to give him a quick hug. "Yes. And I'll look forward to hearing more about Finn and family."

Jesse waited for her at the door. She hurried to him. He touched her shoulder. "Try not to worry. If anything were seriously wrong with Jared. Someone would have called."

"I know," she whispered then shrugged. "It's just, knowing that someone will call and actually being there are worlds apart. She hadn't expected to feel so unsettled about leaving Jared. Even as exhausted as she was, the idea of going up stairs and sleeping in the huge bed without him, left her aching inside.

She followed Jesse to the conference room. He called James. "Jared awake yet?"

"Yes and no," James said.

Jesse frowned. "Switch to video." James's face appeared on the large screen TV. He was clearly in a hospital room. "What does yes and no mean?" Jesse asked.

"Well, he was still out-of-it-groggy from surgery when they brought him to his room, but was so determined to get up and find Rocky that they knocked him back out. Apparently, it's essential that he stay calm and still for the next twenty-four to forty-eight hours. Mom and I are with him."

"Take me back," Rocky told Jesse.

"You sure? You'll be up all night and slow tomorrow. And as James said, he and my mother are there."

She shook her head. "It doesn't matter. I'll get better rest there with him than I will here alone."

"It isn't exactly rational, but okay. Go upstairs and get what you need. We'll leave in ten minutes."

Mulligan left the car at the hospital entrance while he and Jesse walked her to the elevators. Then he left to park the car. Rocky hadn't realized that by returning to the hospital, she was putting them both back on duty, until she overheard Jesse calling his wife to tell her he'd be at the hospital all night. At nine thirty at night the lobby had considerably fewer people around and having them both with her seemed overkill, but she wasn't the security expert. The bodyguard Jesse left with Jared was waiting at the elevator on the fifth floor.

The elevator doors opened, Jesse checked it, then motioned for her to enter. She settled by the control panel and pushed the button for the fifth floor as Jesse got on. The doors started to close.

"Rocky! Wait! Did you get the call about your Da?"

Rocky pushed the open door button to see Maggie hurrying forward. "No. What's wrong?"

"Shit." Jesse grabbed Rocky's arm, jerking her back, as he stepped in front of her. Horrified, Rocky saw Maggie shoot Jesse from a gun hidden in her coat pocket. Jesse's grip went slack.

Before Maggie could shoot again, Rocky shoved Jesse aside, and launched herself at the woman with a full body tackle. She wrapped both hands around the wrist of Maggie's gun hand as they slammed to the ground. Rocky brought her knee up hard as she shoved Maggie's arm down. Wedged between Rocky's knee and hands, Maggie's wrist bones snapped and the gun fired.

Maggie screamed. Rocky got the pistol out of the woman's pocket and pinned her to the ground. People in the lobby were screaming and running wild. Alarms went off.

"Remind me to never piss you off," Jesse said.

"She's deadly," Mulligan said.

Rocky looked up, gapping at Jesse standing there unhurt and perfectly calm, with his pistol aimed at Maggie's head. He had a bullet hole right over his heart. She'd forgotten about the bullet proof vests they all wore. Mulligan stood opposite. He must have walked out the door and came right back in instead of parking the car.

Mulligan took the gun from Rocky helped her up then stared down at Maggie. "Figured we were dealing with desperate."

Nursing her arm, Maggie sat up, tears streaming down her face.

Now that Rocky realized Jesse was unharmed, she knelt down in front of Maggie. It was hard to believe that Maggie was behind it all. Then the pieces clicked. "You're Mary Magdalene, Dougal Oprey's daughter. You knew my mother."

"She treated me like a daughter. She gave me a birthday party. She made me a beautiful dress. And she just left me. She took me to someone's house and left. She left and because I cost him the diamonds, my father beat me every day until he left me with that monster of an uncle who was worse. Those diamonds are mine. I paid for them. You don't need them. You have everything."

"I don't have the diamonds, Maggie. My mother and Da must have hid them somewhere, but I don't have them. How did you find me?" Rocky asked.

"The news segment on Build-A-Future. They showed a picture of Anne. I recognized her then realized you looked just like Finn."

"Who was Riley Scott?

"Riley Dunlavey's son. He and his came over here and joined the Westies. I made the mistake of telling him I found your mother. He showed up here and started taking things over. Your father walked in on us fighting at the office and realized who we were. Riley demanded he give us the diamonds and—"

"That's when my father had a stroke."

Maggie nodded. "When your father tried to speak to you on Sunday, Riley said we were out of time. We either had to find the diamonds before you found out about us and them, or we had to put you out of commission."

Rocky heard a commotion and looked up to see a number of police officers and hospital security men had arrived. Jesse caught her elbow and urged her up. "We need to let the police move in now."

"I just wanted the diamonds," Maggie cried. "I paid for them."

Rocky shook her head, saddened by the pain, devastation, and tragedy that a parent could bring to a child's life. She realized that even though her father wasn't who she thought her father was, she did really have it all. She'd had love.

CHAPTER NINETEEN

Jared knew he'd done it now. He couldn't move. He couldn't think. He couldn't even breathe. He hurt like a son of a bitch from head to toe. This had to be the worst hangover of his life. He felt has if he'd gone to hell and the devil had chewed him up and spit him back out.

And who in damnation was he with now? He felt a woman's head on his right shoulder at an odd angle. As if she wasn't quite all the way on the bed with him. He managed a slight sniff, groaning at the explosion of pain in his left side as the niggling scent of citrus and coconuts tickled his memory. Trying not to breathe so he didn't hurt, he searched his mind…

Rocky! Gasping, he jerked his eyes open and tried to sit up.

"He's awake!" James's voice boomed from across the room.

"God is good! Can you hear me, son?" Jared recognized his mother's voice, but could seem to speak. His throat felt raw. There was a tube in his nose, his throat. What had happened to him?

The weight on his shoulder lifted. "Jared? Can you hear us?"

He shifted his gaze and saw Rocky and nodded.

She clasped his hand in hers. "You were hurt, but everything is all good now. Just rest. We're all here."

He nodded. Shut his eyes then remembered what happened. He gripped Rocky's hand. "Riileey," he croaked.

"Is dead. Now you need to rest and get better. Do you need something for pain?"

He nodded. "First...must...ask."

"Ask me what?"

"Date. Will...you?"

"Are you asking me out on a date?"

He nodded. He heard James laughing and decided he'd punch him later then realized Rocky hadn't answered him. He blinked to clear his blurry vision and saw tears streaming down her face. He gripped her hand tighter, his heart sinking.
"Don't...cry...no...is...okay."

"Yes, yes, yes. Now rest. No worries. We're good."

He sighed and smiled. Moments later, he felt himself drifting away.

Two weeks later...

Jared was screwed. He knew it when he heard the kitchen screen door snap shut—three separate times in the last five minutes. He and his brothers had the habit of giving the aluminum frame an extra push to preempt their mom's "don't let the flies in" shout from wherever she was in the house.

He didn't think it a coincidence that all three of his brothers had decided to drop by the family homestead the very night he was taking Rocky out for the first time, which meant, he'd be sneaking out the bathroom window instead of walking out the front door. He'd be early to pick her up, but that meant they could take their time getting to the marina. On the agenda tonight was a champagne and dinner cruise on the Savannah River—moonlight, music, and stars.

Their first date. Lord he prayed he didn't mess this up. He'd been out of the hospital for a week now, recuperating at his parents' house. He'd enjoyed his mother's TLC and spending time with his father, but was antsy to get back to his own life. He had a number of changes he had to make, because he wanted Rocky in his life.

He'd seen her every day. Twice a day. McKenna Construction had contracted Shamrock Construction to help with the Drake Hotel renovations, and repairing fire damage. The job was almost back on schedule now. Though Jared couldn't return to work yet, he did bring lunch to share with Rocky every day, and they would walk over the site, discuss the progress, and plan the next step. Then she came to see him every night.

It killed him to admit it, but things were not the same. There was a barrier between them. Whether his stupidity had put the walls there, or she was still grappling with the upheaval and violence that had torn apart her life, he didn't know. He just knew that something precious had been lost, and he would do whatever he had to do to get it back.

He had a plan to win her heart. One hundred and one nights of roses and romance before he stormed her citadel again—a take it slow strategy that will show her his heart, and prove to her that she could trust him.

His hands shook as he fumbled with the knot of his tie. It just wouldn't stay right, and he finally gave up fiddling with it. Another minute, and his brothers would be hunting for him. Damn, you'd think it was prom night and they were teenagers again. Surely, all pranks from the past had been forgiven and forgotten.

He winced as he recalled the time he and James had "accidentally" plastered Jackson with the hose as he walked out the door in his suit for homecoming of his freshman year. Jackson had had to drip-dry during the dance, and his shoes were still squishing when he got home at midnight. Then there'd been the time that he and James had soaked Jesse's leather jacket in their mother's best perfume. That had not gone well. He and James couldn't sit for days after the switching their dad gave them, and Jesse had gotten even by getting eau-de-skunk on the inside of his and James's football helmets. They'd stunk on and off the field that whole season.

Come to think of it, he needed to get his ass out of there.

Rinsing a second time with mouthwash, Jared opened the bathroom window, removed the screen, then hiked his leg over the sill. Groaning, he bent in half to slide his way outside. He was still sore and bruised from A to Z it seemed, and it would be a good six weeks before he could consider getting back to his normal activities. But he was alive, he could laugh, and he could love. That was all he needed for now.

"Well, lookee what we have here, bros," came Jackson's slow drawl. "A man trying to escape rather than take his medicine."

Jared snapped his head up and smacked it on the window. "Shit." His head spun for a moment. Jesse and James stood on each side of Jackson. All three were grinning from ear to ear. Jared didn't know what they had planned, but it had to be bad to have them looking so happy.

"Guys, really. You don't want to do this tonight." Jared drew in a breath, trying to stay calm and cool. There'd be no mercy if they knew how nervous he really was.

"I think we do," Jesse said. "Paybacks are hell, bro."

Jared zeroed his gaze on James. "What are you doing, teaming up with them? You've always had my back."

James just shook his head. "Sorry man. I love you, but as I told you before, you're screwed, blued, and tattooed."

Jared held up his hands in appeal. "Listen. You three can pick any other night and screw it up, but tonight is just not it, okay?"

"I'll get his feet," Jesse said.

"Just remember not to be too rough," Jackson said. "Don't want his ass back in the hospital this soon."

"Really," Jared said, breaking into a sweat. "I'm still on the mend here. Let's do this another time.

They all three grabbed hold of him and Jared knew it was useless to fight. If he was back to a hundred percent, he might have given it a shot. As it was, he had to give in and wait for his opportunity to escape, provided he was still presentable for a date by then.

He felt like a trussed pig as they carried him around to the back of the house.

Jesse shook his feet. "How much weight has he lost, Jackson?"

"About ten pounds."

"Bring him on in, boys." John Weldon said.

Jared snapped his head up at the sound of his father's voice. "Dad! Help!"

"Sorry, son. But when it's a man's turn, he just has to take it."

Jared expected his brothers to toss him in the back of the truck and cart him down to the creek or the pig sty. Instead, they carried him into the house and sat him down at the kitchen table.

Jared shifted his shoulders, and adjusted a twist in his suit, as he warily searched the kitchen. Was he about to get a whipped cream pie in the face? The kitchen appeared just as he left it earlier. He had dozens of books opened on the table. All of them were on the history of Ireland and the Roman invasion. When Rocky, Jesse, Mulligan and McNall examined the murals in the Rainbow Room, looking for the diamonds while *he was still in a hospital bed, mind you,* they'd come up empty-handed except for an XX:XVII etched on the pot of gold at the end of the rainbow.

Nobody had been able to crack open the clue, and Jared had been determined to do it while recuperating. So far, no luck.

Jesse leaned in and sniffed. "He smells okay. But do you think he needs a dose of your Old Spice, dad?"

"Maybe," John Weldon said, taking a sniff.

Jared winced and bit his tongue. Old Spice would so kill his designer cologne. He also knew if he said a word in protest, they'd dump the bottle on his head.

"Our, bro, is losing his touch," Jackson said. He's got a spot on his shoe. When was the last time you polished them?"

"An hour ago," Jared said, glaring at Jackson.

Jesse bent down and examined his shoes. "Definitely spotted. Let's take them off." He and Jackson pulled off his shoes.

"Well, would you look at this," James said, tugging on Jared's tie. "His knot is crooked. Can't have that, can we, bros."

"Nope," Jesse said.

"Take it off," Jackson advised.

Shit, Jared thought. "Mom will be back from the grocery store any minute, guys. You don't want to do this."

"I'll do the honors," said his father. Jared just looked up at his father while he undid his tie. He couldn't believe the evening was playing out like this. And that everyone was ganging up on him. This date was so important to him.

His dad paused after he finished undoing the tie. "Now is it right over left or left over right."

"John Weldon, after all of these years, you haven't learned a thing," Jared's Mom said, breezing into the kitchen with a bag. She shoved the bag into Jackson's hands. "Get this ready for me." Then she marched over and took control of the tie. "You do it just like this," she said.

Within sixty seconds, she'd retied his tie and it felt perfectly straight. When she finished, she brushed his cheek like she every night when she tucked him into bed so many years ago. "Just so you know, I couldn't be prouder of you and I love you."

Jared blinked. What was going on?

His father clapped him on the back. "Double what your mother said, son. I am humbled and I am so very thankful, God answered our prayers to return you to us and to heal you."

Jesse tugged on Jared's suit collar and it fell into alignment. "Better get those shoes shiny, James. We don't want Jared to be late."

"What? Me? Why do I have to shine his shoes?"

Jackson and Jesse glared at James. "Because there are two of us and one of you at the moment. Jared's out of the fighting ring for a while yet."

James grumbled, but fetched the shoe shinning kit from under the kitchen sink and set to work.

Jackson clamped a hand on Jared's shoulder. "If you haven't figured it out yet, bro. We're here to bolster you up. My advice to win Rocky is to make her your number one."

Jared's stomach knotted as emotion clogged his throat.

Jesse set a heavy hand on Jared's other shoulder. "First thing, Mulligan says you can be his backup should you ever want to change professions. He sent you this. He only gives these out to an elite few, so consider yourself honored." Jesse handed him a gold coin with a shamrock stamped on it. "And just so you know, I concur. Your every instinct was dead on. That's something that can't be taught. I'm glad you'll be looking out for Jake down the road, if needed."

"Jesse Weldon," Emma admonished. "Don't you go recruiting your baby brother into danger, again."

Jesse rolled his eyes and grinned. "Second thing, I want your and James's karma. Riley Scott had about five aliases. He was a wanted man in several countries with a price on his head, dead or alive. Total fugitive reward is a hundred thousand. Sheridan-Weldon Solutions will be sending you check when the funds arrive. Don't blow it."

Jared's jaw dropped. "What?" He'd learned from Jesse that Riley Scott and his father, Riley Dunlavey, had migrated from Ireland in the eighties, and joined the brutal Westies in Manhattan's Hell's Kitchen area. The mob-like Irish gang had terrorized for years, specializing in murder and torture.

James whistled. "That beats my reward."

James's instincts had been dead on too. The LA couple who'd been so eager to buy the spec house that James had had Jesse run a background check on, had been up to no good. The details were still unraveling, but the plot involved impersonating the man's real wife to steal from her.

Jesse continued. "Third thing, you mess this up with Rocky and I'll—"

"Positive," Emma interrupted. "Remember."

Jesse frowned, looking at a loss. "You get this right with Rocky and I won't pound your ass. Whether she knows it yet or not, she loves you, and was pissed at me for telling you to take a hike. So your chances of winning her over are good."

James brought his shoes back. "Well, I'm going to say something here. And I don't care if anybody likes it or not."

Jared met his twin's gaze and came to grip with the unspoken anxiety tangled up in his heart. They'd been part of a whole since birth, had lived and breathed together all of their lives. Neither of them had really ventured forth without the other until…Jared had seen Rocky in the bar and didn't look away.

James cleared his throat. "I think you're screwed, blued, and tattooed for jumping off the bachelor bandwagon so fast, but if you love her then, she couldn't get a better catch. After all, you are my twin. You're a Weldon who knows how to put everything on the line and step up to the plate when necessary, no matter what the price. So, you go out tonight with confidence, and she had better appreciate you, or she'll have me to deal with."

Jackson and Jesse ragged James. Their dad preened, claiming he'd raised his boys right, and their mom muttered something about the Lord would be the judge of that, but she was smiling. Jared exhaled with relief.

His mother handed him a bouquet of roses and a box of Godiva chocolates she'd just bought. "Give her respect. Bring her love and laughter, be her friend and lover and she'll be yours forever."

Jared headed to the front door for his date with a spring in his step. He could do this. His mother followed.

Just before he opened the door, he glanced up at the plaque posted above it and paused. *"Come to me, all you who are weary and burdened, and I will give you rest."* M 11:28.

"I put that there because of you boys," his mother said. "The best thing a mother can tell her child before he leaves home is that God is always there no matter where they go."

Jared kissed his mother and rushed out the door. He couldn't wait to see Rocky.

"Dessie, I can't find my other blue earring! Help! Jared will be here in any minute." Ever since Jesse had officially concluded her life was no longer in danger, she'd been staying in Dessie's spare bedroom until the repairs to her house were finished.

Trying not to wrinkle her silk dress, Rocky got down on her knees, looking under the bed. She'd already looked everywhere else logical, now she was working on the illogical. She was running late for her date because she'd stayed longer at the nursing home with her father than she'd planned, talking to his new physical therapist.

Her father had spoken twice more over the past two weeks, saying the same thing he'd said before. Keira, unforgivable, stop, pray. Despite Rocky's reassurances that all was well, he was still stuck in a nightmare inside his mind. Rocky was still working with her father's attorney on getting the "after death" papers her father had left for her. Since her father had the stroke the night he discovered who Maggie and Riley really were, McNall had suggested that her father was telling her to stop Maggie whose name had been O'Prey before she'd changed it to Dupree.

Maggie was being held in jail without bond, under accessory to murder and attempted murder charges. She'd insinuated herself into the fringes of Rocky's life over a year ago, quietly looking for the diamonds. She claimed she never meant for anyone to get hurt. But in a conversation a few months back with Riley, whom she had known since childhood, she said the wrong thing. And, Riley, who also knew the story about the diamonds, came looking for Maggie. He took over the search, becoming more and more impatient and violent. Rocky knew that Maggie had had a hard life, but given Pat's murder, her father's stroke, and what they had done and were going to do the Jared and Collin, she didn't have any sympathy for the woman.

Collin had been the biggest surprise. Losing his father and seeing the violence Riley had been capable of, shook him to his soul. He was selling her his father's third of the company for whatever amount she wanted to buy it for, and was in the process of going to the Sudan to help build a church orphanage. He apologized to her again for what happened in the past and for not remembering what he had done. She forgave him and wished him well.

After staying several days, McNall had flown back to Ireland, promising to come back. Rocky returned the promise. One day soon, she'd go to Ireland and met her biological father's family. She wanted to hear more stories of Finn when growing up. She also wanted to find the O'Loughlins in Australia, too.

First she had to figure out her relationship with Jared.

It had changed drastically and she didn't know what to do about it. The first few days she'd known him had been a highly intense, sexually charged rollercoaster that she hadn't wanted to stop when it ended. Now that attraction seemed to be under layers of spun cotton. Still there, still visible, but unreachable and she didn't know if it was her fault or his.

"Did you try the bathroom counter?" Dessie asked. "I remember seeing something sparkly and blue by the toothpaste."

"Huh?" Rocky snapped her head up and smacked it on the bed frame. "Ouch. The bathroom?" She scrambled to her feet before a bounding Pebbles, met her nose to nose. "Of course, I took it off because it got tangled with the curling iron. Where is my brain?"

"Don't know," Dessie said. "I'm wondering the same thing. Why a woman needs a first date when a man's already taken her to the pearly gates is beyond me."

"Dessie! For Heaven's sake. Would you please forget that I told you that? I will never drink Godiva Martinis with you again. They are deadly and you are merciless."

Dessie laughed. "Relax. Your sex secrets are safe with me. And just so we're tit for tat, remind me to tell you about what Mr. Saint did. OMG, I am still vibrating. Page eighty-six of the manual if you're interested in getting a sneak preview before I have time to share. I'm late to work. Don't wait up for me. I hope you and your first date will be hitting multiple home runs by the time I get home. Just keep the stereo going and I won't disturb you. Pebbles knows that when the music's playing she's to stay in her bed."

"You've trained her to do that? How?"

"Multiple dog biscuits, hidden all over her bed." She left with a wave of her hand.

Rocky found her earing and put the finishing touches to her makeup. Then she went down stairs to wait for Jared. Pebbles had parked herself tragically against the front door to await Dessie's return. How a two-hundred pound St. Bernard could look so helplessly forlorn was beyond Rocky.

The longer Rocky waited, the more she worried became about the change in her relationship with Jared. Sure, she'd been upset with him, but coming so close to losing him, had quickly put things into perspective for her. At least, she thought, she had. Maybe all that was needed was a spark to rekindle what she was missing.

Page eighty-six.

Leave it to Dessie. She just had to mess with Rocky's mind. First, Rocky would get Pebbles to move from the front door, then she'd go peek at page eighty-six.

"Pebbles want a dog biscuit?" Rocky went to the kitchen and came back with a biscuit.

Pebbles turned sad eyes her way.

"Hmm." Rocky added a pitch excitement to her voice. "Pebbles want to go outside?'

Pebbles laid her head down.

Rocky decided to turn on the stereo and dump dog biscuits in Pebble's bed. She put on a CD labeled, band, jazz, and rock. Pebbles didn't move. Rocky got the dog's leash, snapped it on, smiled at Pebbles as she held up a dog biscuit, "Let's go for a walk." Pebbles rolled over onto her back.

Glancing out the side-window, Rocky saw Jared get out of his blue truck. Her palms grew damp, her heart hammered, and butterflies swirled in her stomach as she watched him navigate through the faded pink flamingos. Darn. She weighed her options and dashed up the stairs to the Kama Sutra Pocket Guide and flipped to page eighty-six.

Good Heavens! She was not doing a handstand with her heels locked around Jared's hips while he sat on the side of the bed rocking into her tonight. She tossed the book aside. At the last minute she grabbed the bag she had sitting on the nightstand. It wasn't perfect, but it was something. Tupelo Honey. The bottle had been pricey, but she'd been told it was the sweetest, tastiest liquid gold of the South. Stuffing the honey in her purse, she ran down the stairs. Pebbles still blocked the door and Jared was knocking.

Setting her purse on the table, she rapped on the side window. "I can't open the door. Pebbles is in the way."

He peered into the window, frowning. "I think I know where the diamonds are."

"What?"

"Open the door."

She pointed down at the floor. "Pebbles won't move."

Jared leaned in close and whistled. Loud. Pebbles rolled onto her stomach, wagging her tail and got up with a bark.

"Really?" Rocky glared at Pebbles as she opened the door.

Jared came inside. He swept her into his arms, pulling her tight against his chest. He smelled like heaven and felt even better. She clung to him, treasuring the moment.

There was so much she wanted to know about him, so much she wanted to share with him that every minute she was with him didn't feel as if it was long enough.

He found her lips, kissed her hard and swung her around. Then set her down and smiled into her eyes with his. "Did you hear me?"

"Hear what?

"I think I know where the diamonds are?"

"Okay. Where? But I have to tell you I am more excited to see you at the moment than to think about another search that will likely end nowhere."

Jared laughed. "Every man dreams of being wanted more than diamonds."

"Then let me make your dreams come true."

"Do you have a Bible? I think the code is a Bible verse."

"A Bible verse?" Rocky stopped and stared at Jared, her heart pounding. "There's a family bible! My mother specifically put it in my hands the day before she died. She told me it was the greatest treasure of life."

He grabbed her hand and turned back to the door. "Show me."

Rocky snatched her keys from the key rack in the hallway, and they rushed over to her house. She went to the bookshelf, and pulled down the Bible, thankful that it hadn't been damaged in the explosion.

"Where should I look?"

"How many chapter twenty verse seventeen's are there?" Jared asked.

"More than just a few," Rocky said.

"The numbers were Roman numerals, try Romans."

Rocky flipped to the New Testament and found Romans. "There're only sixteen chapters." As she held the book up for him to see, she saw rainbow colored ribbons hanging from a bookmark. Her hands shook as she turned to the page. The bookmark was of a princess riding a unicorn. It marked the twentieth chapter of Luke.

"You're shaking so much, I can't read the verse." Jared reached up and steadied her hand.

"What then is this that is written, The stone that the builder rejected has become the cornerstone."

Rocky frowned.

Jared hooted. "Is there any sort of plaque on the foundation of your office building?"

She grabbed Jared's hand. "On the corner. There is a large marble brick with 1984 engraved on it. The year it was built."

"That's it. It's perfect. *'The stone the builder rejected.'* You mother and father built the office and they'd rejected the diamonds. Diamonds are called stones. *'Has become the cornerstone.'* The diamonds are in the cornerstone of the office building, likely in a time capsule."

Rocky hugged Jared's neck, practically jumping up and down. "You did it! You're right. Oh my gosh! I can't believe it."

He laughed. "Neither can I." He explained how seeing the verse his mother had above the door on his way out tonight got him to thinking.

"Good Lord," she sucked in air. "What am I going to do now? I need to return them to who they were stolen from without involving my new uncle."

Jared kissed her hand. "Don't worry. There's time to figure it out. They've been there for decades. They aren't going anywhere. We've got reservations for dinner to make."

"Let me get my purse." She led the way to Dessis, bringing the family Bible with her. They walked hand in hand. When Rocky went to open the door, it didn't budge an inch. "Pebbles! Let me in girl. I'll give you a doggie biscuit." She pushed on the door. Nothing. She frowned at Jared. "Whistle for me."

"Anytime," he said, grinning. He whistled and the door flung open. She went flying inside and would have bounced off the wall if Jared hadn't caught her. He groaned as she brushed up against his groin. She snapped her gaze to his, and saw the need burning in his eyes. He wanted her bad, but instead of sweeping her into his arms, he inhaled and stepped back. "You ready to go?"

"Yes." She set the Bible on the table and picked up her purse. Why was Jared so retrained? "Where are we going?"

"You'll see."

For having uncovered where her parents had likely hidden a million in diamonds, the conversation as they drove wasn't very exciting. They talked about the weather, the jobsite, and her father's recovery. She kept wanting Jared to be the way he was before, and he wasn't. He was different, and she didn't know what to do about it. She was pleasantly surprised when he drove up to the river and she learned they were going on a dinner cruise.

She'd never been on one before.

"Wait for me," he said. He got out of the truck, retrieved his suit jacket from the backseat, and came around to her door. He opened her door for her and handed her roses and a gold box of Godiva chocolates.

"Thank you." She breathed deep of the roses.

"My pleasure," he said softly and brushed a kiss on her cheek.

Rocky shivered, lifting her lips up for more, but he turned away, and urged her from the truck.

She kept the roses, tucked the Godiva's in her purse, and followed his lead. Twenty minutes later, they were cruising down the river. Stars twinkled in the night sky, a mild breeze caressed her skin, and the earthy scents of the coast flavored the air. They walked around the deck, enjoying the experience before going inside to eat. Crystal chandeliers swayed over the formal dining room, champagne bubbled in flutes, and a live band played oldie-but-goldie music she hadn't heard in a long time.

Jared raised his champagne glass. "A toast."

She lifted her glass.

"To first dates," he said and clinked his flute to hers.

She smiled and nodded.

His gaze searched hers and he set the glass down. "You're not having fun, are you? Hell. Can you tell me what's wrong so I can fix it? I'm sorry about what happened. I'll do whatever—"

Rocky reached over and pressed her finger to Jared's lips. "I just want the Jared that stormed across a bar and swept me off my feet back. I know you've been recuperating, but something's wrong. I don't know how to explain it. I just want the Jared that was so hungry, he couldn't even wait for me to get my robe. The Jared—"

Jared sat back and roared with laughter.

"What is so funny?"

"You. Me. Hell. Life. Here I've been killing myself to be a gentleman. I've a hundred nights of roses and romance planned before I was going to let myself storm your citadel."

"A hundred night's like this?"

"Give or take a bit. The yacht's sort of pricey, but I can do candlelight on a balcony and a stroll down River Street."

"Don't get me wrong. This is all amazing. I've never had such an elegant date. It's beautiful, but if I have to choose between this and you distant, or pizza and you all over me. Give me the pizza." She slipped her purse out from under the table and withdrew what she'd bought for him. "This is for you."

He took the bag, but didn't open it yet. "I only pulled back because I wanted to give you time to know me. To know you can trust me."

"And I was wrong to say what I did. I've had a lot of time to think about this. There're different ways to know a person. Fact-wise in your head, or soul-wise in your heart. Soul-wise you never mis-represented yourself. The intent of your heart from the start was to protect me. Same goes for my parents."

"So, I'm forgiven?"

"Yeah. Just don't make leading me to the wrong conclusions a habit, or I may have to take Jesse up on his references for stupid."

"References for stupid?"

"Apparently it's a common problem with Weldon men."

Jared frowned.

"Don't worry about it now." Rocky reached across the table and pushed the paper bag closer to Jared. "Open it."

He opened the bag and sat staring at the bottle inside. His body shook. "You bought me honey for my biscuit."

"Yes."

"You know what that means?" He looked up and his gaze met hers.

She nearly burst into flames from the sensual heat. She licked her lips. "Yes."

"Come on." He stood.

"Where are we going?"

"The dance floor. It's not like we can jump ship. Hell, it's all I can do to keep from dragging you into a dark corner." He pulled her into his arms and slid his body flush to hers with his thigh so tight against her sex, she nearly whimpered with every step they took. The words to the music faded as he whispered into her ear exactly what he was going to do to her with the honey when the cruise was over.

Whatever barrier that separated them burned in a heartbeat.

Jared was back.

It was the most romantic dinner of her life. It was the sexiest dinner of her life. It was longest dinner of her life.

They hit Dessie's house at a run, having stopped and bought condoms on the way. He'd really taken his plan to heart and had thrown out his supply.

"Which way to the kitchen?"

"To the left. My bedroom is upstairs on the right."

"Later," Jared said, pulling her into the kitchen.

He stripped her clothes off. Dress, bra, and thongs all landed on the back of the kitchen chair. Then he set her on the kitchen table top. "Remember what I told you on the dance floor? How I wanted you to look?"

She nodded. "Do it then. Scoot to the middle and lay back."

She did, feeling like a feast placed before a decadent knight.

"Now spread your legs wide."

She let her legs fall open.

"Wider," he rasped. Clasping one leg he edged her wider until her foot slid off the side of the table, bending at the knee. "Now the other one."

She did as he asked, and shivered at how exposed, and yet, delicious she felt. He stood at the end of the table looking down at her. He opened the bottle of honey, and poured dribbles over her stomach and her sex. Then he poured honey on his finger. He put his finger in his mouth and moaned as he sucked, taking his time.

Rocky frowned. "Uh, Jared."

"Hmm," he said, licking his lips.

"Uh,…is it good?"

"You tell me," he said. He poured honey on his finger and slipped his finger into her mouth. She swirled her tongue over his finger and sucked. The honey was amazing. She sucked away every last drop. He pulled his finger out of her mouth, and she noticed with satisfaction that his pupils had enlarged considerably. So had his erection, given the bulging of his fly.

"Lift your arms above your head. Let me see your full breasts beg for me, Rocky."

She raised her arms to rest above her head and arched her back just a little. He dribbled honey all over her nipples.

"Now close your eyes for a few minutes, and think about me licking you everywhere."

She shut her eyes, and heard him as he stripped of his clothes. She shivered. So ready for him.

"Open your mouth for me," he whispered. She opened her mouth and he inserted a honey covered finger. She licked and sucked eagerly. "Now turn your head and open wider." She opened as far as she could, and a honey drenched hot and throbbing penis slid into her mouth, she moaned with satisfaction, sucking deep and loving the sweet earthy taste of the honey with his masculine musk. His body shivered hard, and she opened her eyes to meet his gaze.

Dark and intense, vulnerable and needy. She couldn't get enough of him. Shuddering as if he was about to lose his last hold on his control, he pulled out of her mouth. Moving to her head, he clasped her hands in his and leaned down and kissed her. He had honey in his mouth, warm and smooth. He fed it to her little by little. She drank from his lips.

Next, he left her mouth, and moved to her aching breasts. He laved each nipple to a hard point with his tongue, then sucked her deep into his mouth. She arched to him, lost within the hot pulse of desire storming through her. She'd missed him so much, needed this magic that only he could create between them. She reached for him, but he pressed her hands back.

"I'm not done yet." He shifted to the bottom of the table, grabbed her knees, and slid her closer to him. Leaning down he licked her sex, swirling his tongue over and over her clitoris, as he lapped up the honey. Her hips bucked with every stroke, and her heart hammered harder and harder. He pinned her thighs down, opening her as wide as she could stretch.

"Come, Rocky. Let me see you come."

"Not without you. I need you inside me. I want you inside me. I have missed you so much," she cried, angling up on her elbows.

He stopped and stood, meeting her gaze. "I've missed you too. You don't know how much. Especially when I thought I would never get to hold you again."

She reached out to him, and he pulled her into his arms, kissing her, deep and long. She met him kiss for kiss. It was if the air and their bodies ignited. He tore open a condom, slid it on, and edging her to the end of the table, plunged inside her.

She wrapped her legs around his hips and they thrust together, sparking a sexual synergy that sizzled through her mind, body and spirit. The shuddering climax that swept her from the tip of her toes to the top of her head, stole her breath, shook her soul, and consumed her entire existence into the essence of him. She wasn't letting go of him any time soon.

Jared let his orgasm flow through each cell of his body, and into the aching recesses of his heart. He treasured the very beat of her heart, every thought in her mind, every laugh on her lips, and every touch of her hand. He knew deep inside that he loved her. A man didn't face his death and not know what he felt for the woman in his life.

He'd been so nervous for the past two weeks that he'd messed up his chance with her. That she would never be able to look at him with the same passion as she had before. He couldn't believe that she wanted him just the way he was, but she did. That simple truth wrapped around his heart like nothing else in his life had before.

He wasn't through showing her how he felt about her, and what he wanted to share with her in life, but there was time. For now, he could have his honey and eat it too, and sometimes that's all a man needed.

Excerpt From WILD IRISH RIDE
WELDON BROTHERS SERIES - BOOK ONE

He should have stayed away, he thought, stepping deeper into the shadows as she drew nearer. He saw she was wearing the damn pearls. Of course she would, it was her day to wear the cursed things. He'd never forget what she and those pearls had cost him. Reporters, like sharks in a feeding frenzy, snapped pictures and yelled questions. Alexi ignored them all. He had to admire that, he thought, his jaw clenching in protest.

Where she was going?

He knew what it was like to be shark bait and Alexi was sailing through the water with her head held high, but even through the light rain he could see she was bleeding inside as she drew abreast of him. Tears streamed down her face and her full lips trembled. She stumbled and reached for something to break her fall, but only grasped air.

Shit. He rushed forward and caught her arm before she hit the ground, his instinct towards her stronger than his will.

"Oh!" She turned and surprise washed over her face. She breathed his name, as if he were an answer to a prayer. "Jesse."

Hell, she still looked too damn innocent and vulnerable for his good. Twelve years and she still had the power to get under his skin even though he knew how deadly she could be. Maybe it was time to turn the tables, collect on what he missed and wipe her from his mind. She couldn't be as good as he remembered her being.

Alexi blinked as heat invaded the chill that had stolen through her since she'd seen the pictures of Roger. She tingled as she looked at the rugged face and chiseled chest of the man who'd just saved her from falling. Half a day's dark stubble covered his rough jaw; and his deep sea-blue eyes, crinkled at the corners from the sun, warily assessed her then stared at her mouth. Tension oozed from him. She had no trouble connecting the man to the wild devil who'd led her astray years ago then broke her heart.

Small towns had their good side and bad side of the tracks, and the wild Weldon boys had been known a time or two to paint their side a bit blacker. Jesse's reputation had been the worst. She hadn't believed that until he'd used her to steal from her family. Over the years, she'd heard from Jesse's mother Emma, who worked at the hospital, about Jesse's stellar military career and security business in Washington D.C. Knowing he'd turned his life around made her glad, but didn't ease the hurt he'd left behind.

"Still a virgin on the run after all these years, Lexi?" he drawled. His voice, as steamy and seductive as Southern summer day, challenged her on an elemental level, a sensual one.

"Almost," Alexi said, letting the last illicit picture she had of Roger fall from her grasp to the ground. She'd only ever been with Roger and *he* didn't count. Not anymore. She sucked in air, latching onto Jesse's appeal. The reporters encircled them. Jesse lifted his hot gaze to her eyes and smiled.

"Almost?" Slow and sexual, his grin spread awareness through her. "Sounds frustrating. Interested in changing that?" He ran his finger under her chin and she caught her breath.

Yes, some part deep inside her shouted. Yes, she wanted to change that. Here was one situation her grandmother couldn't smooth over with a lie. With the cameras rolling, Roger and her grandmother would get a clear picture that Alexi meant it when she said she wasn't marrying Roger ever.

"Yes," Alexi said to Jesse, stepping closer to him. Waves of his sex appeal washed over her. Waves she had no trouble remembering, though she'd only been seventeen when she'd last dipped into them. His nearness and touch sparked something inside of her that wanted to rebel against everything that had just happened to her. "Kiss me," she demanded, loudly.

Jesse arched his brow and asked softly, "What's your game Lexi?" He slid an arm around her and pulled her flush to his bare chest, her breasts to his smooth, hard muscle. Then his mouth covered hers. She gasped at the desire shooting through her as his demanding tongue entered her mouth and his gaze dared her to respond.

She wound her arms around his neck, pressed closer to him, and met his tongue with hers. Surprise that she'd taken him up on his challenge filled his eyes and he hesitated, but only for a moment before he delivered a four-alarm kiss. He bent her back over his arm, inserted his leg between hers and had one hand cupping her bottom, no doubt knocking the socks off the gossip hounds surrounding them. In one kiss Jesse thoroughly ravished her from the inside out and she burned for more. By trying to deliver a message to her grandmother, Alexi wondered what message had she delivered to herself instead.

Jesse ended the kiss, but kept her captive in his embrace as he stared into her eyes. She ran her fingers into the silk of his hair and then surprised herself by kissing him again. His heat chased away the chill Roger had left inside her and she couldn't seem to get enough of it. He groaned then and deepened the kiss. Her hands clung to his broad shoulders, feeling the heat of his bare skin and the strength of his muscled torso. The cameras continued to flash and the world swirled crazily around her as her heart pounded hard at the line she crossed by embracing a half-naked Jesse so intimately in public.

He smelled faintly of aftershave and some indefinable, but intriguing scent. His body, strong and sure, eased around hers, a balm to her chaffed emotions. Yet before she could lose herself in him completely, he eased back and stared hard at her. Emotion and desire collided in her heart, springing tears to her eyes. "Get me out of here, please," she whispered.

Cool cynicism descended into the heat of his gaze. "So that's your angle. You need a hero, even if it's a Weldon." Glancing up at the reporters around them, he cursed. "Well, your highness, these days I charge for services rendered, and I expect to get paid." He scooped her into his arms and rammed through the reporters. "I'll be your hero for a price."

"What do you mean by that?" she asked, struggling in his arms as he headed to the parking lot. Reporters followed.

Jesse stopped a moment to meet her gaze. A sensual promise curved his lips. "We'll take care of the details later. The choice is yours, Lexi. Me or the sharks following us?"

"You," she said, wondering if she'd just made a deal with the devil in Georgia.

Excerpt from *SMOOTH IRISH SEDUCTION*
WELDON BROTHERS SERIES - BOOK TWO

"I'll finish up here. Head Nurse Litton wants you to go home before you end up on a stretcher." Candy lowered her voice so that only Nan could hear. "You work too hard. How you can do double shifts without a complaint is beyond me." The working conditions at Memorial Hospital were not ideal and many of the nurses felt the pressure of having to juggle too many patients with minimal help.

Nan bit her lip as a tinge of guilt heated her cheeks. She wasn't as noble as Candy made her sound, at least, not since Jackson invaded Nan's dreams. Now she not only worked diligently to reach her goals, but she also worked with exhaustion in mind. Too tired plus too tired equaled zero dreams, which meant no Jackson invasions...

Nan blinked, realizing Candy had spoken to her. "I'm sorry. What did you say?"

Taking the baby's chart, Candy shooed Nan toward the door. "You better go home before you fall down. I said that major hunk Dr. Swanson came by the nurses' station earlier asking for you and you didn't even react."

"Me?" Nan blinked with surprise.

"Yes, you. Don't look so innocent. I saw him eating lunch with you yesterday."

"That's only because the lunch room was full and he was kind enough to invite me to his table when I walked by."

"Uh, huh," Candy said with a bright gleam in her eyes that said she wasn't about to be fooled. "Out of all the people passing his table, he just happened to invite you to sit."

"Yes," Nan said. She was far too pragmatic to see Dr. Swanson's invitation as anything but a simple kindness on his part. Brad Swanson was the most renowned neurosurgeon in the Southeast, a medical giant. If Nan had had an "A-list" for Mr. Right, Dr. Swanson's dedication and determination would put him at the top of it.

Sure Candy was making too much of Dr. Swanson's visit, Nan said goodbye to the new mother and baby and left the delivery room. Dr. Schwartz followed her out.

"Nan, congratulations on receiving the Lois Emerson Merit Award again. You deserved to be honored twice in a row."

"Thank you, Dr. Schwartz. I was completely surprised. Once was wonderful. Twice left me speechless." The award was given to honor excellence in nursing care. To Nan it meant she was one step closer to being chosen for the scholarship. That Dr. Schwartz recommended Nan, doubled the honor. Nan greatly admired the woman who balanced a career and a family.

"You've earned it. And I'll be putting my recommendation in for you next year as well. This delivery might not have had as happy an ending, if you hadn't have had the instinct to call me when you did."

"I'm only thankful that both mother and baby are all right."

"Thanks to you. Go home and get some rest."

"You, too."

"No such luck. I left my husband with six five-year-old girls coming over for my daughter's birthday party that should have started an hour ago. Even though he's a flexible kind of guy and completely supportive of my career, I'm sure he's snatched himself bald by now. So I'd better hurry."

Nan laughed as Dr. Schwartz hustled away. Careers didn't necessarily make for a smooth family life. Nan made a mental note to add flexible to her Mr. Right list.

In the nurses' station, Nan keyed a few quick notes into the computer and then logged off for the day. She settled back in her chair and breathed a sigh of relief that was short lived. When her gaze focused on the clock, she suddenly remembered that she was supposed to be at her friend Alexi's house for a potluck BBQ. In ten minutes. She was too tired to rush and too tired to go, which was just as well. Since Alexi was Jackson's sister-in-law, odds were he'd be at the BBQ and she didn't need any more fuel to fodder her nightly fantasies of him.

She hadn't seen him in months, but she could clearly picture every nuance of his bad boy persona. He was the devil who promised heaven in his every move, but offered nothing for the future. She'd grown up under a futureless cloud and she wasn't ever going back there.

Digging her cell phone out of her purse, Nan dialed Alexi's number, braced to face the riot act Alexi was sure to deliver.

"I've got your number, Sugar."

There was no mistaking the deep sensual voice. Nan's heart jumped and an oh-so-hot, sweat broke all over her body. Her voice, caught sideways in her windpipe, squeaked. "Jackson?"

"My name on your lips is a good start. Please Jackson is even better. Ever had phone sex, Nan?"

Air flew from her lungs. An army of hormones attacked her sensibilities and everything else she had too. Liquid fire, pooled, flowed, and stroked.

Oh, my! A quick glance around the nurses' station told her no one had even noticed her. She should disconnect; pretend she hadn't even called. That would be the smart thing…

Instead she griped her cell phone tighter, swiveled her chair to face the wall, and shut her eyes. His voice did things for which she was starved. A moment she told herself. Just a moment to relay her message to Alexi. Then she'd hang up.

"Afraid sugar?" Like smooth Irish cream, his voice glided and curled into a warm knot right where his deep tones stroked the most.

"No." Since she'd forgotten to breathe, she sounded wispy instead of practical.

"Is that a no to sex via a live wire, or no to the fear."

"Both," she gasped, planning to ask to speak to Alexi just as soon as she caught her breath.

"Virgin ears. Mmm, that means I'll be your first. Can't you feel me? I'm right up against you. Feel the heat? My hands on you… my mouth. I can still taste your honeysuckle lips. I keep wondering if the rest of you is as sweet. Do you wonder too, Nan? Wonder how all that explosive attraction would play out between us if we let it loose? Remember the kiss outside the bar against the wall that day? We almost made love right then and there."

Nan gulped for air, she was drowning. Drowning in him again. She popped her eyes open, hoping that the images he evoked would evaporate. They didn't.

"No," she said desperately. "No, I don't remember. I don't wonder. Tell Alexi I can't make it tonight. We're all wrong for each other Jackson, sorry." Nan cut off the call before she heard anything else to tempt her otherwise. She stared at the wall, stunned by how much her need for him had grown since she'd stopped seeing him.

"Nan?" A firm finger tapped her on the shoulder. "Anything wrong?"

She swung her chair around. "Dr. Swanson?" she said, trying to blink his golden blonde image into focus, but a blue-eyed raven-haired devil kept imposing himself onto her retina.

He waved his hand in front of her face. "The one and only, but please, call me Brad. You look tired."

"I am a little," she said, blinking again. This time her vision blessedly cleared and she latched onto Brad's GQ, Armani draped bod with both eyes like he was the last lifeboat before the flood. She gave him her brightest smile. "What can I do for you?"

His eyes widened. "You should smile like that more often. It's quite breath taking."

Nan's jaw loosened with surprise at the personal compliment.

Brad shook his head as if bouncing out of a trance. "Ahem, well, I stopped by to ask you if you'd like to be my date for the charity banquet next Saturday. It's not normally my sort of thing, but I thought if you'd like, we could, uh, go together."

Had Mr. Famous Neurosurgeon just asked her out on a date in the middle of a colleague filled hospital? Nan shook her head to clear out the Jackson oriented cobwebs and saw Brad frown.

"Is that a no because you are working?" he asked.

"No. I mean that wasn't a no to you. That was a no to…never mind. Yes, I would like to go with you to the benefit."

"Excellent," Brad said, giving her the full force of his charismatic smile.

Nan prepared herself for a jolt of excitement, something along the lines of the lightning bolt Jackson had sent shooting through her with his "ever had phone sex" line. To her dismay, nothing happened.

Excerpt from COCKTAIL COVE

FRANKLY, MY DEAR SERIES - BOOK ONE

CHAPTER ONE

*F*or *her thirty-ninth birthday* present, Nikita's husband, Tom, came out of the closet swinging both ways on the sexual pendulum. That was three months ago, just after her nose had detected both a strange woman's perfume and an unfamiliar men's cologne clinging to his clothes.

Her nose never led her wrong and she'd nailed him for his perfidy right in the middle of their 400 square foot custom made his and hers closet. He confessed, dumped the blame at her feet, and took off as free as a bird. She had sat stunned between her Gucci and Louboutins.

Like most women clinging to the slippery side of their thirties, she'd been so busy dodging fat and wrinkle bullets that Tom's betrayal smacked her right between the eyes.

She was still in therapy. She might be perfectly coifed and dressed to the nines in Versace on the outside. But inside, on this doomed day in July when summer blooms lost their virginity to Atlanta's fickle weather, she floundered for a sweaty palmed grip on the conference table's polished edge. The law firm of Cross, Gibbons, and Biddle was nothing but a glorified shark tank. Like most attorneys' offices the illusion of comfort surrounded her, gleaming mahogany, plush carpeting, expensive art—all the little extras to put you at ease before feeding time.

Thankfully, her divorce attorney, Sandra Price wore powerhouse red and looked as calm as James Bond under fire because Tom's smug you're-about-to-be-chum smile had Nik clenching her teeth.

"There won't be any papers signed today," said Bob Cross, Tom's attorney. His sharp teeth flashed making her feel like a surfer on Styrofoam watching Jaws attack.

Nik had never liked Bob Cross and now she knew why. He'd been best man at her wedding and he was as human as a Great White. Cross continued speaking, "My client is petitioning the court for a two week delay in finalizing the divorce settlement."

"For what reason?" Sandra asked, laying her pen down with a snap. "Your client has delayed twice already."

"My client has changed his mind concerning the dispersion of their assets."

Blood drained with dizzying speed from Nik's head. Tom, golden-boy extraordinaire, broadened his smile and Nik bit her lip. Somehow her therapist's advice to forgive and forget wasn't holding up against Tom's tactics.

"Your client violated his marriage vows. He isn't in a position to disagree."

"My client was forced from his home to seek out comfort due to the emotional and physical alienation he experienced from his wife."

"That's a lie," Nik said, half popping from her seat. How could Tom even begin to say something like that? If anything she'd been a golf widow. The man spent more time on the fairway than he spent in their bedroom and that included fore-play as well.

"Relax, let me handle this," Sandra said under her breath, patting Nik's arm. Nik sat and forced her mouth shut as twinges of hurt nipped at her. Tom's smile grew.

When would she ever learn? She'd let the sharks see that she was bleeding.

"Your theatrics are tiring, Mr. Cross. We both know the truth and so will the court. What about the settlement does your client dispute?"

"He'll be left with no viable residence. The house is being sold and your client is receiving the condominium. My client is asking the court for the deed to the lake house, since it has little emotional value to your client and has been a place of refuge for my client over the years of their unsatisfactory marriage."

Icy shock slammed into Nik. She opened her mouth to say something, refute, deny, or scream, but could only choke on the emotion clogging her throat.

Sandra remained the epitome of cool disdain. "Impossible. My client purchased that property in conjunction with her brother prior to the marriage. Your client has no legitimate claim on her share of that asset."

"We'll let the court decide that. Now, in the matter of dissolving their investment properties, my client was the creative force behind these projects. Therefore a fifty-fifty split does not reflect his share of the work involved. My client has a multitude of witnesses and receipts to prove that your client has squandered money on an extravagant lifestyle…"

It was *her* money that had been the capital for those investments. And what right did he have to criticize how she lived? Nik couldn't take anymore. She jumped up and rushed to the bathroom barely making it to the privacy of a stall.

Her heart raced at a dizzying speed, and she gasped for air, fighting off the anxiety that hit her like a truck. From the time she was little, with only English boarding schools and a string of nannies as substitutes for jet-setting parents, Nik had always had a problem with nightmares and anxiety. But instead of diminishing as she grew older, it had worsened during her five-year marriage and now skyrocketed with her divorce.

About the Author

USA Today Bestselling Author Jennifer St. Giles/ J.L. Saint/ Jennifer Saints might have a split personality. Or as a nurse and mother of three, she knows how to multi-task. She writes in a number of genres from gothic historicals, paranormal thrillers, romantic suspense, and sexy contemporary romance. She has won a number of awards for writing excellence including, two National Reader's Choice Awards, two-time Maggie Award Winner, Daphne du Maurier Award winner, Romance Writers of America's Golden Heart Award, along with RT Book Club's Reviewer's Choice Award for Best Gothic/Mystery. She loves hearing from her readers via her website jenniferstgiles.com or you can find her on facebook.com/pages/Jennifer-St-Giles and Twitter @jenniferstgiles

From the Author's Mouth

What can I tell you about me?

I don't play video games or watch horror because I can't take the heat, but give me a kickass thriller every minute of every day and I am there. Be prepared for a Hoover Dam meltdown if you're with me and the movie is sad. So, to avoid disaster, I love romantic comedies.

Never coffee. Always tea. Never beer. Always champagne. There's more, but hey, gotta save some secrets until after the first date, right?

I grew up in Miami. Went to nursing school in Georgia, where I now reside. I raised and home schooled three great kids. I wrote for nine years before I sold a book, which made me a firm believer that a person should NEVER, NEVER, NEVER GIVE UP ON THEIR DREAMS.

I remember my father's remark after a particularly scandalous story about one of my ancestors, a story that involves a conspiracy, treason, betrayal, murder, and execution, a story that after a drink or two in the bar, I might be enticed to share. Anyway, what my father said was, "You can't keep a good man down." And I kind of see that in myself. Not that I am necessarily good, because the definitions of moral words are often relative, but I do persevere, and I am resilient. Nothing in life has ever worked out the way I planned for it too. In many areas of my life, I have yet to reach the level I thought I would, of where I envisioned I would be, but I haven't given up. I won't give up. I continue to work hard and do everything I can to help who I can and to make my dreams come true.

Besides great kids, family, and friends, that perseverance has so far garnered me a USA Today Bestselling tag and twelve plus books on the shelf in a number of genres (contemporary romantic suspense, historical suspense, paranormal suspense, and contemporary romance). I've won a number of writing awards, two National Choice Awards, three Maggie Awards, a RT Book Club Reviewer's Choice Award, the Daphne du Maurier Award, the Marlene Award, and the Golden Heart Award to name most of them. I work with several amazing women in a charity to raise money for a shelter that helps abused and homeless women and children. I've revived my nursing career after a long hiatus, have renewed my license, and have found the right job for now.

I know there are many more great things ahead.

I write romance because I believe that when you boil all of life down to its essence, if you take a human being to the very core of his existence, then you will find that what matters more than anything else is to be loved and to give love.

Life is all about choices and to pull from one of Erich Fromm's quote, *I choose to create and to love rather than destroy and to hate.*

I hope you enjoy my stories.

Go forth, dream, believe, create, inspire, and love,

Jenni (J.L. Saint, Jennifer St. Giles, Jennifer Saints)

www.ingramcontent.com/pod-product-compliance
Lightning Source LLC
Chambersburg PA
CBHW050558260626
47157CB00002B/621